THE MARANN

TALES OF TOLARI SPACE

BOOK ONE

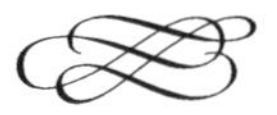

CHRISTIE MEIERZ

Title: *The Marann*

By: Christie Meierz

Copyright © 2012 by Christie Meierz

Edited by Phyllis Irene Radford

Cover design by Kelley York

The author is hereby established as the sole holder of the copyright. Either the publisher or author may enforce copyrights to the fullest extent.

Ebook ISBN: 978-1-961511-77-4

Print ISBN: 978-1-961511-78-1

Hardback ISBN: 978-1-961511-89-7

Published by Novus Mundi Publishing (Publisher), a division of Top of the World Publishing, LLC, with offices at 1008 S. Main Street, Georgetown, TX 78626 ("Publisher").

www.topoftheworldpublishing.com

Printed in the United States of America.

Without limiting the rights under copyright reserved above, no part of this publication may be reproduced, stored in or introduced into a retrieval system, or transmitted, in any form, or by any means (electronic, mechanical, photocopying, recording, or otherwise), without the prior written permission of both the copyright owner and the above publisher of this book.

The scanning, uploading, and distribution of this book via the Internet or via any other means without the permission of the publisher is illegal and punishable by law. Please purchase only authorized editions, and do not participate in or encourage piracy of copyrighted materials. Your support of the author's rights is appreciated.

Publisher's Note

This is a work of fiction. Names, characters, places, and incidents either are the product of the author's imagination or are used fictitiously, and any resemblance to actual persons, living or dead, business establishments, events, or locales is entirely coincidental.

The publisher does not have any control over and does not assume any responsibility for author or third-party websites or their content.

For my beloved

Certain things catch your eye,
But pursue only those that capture your heart.
Native American proverb

FOREWORD

THE MARANN, A SCIENCE FICTION ROMANCE

The origin of Science Fiction writing was in science and the military, and it was a manly thing. There were spacemen, and they did manly things, and if women appeared in the story at all, it was as "arm candy" for the hero. Much science fiction is still written this way.

But some of it is not. Authors like Lois McMaster Bujold, C. J. Cherryh, and the writing team of Steve Miller and Sharon Lee among many others began to combine elements of romance writing with strong and independent female characters, and the men who love them. I confess that I have loved reading these authors and these stories since I was a relatively young man.

Today it is usual to see space operas like the Honor Harrington saga by David Weber with significant romance sub-plots throughout the novels. Part of this is that writers have developed, part of this is that many more women read space opera and science fiction in general, and part of this is the significant crossover of romance writers and science fiction sub-genres like fantasy, urban fantasy, and the like. Writers like C. E. Murphy and Patricia Briggs have easily transitioned to writing urban fantasy with big globs of romance.

About ten years ago, I happened to pick up a novel by an author I'd never heard of. Her name was Christie Meierz. The book was the one you are reading now: The Marann. I loved it, and quickly read all the sequels as they were published. They were all equally good, and continued the promise of the first book.

It was obvious from the first pages that this was not a typical space opera. At first look, the plot rang changes on the story of Anna Leonowen, better known from the musical and movie The King and I. But it is not The King and I. It isn't a story about a British Victorian woman, armored in her certainty that the British society she was born in is inherently more civilized than the Thai culture she is exposed to as the teacher of the King of Siam's brood of children. Marianne Woolsey is dragged out of her comfortable life teaching in a small school in rural Iowa and convinced to take on the job of tutor to the child of the Sural of Tolar. It isn't the romance I expected, though. Marianne and the Sural both have secrets that could keep them apart. You will have to read the story to find out if they do.

In one of those quirks of fate, I was participating in a discussion of science fiction romance on the Facebook page of Sharon Lee when Christie Meierz popped up into the discussion. She mentioned that because of a long illness, she was in need of a new publisher. I popped up and offered Novus Mundi Press. We are now bringing out this special edition of The Marann and the four sequels that were previously published. And even more exciting, we are getting ready to publish the latest in the Tales of Tolari Space: Outcaste.

One of the things that impresses me is that Christie has had some of the best editors in science fiction work on her books. The Marann was edited by Phyllis Irene Radford. Outcaste was edited by Laura Anne Gilman. You can't get better editors than that.

As a fan of Christie Meierz I hope you enjoy The Marann and its sequels as much as I did, and as I do.

Walt Boyes
Vice President, The Heinlein Society
Member Assoc. of Prof. Futurists
Editor, Novus Mundi Publishing

CHAPTER 1

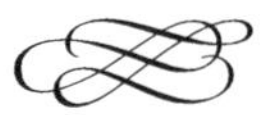

Marianne Woolsey never wanted to leave Earth. For that matter, she never wanted to leave her hometown of Casey, Iowa, where she taught young minds how to wrap their mouths around foreign languages most of them would never speak again.

But here she was, stepping into the business-class seating compartment of an Interstellar Spaceways passenger liner. Of the flight information displayed on her tablet—*Interstellar 4421—Tau Ceti—Gate B08—06:35/25/DEC/2543—4B,* only the seat number at the end was important. In two days, even the date wouldn't matter anymore, not where she was going.

She settled into her place, body yearning for the comfort of her bed but mind abuzz from the coffee she'd drunk to get herself moving after waking at ungodly o'clock this morning. While she waited for the ship to finish boarding and leave Earth orbit, she flipped through the Tolari language vocabulary lists on her tablet, searching for fresh terms to memorize, but found her thoughts wandering off into distraction. Annoyed, she brought her mind back on task, only to meander into fruitless speculation as to how her six large, fancy goldfish fared at her friend Susan's house. Leaving them behind on Earth stabbed at her heart, even if they were just fish.

She shoved the tablet back into her carryall and shifted in her seat, seeking a position to make sleep possible. For this first leg of the trip, Marianne had declined a berth, though the government had offered one. A late Christmas Eve party and an early flight to the Chicago spaceport to catch the station shuttle had collided to result in about four hours of sleep. Now she faced an eighteen hour flight through K-space to Tau Ceti, where she would board an Earth Fleet vessel bound for the Beta Hydri system and the world its inhabitants called Tolar. She wished she hadn't turned down the berth.

A man she didn't recognize stepped over her to get to the window seat, then turned to offer her a large travel cup. The steam drifting from its spout filled the air with the scent of mocha.

"Compliments of Central Command," he said with a wink and a smile. He waggled a government identification card with his picture on it, gripped against a smaller travel cup in his other hand. "Double mochaccino with a hint of peppermint. Happy Christmas."

Marianne groaned. She'd had enough coffee for one day, but chocolate and mint tempted her too much to pass up. She took the cup and sipped at it, closing her eyes in bliss. Then it occurred to her what the man must be doing here, and she flipped them open again to glare at him.

The man's gaze fixed onto hers. Her annoyance at the situation throttled the usual amusement she felt when strangers riveted their attention on her eyes. Her best friend Susan envied the athletic figure daily running gave her, and her friends said she was pretty enough, with even features and wavy light brown hair that reached the middle of her back. Her eyes, though, were a shade of crystalline sky blue that startled everyone and never failed to attract notice.

She preferred it that way.

"Merry Christmas," she muttered. "Are you here to make sure I arrive at my destination?"

"I'm here to make sure you're safe, ma'am."

"I don't need a babysitter. Where am I going to go? Out the airlock for a nice *breathtaking* walk? You should be home with your family. It's Christmas."

He laughed. It was a nice laugh, too. He was a man no one would look at twice—she'd bet real money his forgettable face got him this job—but she would remember his laugh. The rich rumble seemed to emanate from his entire chest. He stuck out a hand.

"Garrison Harding," he offered. "Call me Garry."

She shook the hand and plastered what she hoped was a sincere smile on her face. "Marianne Woolsey. But I bet you already know that."

He chuckled.

"You're entirely too cheerful, Garry." Marianne took several swallows of the minty mochaccino.

His eyes twinkled as he sipped at his own coffee. It was black and had the rich aroma of a dark roast. "I wasn't up late at a Christmas Eve party," he said.

Marianne frowned. Was there anyone in Central Command who *hadn't* kept track of her every move since she got this assignment? "It was my last chance to see my friends for a very long time," she pointed out.

Garry cleared his throat and turned to look out the viewport at the docking ring of Earth Station Hawking, but not before she caught a glimpse of sheepish expression. "Right, sorry," he murmured.

"So why are you here, Garry? It can't be just to make sure I don't run away, when I have every intention of arriving at my destination."

He turned back to her. "Are you quite sure about that?"

"Which, that you're here for some other reason, or that I intend to reach my destination?"

There was that cheerful twinkle again. "The latter."

"I've spent the last three weeks getting used to the idea of being sent to another planet to teach half a dozen Earth languages to an alien monarch's daughter. I'm okay with it."

"Three entire weeks. My, that does comfort one."

She gave him a look. "Why is everyone so suspicious? I never threatened to run away." She took another long drink.

"You should slow down on the mochaccino," he said, ignoring her comment. "It's high top. You might buzz yourself into an alternate dimension."

"I already have. I come from a dimension where I'm cheerfully passing out Christmas presents to lonely old people with no families."

Garry's response was lost to an announcement that passengers were now free to move about the public areas of the ship. He unbuckled himself and got to his feet. Marianne stared at the seat he'd just vacated, wondering what use a seatbelt could have on a spaceship.

"I didn't feel the jump into K-space," she said with a frown.

"It's played up in flicks. You actually can't feel it." He offered her a hand up. "Come along."

She glanced at the hand without moving. "Where?"

"Your berth."

"I don't have a berth."

He chuckled. "Yes, you do." He held up an Interstellar Spaceways keycard.

She squinted. "And you think I'll go there with you?"

Garry tapped a foot. "Oh really, Miss Woolsey, I can't bloody well brief you out here. I planned to impart the information my superiors want you to know until you're too knackered to absorb another fact, then read a good book in the observation lounge while you nap off your Christmas party. Does that meet with your approval?"

"Anything your superiors wanted me to know, they could have imparted to me yesterday, without any risk of innocent or not-so-innocent bystanders overhearing."

Garry's eyebrows lifted. He grinned. "Very good. You've learned a few things over the past three weeks."

Marianne allowed herself a small smile. "Thank you," she said. "I think."

"The dining room then," Garry decided. "Are you hungry?"

She let Garry escort her to the business class dining room. It resembled an oversized train car, with booths sporting tablecloths, breadbaskets, and fresh flowers rather than rows of seats. A viewport graced the wall beside each table, giving diners a stunning view of the featurelessness of K-space, so black it seemed to pull the soul right out of the observer. Marianne glanced out the nearest viewport and looked away, shivering.

Garry declined to let the maître d' seat them, instead brushing past him to the booth at the end of the dining compartment, as far from other passengers as possible. He ordered both their breakfasts before the man could escape. It didn't surprise her when he ordered her usual without prompting.

"You're quite the cranky traveler, Miss Woolsey," Garry said, helping himself to a chocolate muffin in the breadbasket. "Your file indicates you're even-tempered."

"I didn't get much sleep last night." She watched in horror as Garry spread butter on the muffin. "Butter? On a chocolate muffin?" She shuddered.

Garry shrugged and took a bite, nodding and smiling as he chewed.

"What do you mean, 'my file'?"

He smiled and didn't explain. Instead, he pulled a small tablet from his left coat pocket and fiddled with it.

"What are you doing?"

"Making sure anyone who tries to listen gets an earful of white noise." He shoved the tablet back in its pocket and turned his attention back to Marianne. "How much do you know about the Trade Alliance?"

"Um, they're a bunch of weird alien races we trade with?" She shrugged. "There are thirteen now, I think, including us. The Terosha look like giant walking sticks, the Kekrax resemble upright geckos with four legs, four arms, and two tails, and it just gets stranger from there."

Garry laughed. "Fair enough. What if I tell you they *all* warned us to leave the Tolari alone?"

Marianne blinked. "Why would they do that? It's not as if we're going to hurt them."

"They aren't concerned about the Tolari. They don't want *us* blundering around."

"Blundering around what?"

"We're not sure, but we want you to keep your eyes and ears open. Some of our associates in the Trade Alliance think there's more going on in Tolari space than meets the eye. None will say what."

"But the Tolari haven't even invented air travel yet."

"Yes well." Garry paused while a waiter delivered their breakfasts. When they were alone again, he continued. "We have no doubt Tolari technology is backward, though the culture is quite civilized. We want you to find out if there's something else going on, or if our spacefaring friends are simply skittish."

"I'm not a spook." Marianne stabbed her poached egg on toast, took a bite, and smothered her fruit with yogurt.

"No, and we don't want you to be. If the Sural is astute, he'll expect anyone we send to be watching him and reporting what they see, but we didn't train you because it would cause changes in your behavior he would notice. Instantly. The Tolari are keen observers. They can almost read your mind from your body language, and they know if you're lying or hiding something."

Marianne grimaced.

"Yes, we know what a private person you are. Just be yourself. That's all they want."

She heaved a sigh. "That I can do."

* * *

A BUMP WOKE Marianne from a dream about… about... She yawned and stretched—*what was that dream?*—and didn't reach for her tablet to check the time. Garry had talked for hours, alternately pumping her for what she knew and filling her with new information. Her head felt like an overstuffed pillow.

A voice came over the comms. "Ladies and gentlemen, Interstellar Spaceways Flight 4421 to Chi Orionis, with service to Tau Ceti Station and Epsilon Eridani, has just docked. Passengers continuing on to Epsilon Eridani and points in A'aan' space are requested to remain in the ship at this time. If this is your final destination, please gather your personal belongings and proceed to the main airlock. Enjoy your stay, and thank you for choosing Interstellar."

That answered what time it was.

Personal belongings, she thought with a wry grin as she climbed out of the bunk. The only personal belongings Central Command had allowed her to bring were her clothing and a tablet. The tablet contained her personal library along with the entire collection of the Casey Public Library—minus anything to do with technology—and minus music, much to her dismay. The bags with her clothing had been sent ahead to the Earth Fleet ship scheduled to take her the rest of the way to Tolar. She had only a small, worn carryall containing her identification card, her tablet, and a dental hygiene kit. On Tolar there'd be no music, no hobbies, no Tuesday night bowling. She hoped she would be busy enough not to get bored.

She went to the berth's sink and cleaned her teeth, then splashed some cool water on her face. Yawning and stretching again, she gathered up her carryall, left the berth's keycard in a slot behind the door, and entered the sleeper compartment's narrow hallway.

Garry was nowhere to be seen. Marianne made her way to the airlock in the next cabin. As she exited, and the riot of color decorating Tau Ceti station's outer ring assailed her eyes—and air that had passed through too many lungs tickled her nose—a uniformed escort greeted her by standing in the way. He resembled every other Central Command serviceman she'd ever seen: indistinct features, crew cut hair, no neck. That was the point, she supposed. They were interchangeable. She sighed and gave this one her attention.

"Citizen Woolsey," he said. It wasn't a question.

"Yes?" She gazed past him, eyes drawn to the colorful array of shops and many viewports crowding the outer ring. She couldn't see any aliens—that disappointed her—and she could hear only the busy crowd's echoing, multilingual chatter. The shops bustled with activity and bristled with day-after-Christmas sale signs. She wanted to see the alien wares and buy a souvenir, even if the price was outrageous.

"Please come with me, ma'am." He jerked his head toward a tunnel to the central hub.

"All right." Eyes still on the shops, she fell into step beside him. "Where are we going?"

"Sickbay."

She squinted at him. "Why?"

"I'm not at liberty to say, ma'am." He smiled. It didn't extend to his eyes. She fell silent and let him lead her past all the tantalizing stalls and kiosks crammed with colorful items. One stall was little more than a booth containing a life-sized model of a Terosha. A grinning teenaged boy draped himself around it, making kissy-faces while the proprietor recorded the images. The next kiosk held jewelry displays claiming to be A'aan'. Whether or not the kiosk signs told the truth, the bangles and baubles looked exotic. She slowed and peered at three matched filigree earrings in peacock colors. Three?

"Citizen." Her escort's voice was flat. He stood a few meters down the ring, a frown etched on his face. Marianne hiccupped a nervous laugh and scurried to catch up with him. He turned on a heel to enter the walkway between the station's rings.

When they reached the inner ring, he peeled left off the walkway and paused to let her precede him into the sickbay waiting room. Leaving her to a brisk, middle-aged man in dark blue scrubs, he took up a position near the door and stared straight ahead, hands clasped at the small of his back. Marianne bit a lip to keep from laughing at his resemblance to the stereotype of the featureless, brain-numb Central Command conscript.

The nurse rolled his eyes. "You must be Marianne Woolsey," he said, his face brightening into a pleasant smile. *His* smile reached his eyes, and she warmed to him.

"That's me," she replied.

"Right this way, hun." He beckoned her to follow him down a hall and stopped at a door featuring a red sign with bold white letters saying PHASE LAB. He opened the door to usher her in.

"Why am I here?" Marianne asked.

The nurse was more forthcoming than her escort had been. "I was told you're going down to an alien planet. Anyone we send down to the surface gets a locater chip, so we can pull them out if we have to. It's for your own safety."

"I see," she said, and then she shook her head. "No, I don't see. I thought the Sural guaranteed my personal safety?"

"I wouldn't know about that," answered the nurse, "but this is standard procedure. It won't hurt a bit."

"Can I say no?"

The nurse pursed his lips. "You can if you want to turn around and go home. I wouldn't recommend it."

Marianne took a deep breath. The nurse gave a shake of his head so slight she almost didn't see it. She shrugged and sighed. "All right. What do I do?"

His holiday cheer returned. "Lie down here," he indicated a bed with one end pointed at a featureless metal doughnut of medical machinery, "and let me immobilize your head."

She scooted onto the bed and wiggled until she was comfortable, while he positioned her head in the doughnut hole by adjusting the bed.

"This machine will use phase tech to place a locater chip directly onto your brainstem. It will only take a moment. Some people say they feel a sort of mild tingle in their heads, but most don't feel a thing." A pillow of air wrapped her from the shoulders up. "Can you move your head, dear?"

She tried. "Not even slightly."

"Good." He paused. A hum filled the air, followed by a soft click. "We're done."

"Already? I didn't feel a thing."

"Exactly." The nurse smiled as he reached for a switch over her head, and the field holding her head in place dissipated. She sat up.

"Not so fast," he said, putting a hand on one shoulder before she could slide off the bed. "Any dizziness?"

She turned her head and tilted it from side to side. "Not at all."

He put a step stool below her feet. "Get up slowly," he ordered. He kept one hand on her shoulder and gripped her arm with the other.

"I'm all right," Marianne protested as she stepped down onto the floor.

"It's my job to make sure." He dropped the hand from her shoulder, but kept a firm grip on her elbow. "Especially with those heels. You know those are bad for your back?"

She laughed. "So I've heard," she answered. "But I have strong calf muscles. I'm a runner."

The nurse made a rude noise. "That doesn't matter, but I don't expect you to believe it, not with that smug look on your face." He laughed.

The door hissed open. An Earth Fleet officer in khaki stood in the doorway, smiling and bouncing on her heels.

"Citizen Woolsey?" she asked.

"Now *this* young woman is wearing sensible shoes," the nurse said.

She laughed. "I'm on duty, sir," she said, flashing a friendly grin. "You should have seen what I was wearing at *The Elbow Room* last night." She turned to Marianne with a conspiratorial wink, her hands measuring the height of the heels she'd worn. "Pleased to meet you, ma'am," she said, extending a hand. "Sarah Carver, Lieutenant, Third Fleet. I've come to escort you to the *Alexander*."

Marianne shook the hand, smiling back at her. "Pleased to meet you."

"If you would come with me, please?" The lieutenant led her back to the outer ring and into the naval docks, passing through several security checkpoints along the way. She never stopped chattering.

"I understand it's your first trip off-planet," the lieutenant said as they passed through a final checkpoint. "How do you like it?"

"It's amazing," Marianne answered, pointing at the starscape out a viewport.

"I love it out here," the young woman said. "I love this job."

"Do you meet many aliens?"

"All the time. Mostly Den, since their federation is so close to Earth space. And the odd Kekrax, of course—they're everywhere." Her nose wrinkled.

"Do they smell as bad as people say?"

"Oh, not really," she scoffed. "That's just media hype. Most people enjoy having them around. Sometimes they even smell pleasant, and they're kind of comical."

She stopped at an airlock guarded by two armed marines, who came to attention as they approached.

"Here we are, ma'am." She inflated. "The CCS *Alexander,* best ship in the fleet. After you." She tapped a panel on the wall, and the airlock's outer doors slid open.

The Central Command Ship *Alexander,* Marianne discovered as the cheerful lieutenant chattered, wasn't just the best ship in the fleet, it was the flagship of the Third Fleet, with a full admiral on board. The lieutenant's orders had included escorting Marianne to the admiral's ready room as soon as she set foot on board.

Two couples rose from seats at a long conference table to greet Marianne when the lieutenant showed her in. Viewports lined one wall, offering a stunning view of Sol-like Tau Ceti, and a presentation screen filled the space beside her at the door. An elegant sideboard graced the wall opposite the viewports.

The admiral, a trim man with graying hair that obeyed military standards of neatness, stood at the head of the table. A middle-aged woman in a high-waisted gown of cream-colored silk velvet rested a hand on his right arm. A blocky gentleman, in the formal gray of the diplomatic corps and hair the same color tied back in a black ribbon, stood on his left with a much younger woman in a gown of deep rose silk. Marianne waited just inside the door, clutching her carryall and glancing down at the modern and more practical blouse and skirt she wore. Central Command's clothing allowance had been generous, but not *that* generous. The Old Regency style of dress in vogue with the upper classes had cost far too much to consider.

The admiral came forward, extending a hand with a warm smile.

"Citizen Woolsey." He gave her hand a firm shake. "Welcome to the *Alexander*. I'm John Howard. This is my wife, Laura, and Ambassador Smithton Russell and his wife Adeline. I trust you had a pleasant voyage out?"

Marianne shook hands with them all. "I wish I'd had time to look around the station a little. I would have loved a souvenir."

The admiral's smile turned regretful. "My orders are to get you to Tolar with no further delay. Central Command is in an all-fired hurry, and I'm afraid sight-seeing and souvenir-shopping weren't on the approved activities list." He chuckled. "But please, have a seat. We were just discussing you and your assignment."

Marianne took the indicated chair. "Nothing bad, I hope?"

"No, no," he answered with another chuckle. "What's your poison? Coffee? Tea? Juice or soda?"

"Tea would be lovely, thank you."

The admiral punched a button at the head of the conference table. A young man who looked no more than eighteen entered the room and served tea in a delicate china cup with the Earth Fleet insignia on it. After placing a carafe on the sideboard, he gave Admiral Howard a crisp salute and left the room.

Marianne wrapped her fingers around the cup's handle and fixed her gaze on her host. He seemed friendly enough, but the authoritative air he wore and the confidence he radiated suggested he was not a man to be trifled with. "So when do we leave for Beta Hydri?" she asked, taking a sip of the tea. Its delicate flavor spread across her tongue. From New Spain, she thought, or perhaps Britannia. It was good. Very good.

"We've been under way since that door closed behind you," the admiral replied.

Marianne choked a little in surprise and spluttered. With her back to the viewports, she hadn't felt or heard anything to indicate the ship had left its mooring at the station.

"Damned fine crew," he said with a satisfied smile. He poured himself some coffee and took a seat. "Now, bring me up to speed with where you are. What do you know about what you're getting into on Tolar?"

Marianne took another sip of tea. "I'm going to be teaching in the Middle Ages," she said, unable to keep her lips from twitching. Laughter rang around the room.

"Good," the admiral said. "Keep that sense of humor—you're going to need it."

"Alone on an alien planet, I just bet."

"It's not so bad," Adeline said. "They look just like us, and their leader, the Sural, seems well-educated, at least for a primitive."

"I couldn't find a given name for him in any of the material Central Command sent me."

"He hasn't told anyone in the Trade Alliance what his name is," the ambassador said. "Might be a security concern."

"So I'm to call him 'Sural'?"

"*The* Sural," Adeline corrected. "It comes from the name of his province."

"Suralia is a northern province, right up against the ice sheets," the admiral said. "High summer there is like August in Alaska, and deep winter drops to dangerous temperatures. Right now, it's late spring, which is warm enough, but the nights are cold. Didn't Central Command tell you to bring warm clothing?"

"Um, yes," she replied.

The ambassador started to chuckle, a basso rumble like gravel. "They didn't mention how cold it gets or for how long, did they?"

Marianne glanced from one man to the other with an uncomfortable feeling crawling up her spine.

"A Tolari year is just over two Earth years," Adeline said. "The seasons are six months long, and winter gets beastly cold."

"On the bright side, you get a six month summer, with a couple months of warm weather on each side," the admiral added.

"Well," said Marianne, "I'm glad I brought several pairs of long underwear."

The admiral's wife stirred. "I'm sure we can do *something,* if she gets cold?"

The admiral gave his wife a fond smile and patted her hand. "Central Command briefed you on everything you needed to know except the practical day-to-day details. The days are a little longer than ours, just over twenty-five hours, which means you'll only be in sync with ship time once every twenty-five days. Tolar gravity is a touch lower than Earth normal, so you'll have a spring in your step. Details—it's all in the details."

A silvery laugh came from Adeline, the ambassador's wife. "They didn't tell you any of that, did they?" she said.

"No," Marianne admitted. "They concentrated on what they thought I would need to know to be accepted by the Sural."

"The Sural can still choose to send you back," the admiral said. "The first time you meet him, right after you arrive at the stronghold, will be the real test. He'll accept or reject you right on the spot."

"The Tolari make a science of observation," Adeline added.

Marianne nodded. "So they told me. It's almost to the point of mind-reading."

"They also have keen hearing and an absurdly sensitive sense of smell," Adeline continued. "They won't want you to use any perfumes or deodorants while you're down there—things like that can even make them ill. Your clothing is already being deodorized."

"But it's all clean!"

"Not clean enough for Tolari, trust me. Something in our cleaning agents irritates them."

"Almost everything they eat is poisonous to humans, too," the admiral said. "We'll send you down with a food scanner. Scan everything before you put it in your mouth—everything, even if it looks and smells like plain water. There are a few foods we know you can eat—nutritious ones, I'm happy to say—but you're still going to have to take supplements to stay healthy."

"Can't you just phase me down some of our own food?"

"Not much, and not often."

"But—"

"They don't like phase technology," he interrupted. "The Sural won't permit more than a bare minimum, and he won't explain why. He's only going to allow us to phase down vitamin and protein supplements because we made it clear you'll get sick if we don't. We might be able to slip you a gift now and then, but don't count on it. Before you ask, we can't send down a shuttle either. The Sural doesn't want them in his airspace. Your diet is going to get pretty boring, pretty fast."

Marianne smiled. "I'm all right with boring."

The admiral grinned. "Ever consider a career in Earth Fleet?" he quipped. The ambassador and Adeline laughed. Laura just shook her head.

"They're civilized," Adeline continued. "But we have to play by their rules, because they're not advanced enough to play by ours."

"I'll be all right," Marianne said, taken aback at the blithe snobbery coming from a diplomat's wife. It couldn't be all that bad.

The admiral smiled. "I'm sure you will." He looked serious again. "But be careful with the food. Their medical science is primitive. If you get yourself poisoned and can't let us know, they're more likely to kill you than not, trying to help."

"Don't get poisoned." The ambassador lost his smile. "If we have to pull you out, you won't be allowed to go back. It's a kind of cultural taboo—once the Sural has established a relationship with you, he can't allow you to leave. If he does, he can't trust you again, because you might have been tampered with."

"I see," Marianne said, nodding. "Not a very trusting people."

"Not trusting at all," Adeline said. "They've never allowed any other race to return to Tolar after first contact. They are gracious and accept a communications device, then pfft! Goodbye, don't call us, we'll call you. It was a huge surprise to everyone they're allowing a human down there at all."

"Certainly shocked the hell out of the Trade Alliance." The ambassador sipped some coffee. He frowned and put it down. "They still think we should leave the Tolari alone."

Marianne shrugged. "Maybe it really is the physical resemblance between us that intrigues the Tolari."

"That's the astonishing part," the admiral said. "Parallel evolution. Aside from their ability to camouflage and disappear at will, they look entirely human. No one in the Trade Alliance has ever seen anything like it, not even on planets orbiting the same star—much less on planets twenty-four light years apart."

"Do any Trade Alliance races say *why* we should leave them alone?" Marianne asked.

"Not a single damned one," the ambassador answered. "They limit themselves to vague threats, saying we won't like it if we try to bully the Tolari."

"Bully the Tolari?" Marianne blinked. "Why would we bully them? They're not even space-faring. They can't be a threat to anyone."

"Well," said the admiral, "speculation isn't going to answer any questions. We should get you settled into your quarters. Then I'll give you a tour of the best ship in Earth Fleet."

CHAPTER 2

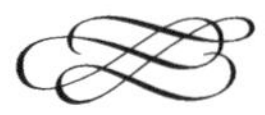

Tau Ceti to Beta Hydri took thirty hours via K-space, even at military speeds. Marianne had a bad case of travel lag as the *Alexander* approached Tolar—it was midmorning ship's time, late afternoon in Suralia, and, according to her tablet, three in the morning back home, and her body knew it. The admiral invited her to the bridge to watch as the ship went into orbit. Coffee and excitement kept her vertical. Just barely.

The bridge monitor occupied an entire wall. At the moment, a growing image of a verdant, Earth-like world filled it, revolving against a velvet starscape. She took in every detail of the spellbinding sight. A large ice cap in the northern hemisphere gave way to green landmasses that looked a little more blue than she thought they should. In the southern hemisphere, where late autumn held sway, the ice cap had shrunk, and the vegetation was yellow.

Awe bubbled out of her. "It's like a jewel!"

A few crewmembers sprouted knowing grins. The admiral chuckled and clapped a hand on her shoulder. "Get a good look at it," he said. "You won't see Tolar again from this angle for a good long while."

An ensign walked up to the admiral and saluted. "Sir," he said, "the shuttle is ready."

"Very good, ensign. Take Citizen Woolsey to the shuttle and see that she's comfortable for the ride down."

"Yes sir."

"Well, Citizen," he said to Marianne, "it's been a real pleasure. Good luck." He shook her hand.

"Thank you, admiral. I'll do my best to make a good impression."

She followed the ensign to a shuttle bay and into a tiny, two-man craft with enough space for herself, the pilot, and little else. The three bags containing her clothing, plus a pack with a portable phase platform and comms unit, filled what little space existed in the back of the cabin, making it even more crowded. She stuffed her carryall into the largest bag, grateful to have her hands free. The ensign settled her in the copilot's seat with an admonition not to touch anything and left her to the good graces of the pilot, a commander of Asian descent who said little, smiled much, and flew the shuttle with the precision of long experience.

Marianne had never flown in such a small craft. The visibility astounded her; she could see the whole universe from the tiny vessel. She sat silent, eyes wide, not caring about the huge, probably goofy smile on her face, trying to absorb everything at once, while the planet grew until it filled the cockpit monitor. The shuttle dove into the atmosphere, juddering in the thick air as it arced over a luxuriant blue-green ocean, streaking toward the Sural's province in the northern hemisphere. His city lay on a coast, against a mountain range. The pilot aimed for a large plateau jutting between the mountains and the city.

As they drew close enough to make out individual buildings, the shuttle turned toward a crescent-shaped ledge the size of a soccer pitch, located perhaps halfway up the plateau's high cliffs. The landscape rushing by slowed until the ledge lay motionless beneath them, and they descended to a landing Marianne almost didn't feel. She shot the pilot an exhilarated grin, then unbuckled and climbed out of the copilot's chair.

The pilot turned in his seat and rose with a pinched expression. "Your pardon, ma'am," he said, "but I can't help you with your bags beyond handing them out to you. I'm not to leave the craft." He reached past her to tap a panel, and the shuttle's back hatch slid open.

She offered him a sympathetic smile. "Don't worry about it, Commander," she said, backing out onto the springy grass as he passed each bag to her. She slung one over each shoulder and grabbed the other two by the handles, one in each hand. "I'm stronger than I look."

He nodded. "Good luck, ma'am." He climbed back into the cockpit and opened a cubby to pull a tablet from it. "I'll be parked here until I receive word whether or not you've been accepted for your post at the stronghold, just in case you need a lift back."

She smiled, waved, and turned to face the world that would be her home for the next twenty-six years.

Gray clouds covered the sky from horizon to horizon, and a strong breeze buffeted the ledge. Above, an enormous, weathered stone citadel she assumed to be the Sural's stronghold loomed on the cliff top. Below, at the bottom of the cliffs, a seacoast city spread along a wide bay.

She sniffed at the air. The breeze carried a tang she couldn't identify—not that she had expected Tolar to smell like Earth. The soil beneath her feet fed and absorbed different plants, and the alien sea beyond the city must possess its own distinct salt balance and its own plant and animal life.

The heels of her shoes sank into the grass. She glanced down—it wasn't grass. It resembled fern, she thought, just a touch more blue than a plant should be. Putting down her luggage, she stooped to run a hand over the ferny bed of vegetation, which yielded and sprang back under her hand. Then a gust of wind sent her digging into a bag to retrieve and don a heavy sweater. Welcoming the extra warmth, she picked up her bags again and walked a little farther from the shuttle, stopping to look around.

"Where is everyone?" she wondered aloud.

A Tolari man burst into view before her. She started, unprepared for this first demonstration of camouflage. The bags slipped from arms and shoulders as she jumped back, a small cry escaping her lips. The man bowed with arms spread to the side and palms forward. Despite her alarm, she recognized the posture as apologetic, according to Central Command's material on Tolari etiquette.

"Forgive me," he said in Tolari. His voice was a pleasant baritone, his dark eyes friendly. He towered over her—he stood at least two meters tall—spare and dressed in a pale blue robe covered with white embroidery. Straight black hair fell well below his knees, gathered at the back of his neck with an elaborate knot. "I mean you no harm."

Taking a deep breath to gather her wits, she tried some Tolari on him. "My name is Marianne Woolsey," she said, extending a hand. The man just stared at it, his eyes flashing with... something. Curiosity perhaps? An awkward pause stretched before she remembered Tolari didn't shake hands—they bowed. She withdrew her hand and did her best to imitate the man's apologetic bow.

"Are you here from stronghold?" she asked, mispronouncing it. Then, trying to get the inflection correct, she added, "Did the Sural send you?"

The man nodded and made an exaggerated gesture toward the cliff face. Then he picked up her bags with easy strength.

"Follow me," he said, his intonation making it a respectful request to a superior.

Must be a servant, she thought, though she'd read a mention of servants wearing black. Maybe he was a guard? She followed him, biting back questions, unsure if Tolari etiquette allowed him to converse with a guest.

They wound their way up a smooth but steep path. From behind him, she had a clear view of his hair, which reached farther than she thought, down to the hem of his robe. Other, simpler knots followed the elaborate braided knot at regular intervals, and she wondered just how close to the ground his hair would reach when brushed out straight. It was the longest she'd ever seen, swinging back and forth across his back as he strode up the path at a pace she had to work to match. She considered herself fit, but back home she ran on relatively flat terrain, since Casey lacked anything like this sort of steep cliff. Hurrying up the path in heels knocked the wind out of her.

When they reached the top, they were still a fair distance from the stronghold entrance. The Tolari, even after carrying her four heavy bags up the cliff at a brisk pace, hadn't broken a sweat. Marianne had, and her feet ached as well. Her escort stopped and stood, patient and attentive, the strong breeze whipping his hair and robes, while she caught her breath.

She gave him a grateful smile through her breathlessness, flicking her gaze to the hem of his robe as it billowed. Trousers and slippers the same color—and perhaps the same silky material—peeked from underneath. Those robes must have been blowing around his legs while he was camouflaged near the shuttle. Central Command really wanted to know how they managed to disappear, clothing and all.

When her breathing had quieted a little, he smiled and said, "This way," gesturing toward the huge stone doors leading into the stronghold keep. She followed him, bracing herself for another stretch of trying to keep up with his long strides, but he crossed the distance at an easier pace. She smiled her gratitude and peered around the cliff top as they walked, edging away from the sheer drop. The lack of a railing made her sweat even more.

The doors opened as they approached—pulled by camouflaged doorkeepers?—and they entered a long, curved corridor of the same dark stone as the outside of the keep. The man put her bags on the floor and winked out of sight.

She stared for a moment at where he had been. No sign of him remained. She looked around, wondering what to do, her attention caught by colorful banners mounted along the walls on each side of the corridor. As she moved toward the nearest to get a closer look, a woman in a plain black robe appeared before her.

Marianne blinked, but didn't startle. Maybe she could get used to this.

"The Sural requests your presence in the audience room," the woman said. "Follow me."

Marianne followed her a short distance down the hall and into a huge open room, rectangular in shape, with the entrance on one of the short sides. Soft mats covered the floor, leading to a raised dais at the far end. Another Tolari in pale blue, with an imposing air of command about him, sat on his heels on the dais, cradling a tiny infant and watching her. As she approached, she recognized the man who had met her at the shuttle. *That was the Sural?* she thought in shock. *The Sural* himself *carried my bags?*

An enigmatic smile curved his lips as she reached the foot of the dais and he motioned her to sit. She slipped out of her shoes and lowered herself to the floor matting, relief rushing through her aching feet. Imitating the Sural's pose, she sat on her heels, waiting for him to speak.

Silence stretched. She swallowed and took a deep breath, bringing to mind the rules of etiquette she'd committed to memory. When Tolari met, the higher-ranking individual spoke first. Farm girl that she was, she had no intention of opening a conversation with the highest-ranking member of the Tolari ruling caste, who sat on the dais studying her without speaking.

"Expect long silences when conversing with a Tolari high one," Ambassador Russell had said during the tour of the *Alexander*. "They like to think before they speak. And they stare. You'll just have to get used to their damned staring."

After what seemed like forever, he nodded and spoke. "I am the Sural." His pleasant baritone rang with authority now.

"It is an honor, high one," she replied in Tolari, then waited, hoping she gave a good impression. The ambassador had been right about the staring. Was it rude to return the stare? Or just expected? She met his eyes, and then glanced away. He could have stepped right out of an antique twentieth century cowboy movie—as one of the indigenous natives—right down to the coppery skin and impassive expression. Her eyes wandered to the bundle in his arms. That had to be his daughter, but all she could see were blankets. If only she could get a closer look.

Silent, the Sural studied the young human woman. Not quite the correct response, he thought, but she was nervous and awed. He extended his senses and touched her with a gentle probe. Like the previous humans he had met, she did not react, sense-blind and unaware. *Good.* He began to explore with more freedom.

Surprise at what he found almost lifted his eyebrows. After his experience with the previous two candidates, both undercover operatives, he had not expected Earth's government to send him what he had asked for: a tutor for his daughter. She also did not broadcast her emotions, as the previous candidates had done. This woman held her presence still, as quiet and reserved as any Suralian. *Lovely.*

Beneath the reserve, she struggled to hold down an anxiety connected to something deeper. His skin prickling, he pushed toward it to the extent he could without physical contact. It ran deep, that anxiety, but it was personal, running far into the past, unconnected to her present situation. She stirred, uncomfortable, sensing the intrusion but lacking the ability to identify it. Chagrined at the unwarranted invasion, he withdrew to her surface emotions; they dripped with apprehension. *Understandable.* He wondered if her government knew what they had sent him.

Doubtful.

Withdrawing back into himself, he let the silence stretch a little longer, keeping his face smooth while he considered. He had studied her qualifications, and they impressed him. She spoke seventeen

Earth languages, including the diplomatic languages of Earth and its five colony worlds—the ones he wanted her to teach his daughter.

Satisfied now she was not another spy for Central Command, he could not resist prolonging the interview with the exotic, beautiful creature. Her eyes startled him and drew his attention. He had seen blue eyes before—it seemed to be a common color among humans, in his limited experience with them. The group making first contact with him had included several blue-eyed humans. None possessed eyes like this.

His gaze wandered across her face. Humans seemed to come in every possible skin tone, along with many other physical variations, such as slanted eyes or tightly-curled hair. This human possessed, along with her striking eyes, quite pale skin, with faint dots across her cheeks and the bridge of her nose.

She was quiet now, drifting in her own thoughts, exhibiting no sign of impatience. *Excellent.* He sent a gentle probe into her anxiety again. A gentle longing for the familiar laced through it, and he suppressed an urge to knit his brows together. If she was not one with a thirst for new experiences, why had she come? Something seemed to pain her, as well. What she hid, however, would take time to uncover.

As he continued to probe, she glanced over at him, her eyes coming to rest on his daughter. Curious interest colored her emotional landscape, warm and maternal. *Good.* She radiated gentleness, and her responses had all been quite satisfactory—from interest in the vegetation beneath her feet to honest confusion when she realized who had carried her bags for her, and now warm curiosity about his infant daughter. Her qualifications and skills, according to Earth Central Command, exceeded those of the spies he had rejected. Yes, this candidate would do.

"I carried your bags from your craft because I wished to observe you," he said, to break the silence. "Your government has sent me other candidates who were, shall we say, not what they said they were."

She blinked. "What else would they be?"

"They were not trained as tutors."

"I am not a tutor, either," she said, nervousness sparking through her. "I was trained to teach twenty or thirty students at one time."

The Sural nodded, and she relaxed a bit. "This much was clear from the credentials your government sent me. Have you other skills than the ones they mentioned?"

She gave a strange shrug, with both shoulders. "They know everything about me."

He gave her a brief smile and rose without disturbing the sleeper in his arms, gliding down the dais steps to lower his tall frame onto the mat beside her. "This is my daughter, Kyza," he said.

The human glanced at him, radiating amusement. With some chagrin, he realized he had allowed his tone to soften and express more than he had intended. She peered at the tiny bundle and extended a tentative hand, stopping just short of touching Kyza to look up again. When he nodded consent, she pulled the blanket open to get a closer look.

His daughter was—and he did not think he exhibited bias in this—beautiful, with long eyelashes and a shock of black hair sticking out in all directions. She pursed her tiny mouth, making sucking movements in her sleep. The human drew a breath and murmured in English, "Oh, how *precious*!"

He raised an eyebrow. She rocked back with a hand over her mouth.

"Forgive me," she said in Suralian, "I meant no offense."

Stupid, stupid, stupid, Marianne thought. *I'm in the stronghold maybe ten minutes and already I'm unforgivably rude.* Her gut twisted, and she fought to keep her face smooth. The briefing on Tolari protocol back on Earth had indicated it was an insult to address the Sural in any language other than his own, unless he had chosen to speak the other language first.

She stared at her hands, stomach in freefall, and waited for him to send her away. For all that she had not wanted to leave Earth in the first place, now that she had, she was just as reluctant to return. Irritation at her own perversity compressed her lips into a line. Perhaps she didn't know what she wanted, but she hadn't spent the past three weeks schooling herself to accept spending twenty-six years on Tolar to turn around and go back after a few minutes. It startled her to realize that the idea of going back to Earth and back to her life wasn't a relief. There were things on Earth she *didn't* miss.

"You have no need to fear me," the Sural said, his gaze still on his daughter. He looked over at Marianne with a more impassive expression. "And you cannot insult me."

She blinked and met his eyes, startled again. He cocked an eyebrow. "Speak your thoughts —" She didn't understand the last word he used. "You will not offend me."

She searched for words. "That is not what I expected," she said.

The Sural uttered a low chuckle. "And what did you expect?"

"They told me Tolari rulers are easy to offend," she blurted out, surprised by her own audacity.

He chuckled again, dark eyes twinkling. "They?"

"Central Command. I am unsure where they got all their information about you."

"Perhaps someone met the wrong Tolari ruler," he said, his face bland. "What else did they tell you to expect?"

She floundered. "Well—it— Should there be guards and aides here? The room is empty, and you sit here holding a *baby*, and—and—"

"And?"

She shrugged. "You act like I am a real person."

"Are you not real?" Amusement tinted his voice.

His reaction seemed to indicate she hadn't used the right word in Tolari—but maybe they just didn't have the concept she wanted to express. Amusing the Sural, she decided, was better than insulting him. She shrugged again, unable to suppress a nervous smile.

He seemed to come to a decision. "Here," he said, laying the baby in her arms.

She sucked in a breath, hands shaking, and cradled the child, who adjusted herself in her sleep and uttered a charming little sigh. Marianne's heart warmed, easing her shakiness. She stroked Kyza's cheek with a fingertip.

"*Shì shàng zhí yǒu mā ma hǎo,*" she sang, an old Chinese lullaby. Kyza opened dark eyes at the sound and fixed Marianne's face with an intense stare. "*Yǒu mā de hái zi xiàng gè bǎo.*"

"She likes you," the Sural said, interrupting the song.

Marianne smiled and rocked Kyza, slow and gentle. "*Ya tozhe,*" she cooed at the baby, breaking into a huge happy grin when Kyza flashed a brief smile. "She smiled at me!" She turned her grin up at the Sural.

"You may stay," he said.

A huge wave of relief crashed through her, and she almost kissed the baby. She stopped herself, not sure if it was appropriate. "You honor me, high one," she said. She beamed a smile at Kyza. The infant still stared at her with dark, slanted—

She gasped and jerked her head up to meet the Sural's eyes. "The shuttle pilot?"

"He has been informed that he may leave."

She heaved a sigh and nodded, smiling, then turned her attention back to the warm little bundle in her arms. Kyza made an unhappy noise and began to stir.

"She is hungry." The Sural made a gesture, and a yellow-robed woman appeared, holding out her arms to Marianne. Marianne placed the baby in the woman's arms and turned back to the Sural as the woman left the room. His eyes were fixed on her, face impassive and unreadable. Another gesture, and a black-robed woman appeared.

"Show the new tutor to her quarters," he ordered. "See to her comfort, and show her how to use the controls in the—" Marianne didn't understand the word.

"Yes, high one," the woman said with a deep bow.

He turned back to Marianne. "Those in black robes are servants," he told her. "You may ask them for any assistance you need. Call out and one will come."

Then he disappeared into thin air. Again, Marianne stared at the space where he'd been. He'd disappeared without a trace—no ripple in the air, nothing. The black-robed woman beckoned to her. She stood to slip her feet back into her shoes.

Her quarters lay in the stronghold's guest wing, a short walk down the curved corridor. It resembled a suite in an expensive hotel. The door from the hall opened into a spacious sitting room, where the servants had already placed her bags. Bookshelves and artwork lined the walls. One corner held a desk positioned to look out the windows onto unfamiliar trees and flowers. On the desk sat a small, exquisite crystal sculpture of what resembled a bird with four feet rather than two. Ahead of her, the sitting room led onto a covered veranda overlooking a garden or park of some kind.

To the left was the door to the bedroom. *Sleeping room,* she corrected herself in Tolari, as she glanced at the bed-sized mat in the center of the rectangular space. In one corner lay the area for which she hadn't understood the Tolari word—a bathing area. The servant led her into it. Walls of the same dark gray stone as the rest of the stronghold, polished to a high gloss, gleamed on all four sides, but the floor looked pebbly and seemed to grip the soles of her shoes. Carved steps led down into a bath large enough to hold two people. Levers and spouts protruded from one end. Once Marianne knew how to use the simple but elegant mechanisms to control the water flow and temperature, the servant left her in peace.

Heated water! Marianne shook her head in wonder. Central Command had told her the Tolari didn't have running water or plumbing. This was both, and it wasn't crude by any definition—low tech, perhaps, but not the simple basins and water pitchers the briefings had led her to expect.

She gazed around her. A door at one end of the sleeping room opened onto the veranda, where it exited into the gardens. She wanted to explore—it looked beautiful out there—but she wasn't sure yet just how much freedom she had, or if it was even safe. Rather than indulge her curiosity, she set about putting her clothes away in the drawers and closets the servant had shown her in the sleeping room. Then, feeling a little whiffy from her exercise on the cliff, she decided to give the bathing area a try.

She played with the levers until the water warmed as much as it would, which wasn't as warm as she would have liked, but it didn't give her a chill. The quick rinse washed away some of her fatigue along with the sweat. She donned fresh clothes and contemplated the stale clothing she had just removed. Central Command had given her no information on how the Tolari did their laundry, and she had no idea what to do with it. As she pondered, the black-robed woman appeared in front her again. She started.

It might be harder to get used to this camouflage thing than she thought.

"Forgive me," the woman said with an apologetic bow. She waited for Marianne to catch her breath. "I will take your robes for cleaning."

Marianne nodded, feeling a little foolish. "My gratitude," she said.

"It is my honor," the woman said, leaving the room in a more conventional manner.

* * *

SMITHTON POURED HIMSELF A WHISKEY. He'd just received word the shuttle had lifted—and left Marianne Woolsey behind.

"We did it!" his wife exclaimed, face glowing. "We got someone in there."

He grunted and sipped the drink. "How useful she'll be is another question."

"Oh Smitty." Adeline pursed her lips. "Don't be such a stick. She'll do fine."

The door chime sounded. Adeline swayed off to see who it was.

"Come in," he barked, before she could get halfway there. The ship's AI opened the door on John and Laura Howard—as he expected. He caught John's eye and raised the glass. "Drink?"

"I'm on duty," John replied. "Early for that, isn't it?"

Smithton took a sip.

"I'll make coffee," Adeline said in a bright voice.

The admiral lifted a hand. "The ship's processors—"

"—make wonderful tea and ghastly coffee," finished Laura. "I don't know how you drink it." She shot Adeline a smile. "I'll help."

The women disappeared into the suite's small kitchen with a swish of their long dresses.

"Well?" Smithton asked, sinking into one of Adeline's well-padded sofas.

John took a seat in the one chair which wasn't overstuffed and examined the fingernails of one hand. "Well what?"

"You owe me a week's pay."

His friend's expression turned sour. "Who'd have thought Central Command would keep their mitts off the girl?"

"Anyone who could put two and two together. Come on, pay up. You bet the Sural would reject Miss Woolsey just as he did the other two candidates. You lost." John pulled a card from an inside pocket of his uniform jacket, flipping it across the coffee table. Smithton caught it and swiped the back with a finger. He grinned. "You got a raise. I'm going to buy Addie something shiny with this."

John laughed. "You do that."

"Do what?" Adeline came through the door from the kitchen carrying a porcelain coffee service on a gold tray. Laura followed with a small silver plate piled with cookies.

Smithton let his grin broaden. "Buy you a nice bauble with a week's worth of John's pay."

"What did you two argue over this time?" Laura asked. She put the plate on the coffee table and sat on the arm of John's chair.

John snaked an arm around his wife and leaned forward to grab a cookie. "I was sure I'd be shipping Miss Woolsey back to Tau Ceti by now."

"Oh ye of little faith," Adeline scoffed, as she set the gold tray beside the silver plate and started serving coffee.

John mumbled around a cookie. "What made you so sure this one would pass the Sural's muster?" Adeline handed him, then Laura, steaming cups.

"She's really just a teacher from a tiny high school somewhere in Iowa," Smithton said. "Speaks an ungodly number of languages and practiced them in the Babel cloud where someone noticed. She's only twenty-seven. No secrets and clean as a babe in arms."

"Hah! You had inside information!"

He sipped his whiskey, unperturbed. "You had access to it if you'd bothered. Besides—you don't need your Earth Fleet salary any more than I do, though I do like to decorate my wife with it when you lose."

John snorted and stuffed another cookie in his mouth. Laura poured milk from a creamer into their coffees.

"She seemed like a nice young woman." Laura slid a cookie from the silver plate and nibbled at it. "I'm glad the Sural didn't send her away."

"We all are," John said. "But now the real work begins."

CHAPTER 3

The Sural remained camouflaged in the audience room, observing the human woman as she left for her quarters with a servant. Some disinformation had provoked her reaction when she forgot herself and spoke English—she had expected a summary dismissal for a child's mistake. She *was* little more than a child, at least in his people's terms, and it seemed she required some re-education.

He wanted to uncover her secret, but he suspected that would take time—seasons, perhaps years. What she hid lay so deep it could only be personal, and it would require winning her trust to uncover it. From what he could sense, that would be no easy task. Still, the humans had chosen better than they knew. This Marianne Woolsey possessed a natural reserve and an appealing clarity of spirit. His daughter would do well with such a companion.

He dropped his camouflage and made his way to the open study off the audience room to read reports until the new tutor finished settling into her quarters. The stronghold seneschal rose from a chair near the desk as he entered the room.

"This candidate is satisfactory," the Sural said.

The man bowed. "Yes, high one."

When the seneschal did not move to leave, he asked, "You have more to say?"

"Is the human permitted to leave the plateau?"

"I do not hold her captive."

"If she should wander into the city—"

"She will see what I wish her to see." He flicked a dismissal with one hand and turned his attention to a report while the man bowed and left. When a servant came to inform him that his new guest appeared to want to explore the gardens, he went out to intercept her.

She stood on her veranda, gazing out into the gardens, when he walked out from behind a tree and into her line of sight. Hands clasped behind his back, he relaxed and dropped his air of authority, becoming more like the man who had carried her bags up the cliff and little like the imposing ruler he affected in the audience room. He offered a friendly smile. Her answering smile became uncertain as he neared.

"Would you care to see my gardens?" he asked, schooling his face back into impassivity.

"Yes, many!" She stopped. She had used the wrong intonation and seemed to realize it. She tried again. "Yes, very much."

"Your language ability is impressive." He led her out amid the flowers. The late afternoon sun hid behind the clouds, but summer would come soon. The cora trees had long since come into full leaf, and small pale blooms sprouted from the ground cover. He looked down at the flowers and took a deep breath. Their delicate fragrance filled the garden.

"The groundcover requires a cold winter to bloom," he said. "Can you smell it?"

The young woman sniffed the air, and her face fell. She shook her head. "No, high one. The information Central Command gave me indicates your sense of smell is much more sensitive than ours."

"So it seems." Comparing their sensory abilities was, perhaps, not the best topic to pursue. He veered away from it. "When did you begin to learn my language?"

"Three—" She fell silent, struggling to find a word "Perhaps twenty or twenty-one days," she finished. "We would call that three *weeks*." On the last word, she dropped into English, and he sensed her anxiety spike.

"So little time." He offered a reassuring smile, but rather than quell the anxiety, he seemed to prolong it. He smoothed his face, and her tension eased.

The woman was a puzzle.

"There wasn't enough time to give me a full vocabulary implant, but I have the essentials, and I have a—" she stopped, squeezing her eyes shut as she sought the proper word and intonation. "I remember everything I hear," she finished.

"A useful ability for one who specializes in language," he said.

Enjoyment begin to color her presence. She took a deep breath, tension dissolving from her as she exhaled.

"You are free to wander the gardens whenever your duties permit," he added. "It is quite safe."

She looked around her and sighed, her shoulders loosening and back straightening as she relaxed. Concentrating on exercising her language skill seemed to be enough to take her mind off the identity of her conversation partner, despite her obvious travel fatigue.

They neared a small cora tree in full bloom, its leafy branches covered with small white flowers. A gathering of flutters burst into the air, a riot of color swirling away, alarmed by the approach of a stranger. She stood still and, much to his surprise, faded from his senses a little, in an apparent attempt to lure the flutters back. He had not imagined a sense-blind human could possess such an ability.

A few of the creatures returned, hopping about in the tree's upper branches, agitated and scolding.

"What are they?" she asked.

"We call them flutters," he said. "This kind can live only in cora trees." He held out a hand and reached out to one with his senses, holding its primitive emotions captive. It flew onto his fingers and sang. She made a small, delighted sound, clapping her hands in front of her face. He kept the creature's senses still, soothing it, and brought his hand down to her eye level.

The little creature's plumage shimmered in vivid shades of red, blue, and green, punctuated with bright white eyes and a black, conical beak. It gripped his fingers with its four feet and fluttered its wings, a small, living jewel. His human guest extended a hand to stroke its breast with a finger. The flutter crooned, and a delighted smile came to her lips. The Sural's gaze fell on her face, and the smile captured him. A desire to let himself sink into those startling, luminous eyes stirred to life.

No, he told himself. He loosed his grip on the flutter's senses and it flew off, scolding. His guest laughed, her remarkable eyes following its progress through the garden. He withdrew back into himself, reflecting. She could not read him, he reminded himself. Humans were unaware of the world outside their own senses.

A guard behind her flickered, reminding him of the time.

"It is time for the evening meal, proctor," he said, turning to head for the refectory's garden entrance.

"What was that word?" she asked as she fell in step beside him. "You used it before, in the audience room."

"A title we give to private tutors. *Proctor.*" He hid a smile. To educate his daughter, this new tutor needed to communicate well with him. That she felt comfortable enough to ask him a trivial question made a promising start.

She mouthed the word, and then uttered it under her breath, running through all its intonations and inflections. She spoke with a pleasing accent, but although she could understand him and make herself understood, she would need to learn a great deal more of his language if she was to be his daughter's tutor.

He could think of no reason to disturb the family tutor with such a short-term venture—a linguist with a fair grasp of his language and an eidetic memory could become fluent before the end of the season. He would teach her himself.

"Well done," he said as they reached the refectory.

He led her into the large room, filled with round wooden tables surrounded by elegant but simple wooden chairs. Stronghold staff occupied many of the round tables, wearing robes in the colors of their castes, from black to dark brown to pale yellow to deep blue. Their quiet conversation created a pleasant background murmuring.

In the center of the refectory, on a low dais, the long, rectangular high table stood. At one end sat his heavy, elaborately-carved chair, with simpler chairs lining the long sides. Tables laden with food trays populated one end of the room, where swinging doors led to the kitchens. The new tutor frowned a little.

"High one," she said, "I need to return to my quarters."

He raised both eyebrows at her. "Is there a difficulty?"

"My food scanner," she said. "I need it to tell me what I can eat."

He nodded and signaled a servant. "Bring it," he ordered.

"Yes, high one," said the black-robed servant, disappearing. Since the refectory occupied the guest wing, he reappeared only a short time later, holding the small, thumb-sized scanner.

She accepted the device and tapped one end to activate it.

Engrossed in checking its settings, she failed to notice that the Sural and every Tolari nearby winced. It seemed human hearing could not detect the grating whine the device emitted. The Sural made a casual gesture for tolerance and led her toward the food. Relief blossomed behind him when the irritating sound moved away.

Trays covered the tables near the kitchens, loaded with fruit, greens, individual bowls of a thick soup, and grain rolls. Steaming carafes and empty mugs sat to one side.

"This is tea," he said, indicating the carafes. "From a flower we grow in cool river valleys. Suralia has many tea flower plantations."

She passed her scanner over a carafe, and a light on the device blinked green. This seemed to be a positive finding, for with a smile, she poured herself a mug and sipped at it.

"Wonderful!" she exclaimed.

He ventured a smile of satisfaction, which elicited no anxiety from her, and moved along the rest of the trays in turn. She scanned them all, finding a grain roll and a piece of fruit that the device proclaimed safe. The soup, he explained, consisted of vegetables and roots. The scanner flashed red, which apparently indicated toxicity.

She juggled the food and the scanner, but he took the tea from her to free up a hand. With a grateful smile, she bowed her thanks. Then she turned her attention to the scanner and, much to his relief and that of everyone in the refectory, deactivated it.

"It is my honor," he murmured, accompanying her back to the high table. When he had settled her in the chair at the left hand of his own, he went back to the tables of food to select his own meal. In a low voice, he ordered a servant to remove the new tutor's device during the night and have it repaired to no longer emit its irritating noise. Then, returning to the table, he took his place in the heavy chair to find she had waited for him to begin her own meal.

"A human custom, to wait?" he asked.

Marianne nodded, taking in the astonishing amount of food in front of him. His eyes glinted as he started on his meal, and she turned to her own. Mimicking the eating habits she saw around her, she tore the grain roll in two and took an experimental bite from one half.

The glaze was sweet, and the bready interior delicious and herby, but moments later a *fierce* afterburn lit a fire in her mouth and throat. Gasping, she grabbed her mug and took a long drink. The fire went out, much to her amazement. She panted, catching her breath, glancing at the Sural to find him regarding her with concern written across his face.

"Are you in distress?" he asked.

She nodded, then shook her head, then coughed a little and started to laugh. "I will be all right," she said. She panted and fanned her mouth. "I don't know the Tolari word."

"What is your word for it?"

"*Spicy hot,*" Marianne answered in English. "Like a fire in the mouth," she added in Tolari.

"We do not have this concept."

She shrugged. "I can become accustomed to it." She drew her brows together as she examined the piece of fruit she had brought back from the tables near the kitchen. It was purple and about the size of a man's clenched fist. "How do I eat this?"

The Sural offered a hand, and she passed it to him. He demonstrated where to begin peeling and started it for her before handing it back. "Peel half, then eat," he advised.

She followed his directions and, taking caution from her experience with the grain roll, took a small first bite. Her eyes popped at the sweet and unusual flavor. "Sweet," she said. "Like a *banana.*" She took another bite, nodding and smiling as she chewed.

The Sural gave a satisfied nod and picked up his soup, drinking from the bowl. He alternated the soup with substantial bites of grain roll, which he often dipped in the soup first.

"Do you have—" She paused, searching for words. "Small tools to eat food? Or small flat trays to hold it?"

He lifted an eyebrow at her, smiling and shaking his head. She returned to her grain roll, eating small bites with liberal amounts of tea. Despite the heat-reducing properties of the tea, the spiciness added up. She leaned back with her tea after finishing half the roll, her stomach's complaints reduced to something she could ignore.

The Sural stared at her, sipping his own tea, his eyes studying hers. She tried and failed to hold back a grin. Even aliens, it seemed, couldn't help noticing her eyes.

"Do you think you will be content here among my people, proctor?" he asked.

She leaned back to think. As tiring and overwhelming as the last two days had been, she wanted to bounce out of her chair and dance. She had gained the Sural's acceptance where others had failed. "Yes, I believe I will." The answer surprised her. "I'm glad I came."

He gave her a sharp look. "Did you not want to come to Tolar?"

"Well," she began, shifting in the chair. Had she given it away somehow that she hadn't wanted to leave Earth? Anxiety jabbed her in the stomach. "Well."

The Sural seemed to focus on her. She fidgeted with her unfinished roll.

"Do not fear me," he said, his expression becoming serious. "I will never harm you. I have pledged my life on it to your government."

"You can send me away, though."

"I have said you may stay. I neither give nor change my word at whim."

She paused. If she said the wrong thing... she didn't know if she'd spark an interstellar incident. "I—" she started.

The Sural waited. He seemed to have an inexhaustible supply of patience... so far.

"I never wanted to leave Earth," she murmured, looking down at her hands.

His face lost some of its impassiveness. "I understand what it is to love one's home," he said.

She gave him a quick glance, then looked back down to her hands and nodded. "It was a great honor to be chosen for this mission." She took a breath. "But I never sought it."

"Why then did you come?"

"Central Command chose me. I had no choice. My government said if I came and you sent me back, there would be no..." she searched for the word and didn't find it, "bad actions."

The Sural went still. "Repercussions," he said. His voice had gone flat.

"Repercussions," she repeated, nodding. "But if I refused to go, I would regret it."

"They threatened you?"

Marianne looked up. His face betrayed nothing, but he seemed... outraged.

"Not exactly. Central Command never threatens. It would be bad —" she couldn't find the word, "—reputation." He shrugged a shoulder, appearing unsure what she meant. "They make it clear your best interest is to... *um*... accept their offers."

The Sural took a long drink from his mug and set it down. He stared at her—no, he stared *into* her, with a penetrating look that seemed to pierce her soul. She shifted in the chair again and looked away.

"Do *you* wish to tutor my daughter?" he asked, after a time. "Do you wish to stay of your own accord? If not, I can send you back to your admiral and request another candidate. Perhaps Central Command will then send me a tutor who desires to stay."

She started a little. "It was hard to leave the life I built for myself in Casey," she said in a soft voice, "but I cannot say I *want* to go. I never planned to leave Earth—I never planned to leave Casey—my home—but..."

Her eyes drifted to the garden windows. It wasn't so *very* different here. Tolar had trees, flowers, something like grass, even birds. She set her jaw. If she left now, she'd never know if she could have made a go of it. She drew a deep breath and looked him in the eye.

"Yes, high one. I do want to stay and tutor your daughter."

"Excellent!" he said, with a smile she thought might be warm beneath his chilly exterior. He gestured with his hand to include the whole room. "My home is your home."

Mi casa es su casa, she thought, stifling a relieved sigh. *Crisis averted.* It seemed to her she'd come close to dismissal twice. This assignment might end up harder to keep than she thought.

Her gaze wandered back to the windows, to the tree where she'd startled the colorful, bird-like creatures, the flutters. Their chatter drifted in through the open garden door, sounding like budgies. She shook herself. *No. He said he doesn't change his mind lightly.*

"Does something else trouble you, proctor?"

She pulled her attention back to the Sural. He stared at her, brows drawn together, concern darkening his mahogany eyes.

"No, everything is fine," she said, picking up the half-eaten roll and taking a bite. She chased it with tea to neutralize the spiciness. Tolari bread would take some getting used to.

He didn't let it go. "You seemed distressed by your thoughts."

"I have a lot to think about."

"Because you left a great deal behind."

She tried not to flinch and failed. That struck home. Her friends, her house, her job—even all those Christmas presents. Central

Command had allowed her to bring none of it with her. "I miss..." she inserted the English word, "Christmas."

"Who is Christmas?"

Now she laughed. "Christmas is a what, not a who. A big celebration near the beginning of winter. People spend time with their families, exchange gifts, eat and drink together. We are celebrating that time now on Earth."

"I see," he said, nodding. "Then perhaps you will enjoy our seasonal celebrations—they may be similar. We have music and dancing, and friends share meals and drink together."

"Drink? What do you drink?"

"Spirits. To relax the body and lighten the heart. They are made from grains and mixed with fruit."

Alcohol. It had to be alcohol, or something like it. The Tolari drank? That was nowhere in Central Command's information about them. "When is the next celebration?"

"High summer."

She did a quick mental calculation. That was four months off. "I look forward to it."

* * *

LIFE ON TOLAR quickly settled into a routine. Nurses brought Kyza to Marianne many times a day. She read to her, talked to her, sang to her. She began to grow comfortable carrying around a powerful ruler's child and presumed heir. Attentive nurses whisked Kyza away before Marianne was even aware the infant had begun to grow restive or hungry, to bring her back when she was quiet and receptive.

She wondered who, and where, Kyza's mother was, but it didn't seem appropriate to ask.

In her free time, she studied the language, roamed the stronghold and its grounds—which together covered an area the size of a small town—or read books. Central Command had packed her tablet with not only the collections of the Casey Public Library, but also a complete and up-to-date archive of comparative linguistics, one of her favorite hobbies.

As days and then weeks passed, she grew accustomed to conversing on familiar terms with the Sural. She had imagined she would seldom see Tolar's sovereign ruler. Nothing could have been further from the reality of the quiet, even gentle, leader in embroidered robes of soft, pale blue. His patient kindness toward her was puzzling, as he showed her his world from the boundaries of the stronghold plateau, taught her his language, observed without expression everything she did in his presence and seemed to derive satisfaction from her delighted reactions to new things. Days passed in which she caught no more than glimpses of him between meals, and then it would seem he spent all her waking moments with her, asking questions about her impressions and what she had learned about Tolar and his people.

Reports had to go to the ship on a regular basis. A comms unit occupied the desk in her sitting room, but the Sural had indicated from the beginning he took a dim view of using it without restraint as humans tended to do. She couldn't imagine how it affected him, at the Tolari's pre-industrial level of technology, but she left it unused in consideration for his preference. Instead, she wrote out reports on her library tablet and transmitted them to the ship in the early morning before she went to take her morning meal with the Sural. He seemed to know of her transmissions, asking an occasional question, with a crooked smile, as to what she had reported to 'her' admiral, but he didn't object.

The reports themselves varied, from detailed analyses of Tolari social structure and its caste system, to speculative reports on Tolari child development based on her observations of Kyza, to reports on the flora and fauna she discovered in the gardens. She described the Tolari diet, noting she had never observed them eating animal-derived foods, seeming to subsist on fruits, grains, nuts, greens, and vegetables. They drank teas, fruit juices, and flavored waters.

As her command of the Sural's dialect solidified, she began to have animated discussions with him about Tolari political and social structure, trying to pin him down on what his exact role as planetary ruler entailed. In the end, she decided she didn't have the background or education to understand. He ruled his province, and he ruled his planet, but he had little say in the rule of other provinces. They were autonomous, though their leaders held lower rank in the ruling caste than he did, and there seemed to be limits to what he could order them to do, though within those limits they were bound by honor to obey him. Their alliances shifted. The Sural's allies were often enough his enemies' allies, and the enemies of his enemies were not always his friends. There had to be a piece missing. She couldn't figure it out.

"I am *Suralia*," he answered her one morning after she asked him, yet one more time, how he could rule the planet but not its provinces.

"Eh?" she said.

"*I* am Suralia."

"You are Suralia." Repeating the words didn't give them any more meaning than when he said them.

"Yes."

She shook her head. "I do *not* understand. How can you *be* your province?"

He put a hand, fingers spread, on his chest. "I am Suralia, and not any other." His expression was amused, and his lips tilted. "The province is my life, and my life is the province. We are one, I and my people. Their lives belong to me, and my life belongs to them. I cannot *be* another province if I am Suralia."

"If the province is your life, what would happen if Suralia were destroyed by some kind of disaster?"

"I would walk into the dark."

She blinked. "What is *the dark*?"

"You call it death."

"You would commit suicide?" she gasped.

"I would stop my heart and neural activity, yes."

"You can do that?" She gaped.

He nodded.

Marianne slumped against the chair back. "Then what happens when *you* die?"

"My daughter rules Suralia after me, if she passes the trials."

"So your people would survive your death, but you would commit suicide if they died?"

"They would walk into the dark if I died in dishonor," he corrected.

"What, all of them?"

"Provincial rulers carry a heavy responsibility."

"To put it mildly!" she exclaimed. "How many people live in Suralia?"

"At present, the population is approximately four hundred twenty-five thousand men, women, and children, most of them in the city below."

“Oof,” she said, letting her breath out in a gust. “I begin to see why your honor is so important to you.” She paused, afraid to know, and then asked, “Has that ever happened? A whole province going into the dark?”

The Sural nodded. “Twice in our history. The more recent instance occurred over a thousand years ago.”

Her mind balked at mass suicide on that scale. “More than two thousand standard years,” she murmured. “What about the children?”

“They follow their parents into the dark. Even infants can follow a parent into the dark—it is an innate ability. We develop the capacity to control it sometime in our fourth year.”

Seven or eight years old, in Earth terms, she thought. She shook her head and sipped some tea, thinking. “On my world, suicide is a crime.”

The Sural choked on his tea. He controlled the reaction, but for a brief moment, she had never seen him so surprised. Then he stared at her, every bit of expression gone from his face.

She gave him a rueful grin and shrugged. “It *is* legal in a couple of the colonies, though—New China World and Far India.”

The Sural ate the rest of his meal in silence, continuing to stare at her. “Summer is a busy season for the Sural,” he said when he finished. “I have much work to do.”

Something brushed against her as he left, though the table lay between them. She frowned at his retreating back, and then shook it off.

CHAPTER 4

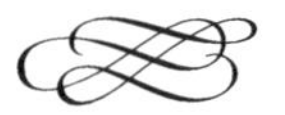

On a day in midsummer, Marianne woke to find the stronghold almost empty.

"They have gone to the summer festival," a servant said when she asked where everyone had gone. "The Sural left orders for you to be escorted to the city should you wish to participate."

As if I'd miss this. Marianne rushed to change into comfortable shoes for the trek down the cliffs.

The city center's main avenue was full of—May poles. *May poles,* with Tolari dancing around them in patterns.

Apothecaries in yellow holding black ribbons attached to the top of a pole danced and wove with indigo-robed scholars holding yellow ones. The pattern taking shape on the thick pole, about twice a man's height, looked like nothing so much as a vertical bumblebee. Farther down the avenue, at the next pole, dancers in pale blue, dark green, purple and black wove ribbons of pale green, dark purple, gold, and silver.

Tolari milled about between the many poles lining the avenue. Some strolled with children clinging to them, others walked arm in arm, still others clustered in groups. Blue, yellow, green, purple, mauve, black, and more; an explosion of color filled the streets. Most of the dancers and passersby, male and female alike, wore flowers in their long hair.

Even the clothing on display had more variety than the robes the stronghold's somber workers wore. Although the same castes wore the same colors, some individuals wore robes so short as to be better described as tunics. It made sense to Marianne, since the long robes everyone wore on the plateau couldn't be practical for many activities, but... she wasn't sure what she had expected.

People *smiled.* Looked happy. Had animated conversations with each other. It was so unlike the somber atmosphere on the plateau. She glanced up at the edifice, looming above the city, wondering what could have happened to create the gloom up there, and wondering whether the Sural would tell her, if she asked.

She toyed with the idea as she strolled along, admiring the beribboned poles, then shook her head and snorted to herself. The Sural had been more forthcoming about Tolari culture than she had expected, but asking after his somber demeanor was more than a little personal. *Tell me, high one, what happened to make you such a cold fish?* She shook her head again, a smile elbowing its way onto her face. No, she'd leave that one for a few *years* down the road.

Movement caught her eye. People skipped in circle dances to lively music emanating from a sunken theater at the square's center. She headed toward it. A woman in the mauve of the musician caste played an instrument looking and sounding much like a Celtic harp. Fingers dancing on the strings, she smiled as she played—a Tolari smiling easily!—while the crowd in the theater reacted to cues Marianne couldn't see or hear.

Puzzled, she stood listening and watching. What *was* it they reacted to?

"Do you enjoy yourself?" The Sural's voice came from behind her.

She spun to find her nose almost touching the tall Tolari leader, who carried his infant daughter across his chest in a sling. A nurse stood nearby.

"Yes, very much," she answered, backing up a step. She could swear he enjoyed disconcerting her just then, though his face was, as usual, impassive.

Then his lips twitched.

Marianne cleared her throat. "Your daughter is sleeping through her first summer festival."

He turned a warm smile on Kyza. Marianne shook her head. The Sural, smiling in public! Almost, she asked him why he was so subdued in the stronghold. Then prudence came to the fore and stopped her tongue.

He caught her eye. "Walk with me." He swept one arm toward a street lined with booths. A light breeze from that direction brought mouthwatering aromas. "Have you any questions?"

"That music," she said. "There was something... different about it."

He chuckled. "Of course. It is Tolari."

"What I meant was—"

"High one?" A small girl in a brown robe bowed to the Sural. Marianne thought she might be five or six, in Earth years. She held up a circlet of yellow and orange flowers toward the Sural. "I made a flower circle for you, high one."

He stooped on one knee before the child, a gentle smile playing around his mouth. "You honor me, child," he said, as the little girl stood on her toes to place the circlet on his head like a crown. "What is your name?"

The little girl seemed to have run out of courage, but a man in brown answered for her. "She is Yreth, high one. She has eleven seasons."

Five and a half, Marianne thought.

"And this is Kyza," the Sural said to Yreth, loosening the sling so the girl could see. "I hope she will be the next Suralia. See? She is only in her first season."

Yreth's face took on a serious expression. "She should wake up or she will miss the festival."

"You may be correct." The Sural gave the girl's nose a gentle tap. "But now you should return to your father, or you also will miss the festival."

Her mouth formed a small O, and her eyes went wide as she turned to run back to her father. "Fafee!" she cried. "I want to see everything!"

The Sural chuckled and nodded at the man before turning to continue on his way, grateful the child had distracted Marianne from asking about the theater crowd reacting to the musician with the powerful gift. With one hand, he settled the flower circlet in his hair. In truth, he had found the child's offer of it heart-warming.

He should not have startled Marianne, but the prankish festival mood in the city had overcome him. It did, however, help to set the human tutor a little off-balance, making it easier to redirect her attention. The child had done the rest. Marianne seemed to have forgotten about the music.

"Do you think there will be anything here I can eat?" she asked, her eyes on the booths along the street.

"Possible," he replied. "Did you bring your scanning device?"

"Right here." She patted her... he had heard her call it a *skirt*. Like robes, the peculiar half-garment possessed pockets, and she seemed to have tucked the food scanner into one.

The dark green *skirt* fell from waist to ankles. Tucked into that, she wore a white garment covering her upper body and arms. The color combination was outlandish—laborers wore that shade of green, and no one but the Jorann wore white. Since no human belonged to any caste, his daughter's tutor should, by all logic, wear Suralia blue. Instead she wore a different color every day. It was... strange and exotic, much like the woman herself.

A pleasant hum filled the air. Marianne walked along the street, scanning the food at each booth, the little device blinking red. He followed, nodding at the cooks and the bystanders who bowed as he passed, observing as Marianne smiled and exchanged words with them.

"Phooey," she muttered, as she reached the last booth and the device still blinked red. The street opened onto another, smaller square, this one hosting entertainers. Her face brightened. "What is that?"

In the courtyard's center, a musician sat within a semi-circle of conical drums. He started up a beat, and a few heartbeats later dancers joined him, gyrating and leaping in a complicated pattern. Marianne hurried forward to stand with those watching the display, delight shooting through her.

He had not moved from the square's edge when the dancers finished their performance and the spectators formed a circle to dance around the drum musician. Kyza slept through it all, while the nurse stood beside him, keeping her senses fixed on her slumbering charge. Marianne returned, pleasure flashing in her eyes.

"Join them," he said.

She glanced back, biting her lower lip. He sensed longing in her. "I would need to learn the steps first," she replied.

"This dance is simple. I will teach you." He pulled the sling over his head, taking care not to wake his daughter, and gave her an empathic caress before leaving her cradled in the nurse's arms. "Come," he said, as he turned toward the circle dance.

The steps were, as he had said, simple, and Marianne danced with enthusiasm after a few repetitions. When she needed no further instruction, he gave himself up to the dance, relishing the rare opportunity to interact with ordinary Suralians.

* * *

MARIANNE LOUNGED IN A GARDEN GAZEBO, savoring the crispness in the air from the approaching autumn. The graceful pavilions in the garden had become her favorite place to spend time when she was not engaged with Kyza. The Sural had joined her to continue a discussion begun over the morning meal. Discussion finished, they had fallen silent, listening to the flutters singing and chattering in the cora trees.

The Sural lifted an eyebrow and gave her the penetrating look she'd found so unnerving when she first arrived. "What were you reading when I joined you?" he asked. In English. His accent sounded like a cross between Scandinavian and New Mandarin.

Her eyebrows tried to meet her hairline. "You speak English?" she exclaimed.

One side of his mouth tilted upward.

"When did you learn English?"

"The winter after your people first made contact with us."

"*How* did you learn it?"

"The A'aan' were happy to provide us with the learning materials," he said. "Just as they were happy to provide similar materials on our language to your people."

"Well," Marianne said. "Well." She blinked and opened her mouth again, but no other word came. She closed her mouth with a huff.

"Read to me from your tablet," he said. "One of your poets."

She spent another moment huffing at him, then at random chose a twenty-second century English poet, Gaidon Damerell, known for his exquisite sonnets about love and nature. The Sural leaned back against the gazebo, eyes closed and long legs stretched before him, listening with a small smile on his lips.

As she read, Marianne tried to stick to Damerell's poems about nature. Reading a love sonnet to the Sural seemed inappropriate, so she skipped those. When she stumbled into one that began on a pastoral theme but turned erotic, her voice hitched, and he opened an eye, his face impassive.

"What do you find disturbing?" he asked, still speaking English.

Blood rushed to her face. "It's... um... it's not appropriate," she stammered. "Not by human ethics. To, uh, discuss intimate topics with—with an employer. Or someone from a much different social class."

His eyes glinted. "Compared to my people's love poems, that was chaste."

"I would be more comfortable if you permitted me to choose another."

He shrugged a shoulder. "Proceed as you like."

* * *

In the autumn, Kyza turned into a noisy, grabby toddler who followed Marianne around the stronghold, chattering and babbling, switching from one language to another: the human languages Marianne had come to teach and the Sural's own dialect of Tolari. Marianne wondered if the tot believed she was her mother, but it was also obvious she adored her father. She preferred him to anyone else present, begging to be carried, rubbing her forehead on his cheek, crawling all over him when he sat. He tolerated it all—more than tolerated it, seemed to revel in it. He was gentle and patient with his active, curious daughter.

Winter brought treacherous temperatures, putting an end to time in the garden and, indeed, to any movement out of doors. Marianne's usual haunt moved to the guest wing common room, which contained a small library. Not all the books on the shelves were in the Sural's dialect, and Marianne began to spend her free time puzzling out books written in a simple dialect close enough to Suralian for her to understand it. When she felt she had mastered the language, she gave it a try on the Sural.

He eyed her with growing amusement as she spoke, then burst into the first honest laughter she'd heard from him. Sporting a crooked grin, he composed himself and said, "You sound like a Paranian. I shall have to find some books from Detralar. Detrali is even more amusing to most Tolari." He stifled a chuckle, his eyes sparkling.

"Why is that?" Marianne asked.

He shrugged a shoulder. "It is."

"You have—biases—on Tolar?"

"Not in the same way that you have explained human biases," he answered, "but we find our cultural differences highly entertaining."

"Hmm," she said.

He raised an eyebrow at her.

"Does anyone find Suralia... entertaining?" she asked.

His mouth twitched. "Not while I live," he answered.

Marianne laughed. The Sural watched her, mild amusement crossing his face.

"We do have a reputation," he continued.

"For what?"

"Coldness."

Marianne bit her tongue.

"Speak your thoughts, proctor."

"Um," she said. "I can see why."

He cocked his head.

"I mean—well—you all walk around looking disinterested and impassive most of the time, except during your festivals. You in particular—you're pretty emotionless."

The Sural lifted an eyebrow. "We are what we are. But I admit the plateau is a colder place now than it was in my grandmother's day."

Marianne's breath caught. "What happened to cause that?"

"The last attack. Everyone in the stronghold died."

That explained the gloom. "Oh." She rocked back on her heels. "Forgive me."

He waved it away with a hand and started to pace. "You would call it two generations ago," he said. "We have strengthened Suralia's defenses since that day. Another such attack could not succeed."

She bit her lip, a nasty sensation crawling up her spine, as the reality of Tolari interprovincial conflict smacked her in the face. He glanced over at her.

"Have no concern, proctor," he added. "My enemies in the ruling caste seldom make an attempt on me now. But even could an attack succeed, an invading ruler is more likely to capture and hold you than to harm you." He eyed her. "You are not one of us. Capture would not dishonor you."

"That's not comforting," she said.

"Human worry is needless. We prepare and do what needs to be done. And what needs to be done, perhaps, is to search my personal library for books in Detrali." He bowed, mouth twitching, and strode off.

Marianne dug into the books he brought back. It helped her mood to occupy her mind as the weather grew colder and the stronghold became entombed in ice and snow, but the dark and the cold grew pervasive and unsettling. Without the solace of the gardens and the chattering flutters, Marianne fell into a continuous gloomy mood.

She attributed it to the short days at first. The sun was in the sky for perhaps eight hours, rising after the morning meal and setting by the evening meal. After some thought, she realized she had been on Tolar for something more than a standard year, cut off from almost all contact with the ship. She had grown lonely, much to her own surprise. She'd never experienced much loneliness. School, college, and then her job as a high school teacher had kept her busy, and the social interactions of the teacher's break room, Tuesday night bowling, and, to a lesser extent, volunteer work and language practice in the Babel cloud's virtual parks and cafés, had fulfilled her slight needs —but none of those could be had on Tolar.

To her frustration, she couldn't find a way to socialize with the stronghold's other inhabitants. Both status and rank mattered to them. No one in the keep had anything like Marianne's combination of false rank and no status, and they didn't know how to respond to her. She had no common ground on which to strike up a friendship with the women among the servants, guards, nurses or cooks.

The Sural may have been content to live in splendid isolation, but she felt alone and cut off. And he seemed to sense it.

"Proctor, something oppresses you," he said, broaching the topic during the evening meal. They ate alone in the refectory.

"I'm fine," she said.

He raised an eyebrow, waiting with his usual patience. She fiddled with her food. She looked up to find him staring at her. "Forgive me, high one," she murmured.

He raised the other eyebrow. "For?"

"I don't need much, but—I need more..." she stumbled.

He cocked his head. "More of what?"

"I miss—I miss just... just talking with another woman." She winced. Talking about this made her feel naked. Taking a breath, she pressed on. "Girl talk. We—we need to talk to each other sometimes, just women. Unburden our hearts. I never realized before just how much I need it."

He nodded, a thoughtful look in his eyes. "I understand. By limiting your contact with the ship, I have deprived you of something you need to be content."

"I've always thought I didn't need anyone. I was happy by myself in Casey, living alone. I guess I wasn't as alone as I thought." She fell silent, staring past him, at the dark outside the windows.

Something like compassion warmed his expression. "Very well," he said. "For the sake of Kyza's tutor, there shall have to be less peace in the Sural's airwaves. You may contact your ship each day when it is in orbit."

She turned back to him, a huge smile bursting onto her face. "Truly?" she blurted.

"Indeed. It would be best if you chose a regular hour to do so."

"Thank you, high one," she said, and jumped up to run off to her quarters. Once there, with shaking hands, she powered on the comms and explained her call.

"Who won the Super Six?" was her first question when Adeline Russell came on the screen.

Adeline's eyebrows shot up. "That's the *first* thing you want to know?"

Marianne nodded. "I *love* interplanetary pro cycling."

"Just a second, I'll look it up." Adeline looked away from Marianne for a moment. "Brad Yates."

"*Yes!*" Marianne exclaimed. "He looked *so* promising before I left!"

Adeline just shook her head. "Whatever makes you happy," she muttered.

"What about my friend Susan? Do you know if she's… I don't know, angry with me, for not calling?"

"You shouldn't have told your friends you would keep in touch," Adeline said with a frown, "but yes, she's fine. She's dating the Spanish teacher we sent to replace you."

Marianne blinked. "What, really? What's he like? Is he treating her right?"

Adeline laughed. "Relax, Marianne, he's perfect for her, all sexy and Spanish."

"A real Spaniard?" Marianne broke into laughter. "That's perfect!

At least he's not the boy next door. She really didn't want to marry him."

Thereafter, Marianne called the ship, if it was in orbit, every morning after transmitting written reports to the admiral and the ambassador—if it wasn't too late in the night, ship's time. The ship patrolled nearby for three terrestrial months at a time, then headed back near Earth for a month. When the *Alexander* orbited the planet, it helped Marianne keep track of Earth time. She was prone to lose track on Tolar, where the twenty-five hour days threw her off and the Tolari counted time in terms of seasons or years, if they counted it at all.

For most communications, she chatted with Adeline, who functioned as the ambassador's administrative aide. When Adeline was unavailable, she spoke with the admiral's calm and motherly wife Laura who, though not the brightest star in the sky, was insightful and wise. Laura had children Marianne's age and could see right through her. That was a little disconcerting, so she preferred to chat with Adeline—or Addie, as she wished to be called.

"Kyza is learning to eat at the refectory table with us," she told Adeline on one winter morning when the temperatures in Suralia fell lower than usual. "Though all she does is climb all over the table, grabbing and chewing on her daddy's food, while her nurses have to scramble to keep her from falling on her head."

Adeline laughed. "She sounds indulged."

"You could say she's a bit spoiled," Marianne admitted. "But the Sural doesn't let her do anything that would bring her to harm. She's not allowed outside the keep, however much she wants to go play in the snow. The cold out there is dangerous, even for them. Deep winter, they call it. And the glaciers are growing. They don't make it to the stronghold plateau, but they're close enough."

"I see you're wearing a Tolari robe," Adeline teased. "You're not going native on us, are you?"

Marianne shook her head, laughing. "It's cold in the stronghold—well, to me anyway—and these robes are warmer than anything I brought with me."

"Really?"

"There could be a good market for this fabric on ice worlds. Something to think about trading for, or maybe teaching them to mass produce. I don't know what it's made of—the Sural becomes cagey when I ask. It feels thin and lightweight, like silk, but it's fantastically warm. I'm wearing a pair of their slippers, too, though they don't fit right in the toe. Tolari don't have toes."

"What huh?"

"Imagine if the skin between your toes all fused together but the bones were still there, with the same joints. Still useful for balance because the big toe bone is the same, but less individual flexibility. They can't bend just one part, the whole assembly flaps. And they don't call them feet. They call them peds."

"Huh," Adeline said again. Marianne could see her making notes. "How'd you find this out?"

"Kyza used to pull off her slippers to suck on her peds. And chew on them too, but she stopped doing that when she started getting teeth." Marianne grinned, remembering the surprise on Kyza's face the first time she bit herself.

"Looks like you're happy down there."

"It's tolerable," Marianne said.

"No, you're happy, I can tell."

"Addie, now you're as bad as Laura."

Adeline laughed.

* * *

THE SURAL LEANED back at his desk, thrumming with satisfaction. His daughter's tutor *was* happy, now that she had the social contact she required. She had emerged from her gloom and smiled her captivating smile more often. An image of that smile played across his mind's eye, and his own lips curved of their own accord.

He shook himself. She still hid something, though she was not a trained operative. It was obvious she had been ordered to report everything she learned—he had expected Central Command to use any human they sent as a passive spy—but she lacked any covert training. No, something troubled and even pained Marianne. He could sense it when it came to the surface now and again.

On occasion, he attempted to lead her into talking about it, but when the subject turned to adolescence and relationships, she would become evasive and close down her emotions. He was convinced she had never formed an intimate attachment with another individual. In fact, she seemed to have no attraction at all to others. *The Spinster*

Schoolmarm, he had heard her call herself, for all that she was so young by his people's standards—twenty-eight human years was a season less than fourteen on Tolar, barely past childhood on a world where the young came of age at thirteen.

His thoughts turned to Kyza. His daughter delighted all who came into contact with her. In the family wing's privacy, he could play with her and let her laugh with abandon. He wished he could share that with Marianne, but what he did not wish the humans on the ship to know, he could not allow her to see. It might force her into choosing between her loyalty to her people and her growing loyalty to himself, at least for the present, and it necessitated keeping his own emotions under tight control so that Kyza never displayed strong feelings when Marianne was present. He regretted the deception, but the humans had to continue believing for now that his people were cold and heartless. They would learn otherwise soon enough, but it suited his purposes to delay the revelation.

Kyza began to stir, sending tendrils of need through the parental bond he shared with her, unusual as it was for a father to be bonded to an heir so young. In the normal course of their development, infants bonded to the women who bore them, regardless of whose heir they were, for their first six or seven seasons of life if they were boys and closer to ten seasons if they were girls, but the woman who mothered Kyza had died soon after giving birth. The tragedy had forced him to attempt bonding with his newborn daughter.

The leader of Suralia's science caste, a woman of great strength and intellectual genius, had mothered Kyza. Her consent to his request for an heir represented a great honor, but he had not chosen her for high caste rank. Genetic analysis indicated she could give him an exceptional child—one who could, perhaps, survive the great trial. That had been his primary consideration—but he had not expected it to cost the woman her life.

By law, because he belonged to the ruling caste, she had lived in his stronghold while she increased, joined by her heir and her bond-partner. The same law would have required her to continue there until Kyza was ready to transfer her bond to him—had the woman lived.

He had been present, as stunned as the apothecary—who expected to save her—when the woman had succumbed to shock after suffering a massive hemorrhage during the birth. His daughter then, on instinct, tried to follow her into the dark. Shaking himself out of the empathic daze death could cause the unprepared, he had wrapped his senses around Kyza and surrounded her with love before she could shut herself down. She had struggled against him like a flutter trying to escape a net, seeking to follow the mother she knew in the womb.

He had refused to let go, and the contest of wills had continued for much of a day. Kyza was exhausted and close to the dark when she turned back and bonded to him, allowing him to comfort and cradle her into a warm, contented glow. She had opened her eyes and lived. He had wept with joy, even while the woman's bond-partner had sobbed in devastated grief and followed his beloved that night into the dark.

It was a pity he needed the humans to believe his people were cold and emotionless.

CHAPTER 5

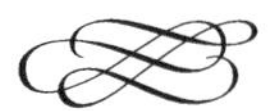

Midnight. Marianne ran through a cornfield, lungs burning, terror forcing whimpers from her throat. Running as fast as she could, she dodged among the corn stalks, trying to slip out of sight, trying to lose her pursuer. Faster—faster—heedless of the leaves slashing at her face and her bare arms. Then her foot caught on a clod of earth and she sprawled on her face in the fragrant soil.

She screamed and scrambled to her feet. The Sural would protect her. The Sural had promised to protect her. The Sural... where was the Sural? Marianne searched the darkness as she ran and found him, far down the row, turning to look at her. She reached out her arms to him just as her ankle twisted in the shallow rut formed by a fallen cornstalk, throwing her to the ground a second time. She screamed again and woke with a cry, a red haze fading into the darkness before her eyes. Panting, sweat pouring from her body, she sat up and remembered where she was: in an alien stronghold, on an alien world, where there were no cornrows and no one to chase her through them.

The Sural awoke with a start and sat bolt upright, staring into the darkness, through the walls, straight across the stronghold to the spot where Marianne lay asleep in her quarters—or rather should have been. She was awake, radiating psychic agony.

He had felt her reach out to him. He could feel her now, wanting him to protect her from... something. Something evil that had happened to her long ago. He reached out to her through the tenuous connection she had—astoundingly—forged across the night, letting strength and comfort flow through it, hoping she would not sense it was him.

Marianne slumped back onto her sleeping mat and dug the heels of her palms into her eyes. In the space behind her eyes, she could almost see the Sural looking at her. Desperate for any sort of contact, even imaginary, she let herself sink into thoughts of him, imagining him holding her close to comfort her, imagining—

NO! Every fiber of her being screamed, shutting down the fantasy with a snap. She arched her back and slammed her head and fists into her mat, eyes squeezed shut. Then she curled into a tight ball of desolation and sobbed.

Guards all over the stronghold flickered from the empathic blast, and the Sural's head whirled in pain, his senses scalded. Kyza woke, screaming in fright, seeking her bond with him. He scooped her up from her cot to cradle her in his arms, soothing her, heedless of his burned, aching senses. Working to shield Kyza from his own pain, he communed with her, letting awareness of the surroundings slip away as Kyza drew strength from him.

Marianne had accepted comfort from him, if only for a moment. What had triggered the terror and the powerful emotional blast, he could only wonder. It had to be connected to the pain she hid. He was convinced of it.

* * *

DURING THE NEXT morning's meal, Kyza interrupted her busy exploration of the high table to throw herself into the Sural's lap and curl up against his chest. He cradled her there, eyes closed, allowing her to commune with him despite Marianne's presence at the table. After a few long moments, Kyza pulled away and climbed back onto the table, taking some of his meal with her.

When he opened his eyes, Marianne gazed at him with a wistful expression. He smiled at her. Lack of sleep tinted her eyes red, and he could see signs that she had wept.

"Rest today," he said in sudden decision. "Ask a servant to show you to the library. The one in the family wing."

"Yes, high one," she said, nodding, weariness in her voice.

"I cannot stay." He stood and gathered up Kyza. "I must work. Are you distressed?"

"I'm fine. I'm just tired. I didn't sleep well."

"Perhaps you should have a talk with Adeline Russell or Laura Howard."

She gave one of her odd, two-shouldered human shrugs and made a visible effort to brighten up, offering him a tired smile.

"I'm fine, honest," she said. "And I've already spoken with Adeline this morning, but thank you for giving me the day off."

He made a slight bow and left, taking Kyza with him.

In truth, his duties were light at this time of year. His people became sluggish, distracted, and sleepy during deep winter, when the days were short and the cold deadly, and they accomplished little anywhere in the province. He himself needed no stimulants to remain alert, but most of his advisors did. He had little use for them in their winter lethargy, so each year he drew up plans for the spring during the previous autumn. Since the winter had set in, he had no duties beyond overseeing the stronghold's day-to-day operations. Those few of his aides who remained alert kept an eye on activities in the southern hemisphere and sent him reports if alliances shifted. It was always a restful season, in which he could study or indulge in pastimes.

He handed his daughter to a nurse and camouflaged, returning to the refectory as Marianne finished her meal. She asked a servant to show her to the library, as he had suggested. When she disappeared around the passageway's curve, he dropped his camouflage and went to his study to read the small number of reports waiting for him.

* * *

When the short day dawned, the Sural strolled into the library to see how Marianne fared. She hunched over a book, so absorbed she failed to notice him enter the room. He sent a delicate probe into her surface emotions and found she was using the book to soothe herself. He scuffed a ped against the matting.

She looked up at the sound and turned, a wan smile coming to her lips when she saw him. He took a seat across the table and glanced at the book she held.

"Vetralen is a modern poet," he said. "He still lives. Very good."

"Have you read his work?" she asked.

He ignored the question. "What happened in the night?" he asked instead.

She paled. "You know about that?"

"You woke most of the stronghold."

She winced, and he sensed disbelief mixing into chagrin, embarrassment, and... fear. "Forgive me, high one."

"What was it?" he persisted.

"A—" She stopped, lips parted, then clamped her jaw shut and frowned. "Nightmare," she said in English. "A bad dream," she continued. "Very bad dream."

He let his expression soften. "Tell me," he said.

"I was—" He sensed her consider trust, but a surge of anxiety wiped it away. "Forgive me, high one," she continued. "I would rather not talk about it."

His heart contracting, he suppressed the heavy sigh her distrust inspired and tried a different tactic. "A strange word, *nightmare*," he said.

She nodded, relief shuddering through her at the change of subject. "It comes from *mara*, a Scandinavian word for a spirit sent to suffocate people in their sleep. But many English speakers imagine the nightmare of myth and legend as a dark horse with glowing eyes and flaming hooves, bearing evil dreams."

"You have many animals on Earth."

"Yes, millions of species. The largest live in the oceans."

"And your people sometimes bring animals into their homes," he said. "I find this difficult to imagine."

She grinned. "Dogs or cats, often both. Birds are common, so are fish, sometimes rodents, even reptiles, insects, arachnids." She laughed a little. "I guess it must seem pretty strange to you."

He nodded. "We have no land animals larger than a scurrybrush," he said. "However, we do have immense creatures in our oceans."

Her face grew wistful as she seemed to sink into memory. "I had a dog when I was a girl. A pug."

He raised an inquiring eyebrow at the unfamiliar English word.

"A breed of dog," she explained. She sighed. "My little Gretchen. I loved that dog."

"Gretchen?"

"My dog. That was her name."

"You gave it a name?" Both the Sural's eyebrows tried to reach his hairline, and his eyes went wide.

She laughed. "Of course."

"I am perplexed."

Amusement displaced some of her weary sadness. "Sometimes I forget you're an alien," she said. Then she remembered where she was. "To me. You look so human." The atmosphere grew awkward.

He lifted a shoulder. "You look Tolari," he countered, his face unreadable.

Marianne swallowed. "So, high one," she said, trying to get past the awkwardness, "do you still want your daughter tutored by a woman who would sleep with a dog?"

He smiled. "Yes, proctor, but why would you want to sleep with an animal?" It surprised her to see him shudder a little.

"I don't know." She tilted her head to one side. "We just—I don't know. Maybe it's just the comfort of touching another warm, living being. Touch is important for us, and it's vital when we're children. Our babies can die if they aren't held enough."

"And your adults?"

"Adults can live without it."

"But not well."

"I don't know about that," she said. "I do just fine."

He cocked an eyebrow.

"I do!" she protested.

He inclined his head. "As you say," he yielded.

She grumbled, shifting in her chair and twitching her shoulders, then sighed.

"Read to me," he said.

He inflected it as a request, not a command, but she was happy to carry it out. Reading to him reminded her of poetry exchanges in the Babel cloud. "Of course, high one."

Grateful that Vetralen composed nothing but delicate word pictures of nature scenes, she chose a poem describing the High Fralentolar Mountains. The Sural leaned back, closed his eyes, and stretched out his long legs.

He must be bored senseless, she thought as she read, some of the tension draining from the muscles in her neck and shoulders. She took a deep breath, grateful for the relief. Perhaps that was why he'd asked her to read to him: it relaxed her.

Something flickered at the corner of her eye. "What was that?" she said in English, putting down the book.

"A guard." The Sural's eyes opened and fixed on her.

She swiveled in her chair, searching the room, but saw nothing. "There are guards in here?"

His face became bland. "Yes, two in this room. They are camouflaged."

"Where else do you have guards?" Her hands started to shake.

The Sural gave her a sharp glance, his eyes darkening with concern. "There is nowhere in the stronghold out of range of a guard. The safety of the Sural and his daughter—and his guest, the human tutor—all demand it."

"They're everywhere? In *every* room?"

"Yes, every room."

Her heart seemed to stop. "You mean—you mean there are guards in my *sleeping room?*"

"Yes, of course."

"And—and they've watched me dress, and bathe, and—and—" Her throat closed.

"Proctor." His voice was low and soothing. "For us this is a comfort, not a source of distress."

Her stomach clenched. "We'll just have to agree to disagree about that." She grated the words out.

"Why does this anger you?" He rubbed his eyebrows.

"I've been exposing myself to them every time I change my clothes or bathe!" she exclaimed. "And—and how many of them are *men*?" She jammed her hands into her armpits to stop their shaking.

"Proctor," he said, his voice still gentle, "your government informed me before you arrived that some humans have modesty inhibitions and that you may be one of them. The guards in your quarters are women."

Marianne took a deep breath and expelled it, letting her hands fall into her lap. She slumped back in her chair, feeling foolish. "Oh," she said. "Oh. Thank you, high one."

"My honor," he murmured.

She looked up at him and said, "I'm sorry." She looked away, stifling the grumble that tried to escape.

He smiled and gestured toward the door. “The guard was reminding me it is time for the midday meal. Would you accompany me?”

“Yes, high one,” she said, getting to her feet.

His enigmatic smile appeared. It was maddening.

CHAPTER 6

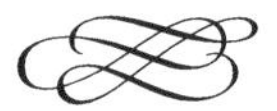

The arctic cold of Suralia's deep winter gave way to the beginning of spring and its more survivable temperatures. The flutters emerged from the hollow interior of the cora trees, waking from their winter hibernation, and new growth began to poke through the snow. Marianne stood at her sitting room window, watching Kyza show her father a bemittened hand full of snow. On this morning, the Sural had taken his daughter outside to frolic in the garden before the morning meal. Kyza was a few months short of two standard years now, and she'd become inquisitive, fearless, and most of all, verbal. While Marianne couldn't hear what the Sural and his daughter said to each other, Kyza's lips moved without a pause.

Grinning, Marianne turned away from the window and activated the comms unit. It was time to contact the *Alexander*.

Adeline seemed in a mood to tease. After the preliminaries of confirming the ambassador had received Marianne's written report, she didn't waste any time getting down to it.

"The Sural spent an awful lot of time with you when the stronghold was socked in with ice and snow," she said.

"He doesn't have much work during the winter," Marianne replied. "They let up on their plotting and scheming when the weather closes in—it's not honorable to take advantage of a sluggish and sleepy enemy. No sport in it. All he has to do is run the stronghold and read a few reports. Talking to me was probably more interesting than watching the frost creep up the walls."

Adeline laughed. "I just bet it was," she replied. "Especially to a man."

"Addie! He's an alien!"

"He's a pretty handsome alien, if you ask me. Like classic Greek god handsome. Don't tell me you never noticed?"

Marianne pressed her lips together and grumbled. "It's unprofessional."

"You know, being gods didn't stop them from dallying with beautiful human women—and you're pretty enough to qualify. Maybe the Greek gods were the Tolari gone space-faring, and the Sural is just biding time before he becomes a dark Adonis and sweeps you off your feet. Or actually, he's their ruler—maybe he's Zeus."

"Nonsense!" Marianne's face heated. "He treats me as if he were a monk. He might be one, for all I know—I never see his wife, or concubine, or whoever Kyza's mother is. He never so much as lays a finger on me. He's very careful."

Adeline's lips formed an O. "Ooh, *careful.* That sounds promising." She winked.

"Addie! It's not appropriate! He's my employer, and anyway, I'm just a schoolteacher descended from generations of dirt farmers."

"Suit yourself," Adeline said with a shrug. "But if it were me—I'd get a little closer to see what happens."

"You're a minx, Addie," Marianne scolded.

Adeline sighed and struck a pose with the back of one hand on her forehead. "My secret is out!" she exclaimed in dramatic tones. Then she leaned toward the monitor and said in a low voice, "It's a good thing Smitty can keep up with me, or I might just come down there and try to take that Sural of yours away from you."

More blood rushed to Marianne's face, and Adeline's laugh turned gleeful.

"Oh Marianne, you're so much fun to tease. You and Laura. You both blush so predictably."

Marianne forced herself to laugh and turned her head toward the door to the hall as if someone stood there. "I have to go now, Addie. Say hi to Laura for me, will you? Tell her I'd like to talk to her tomorrow."

"I'll do that."

* * *

A FEW DAYS after the spring festival, the Sural announced he would accompany a group of laborers back to a tea flower plantation not far from the city. Since he intended to take Kyza with him, he asked Marianne to come along.

Marianne packed a bag and hurried into the corridor. The Sural stood near the great doors, opened to the morning sunlight, with Kyza slung across his back and drumming on his head. Two nurses and several servants gathered just outside, all carrying packs or shoulder bags.

The Sural set a pace the rest of the party could match and still be able to maintain a quiet conversation. The trek down the cliffs Marianne knew well, but rather than continue south into the city, they joined up with a farmer and a party of wandering agricultural laborers, all in dark green robes, and turned west onto a packed dirt road. The vegetation changed, becoming scrubby as they left the city environs and headed into the hills of Suralia.

Small creatures lurked in the bushes. She caught occasional glimpses of them breaking from cover when one of the party wandered too near a hiding place. Most were furry animals resembling six-legged squirrels. Some bounded away like tiny kangaroos. A few turned out to be ground-nesting flutters. Kyza squealed at each one.

"Fafee!" she cried, pointing and bouncing in the sling. "What that? What that?"

The Sural named the creature for her, and she went back to making a mess of his hair. Marianne made a mental note of the names for future reference. The stronghold library might have a book on local fauna.

The party reached the banks of a river at late morning. It coursed through a valley filled with orderly rows of bushy, waist-high plants, punctuated by groups of cora trees.

"Tea flower," the Sural said. "And the cora trees will be familiar to you. We will stay on this plantation until the trees are netted."

"Why do you net the trees?" she asked.

"To save the fruit from the flutters."

The road crossed the river at a graceful stone bridge, passed through the tea flower plants—which didn't possess anything Marianne could identify as flowers or flower buds among their spiky foliage—and turned north to run along the steep hills on the other side. A few stone buildings with tile roofs dotted the lowest of the hills.

The farmers served a midday meal when the group arrived. The servants who'd come with the Sural unpacked their shoulder bags and packs, revealing cloth-wrapped packages of medicines and seeds, which were carefully laid away in the nearby dwellings. Meanwhile, the oldest of the stronghold servants set about cleaning and reknotting the Sural's hair, which Kyza had smeared with her midmorning snack as well as pulled in all directions. Two farmers living on the plantation had small children, who discovered Kyza with much noise and enthusiasm. The three crowded together to eat under the tables, monitored by the nurses.

After the meal, the work began.

The laborers carried large woven nets from low storage buildings beyond the hilltop and laid them in piles near the clusters of trees. Then came the really interesting part, to Marianne's mind—the children ran around a tree, shrieking and flapping and scaring off the flutters, at which point the laborers used long wooden poles to fling the nets over the tree. They repeated the process until all but one tree in the cluster lay covered—for the flutters' sake, the Sural explained.

When the children grew tired, the servants took their place, using tubes of a strange, flexible wood to beat the trees and frighten the bird-like creatures into the air. Marianne joined in, wielding one of the light-weight tubes like a sword and provoking smiles and laughs from the Suralians.

By the end of the afternoon, they had netted three clusters of trees. After the evening meal, everyone hiked to the next hill. It boasted a crown of stone seats around a bare circle of dirt, in which the servants built a fire.

When darkness fell, the singing began.

* * *

THE SURAL STOOD in the darkness, camouflaged and barriers shut. His daughter lay abed, walking the far shores of sleep in a pile with the other two children. Everyone else—save one nurse watching the children—sat around the fire singing. He lingered in the shadows to observe.

Two farmers, a man and a woman, traded turns singing the verses. He positioned himself where he could make out Marianne's voice among the others as the entire group sang the refrain—with her eidetic memory for language, she had learned the refrain on its first occurrence and joined in on the second. She sang, and laughed, and he had never seen her so relaxed. When the laborer sitting at her right hand rose and left the circle during a lull in the singing, the Sural wasted no time taking the man's place.

"Where have you been?" she asked, her voice resonant with high humor.

He smiled—she was very relaxed, indeed. "Watching."

She snorted.

"Do you enjoy yourself?" he asked.

"Very much. Netting the trees looked like a lot of work, though. Is the fruit that important?"

He shook his head. "Not the fruit—the seed within. Its oil cures a plant disease that can destroy several important crops."

"Oh I see. So you do this every year?"

"Not I. My father used to bring me here as a boy, but I have not returned since I took power. The Suralia my grandmother preferred to visit the plantations farther north and west toward Detralar, in the Kentar Valley."

He stared into the fire and leaned forward, elbows on his knees, fingers laced.

"High one?"

He swiveled his head toward her, and his heart gave a hard thud. Marianne's eyes reflected the firelight, and her hair, loose around her face, glowed. His mouth went dry.

"I just realized—you didn't bring any guards," she said. "Aren't you in danger?"

He gathered his scattered thoughts. "No," he replied. "Not at present."

She sighed. "I will never understand Tolari politics."

"Perhaps you will, in time."

Across the fire, someone began to sing.

* * *

WHEN EARLY SUMMER ARRIVED, Kyza stopped climbing on the refectory tables and found a new game.

"Fafee!" she cried one morning, standing on a chair to lean against the table toward her father.

"Yes, Kyza?" He looked up from his meal.

Kyza took a deep breath—and disappeared.

The Sural lit up. "Kyza!" he exclaimed with a huge, delighted smile, pride written all over his face. Kyza popped back into view, giggling and laughing so hard she nearly fell off her chair. He stood and swept her into his arms, taking her out of the refectory with a swoop and a spin.

Marianne watched them go, eyes wide, jaw slack. Kyza's giggles retreated down the corridor.

That was... normal, she thought.

* * *

THE SURAL COULD NOT CONTAIN his grin. Kyza was young to have discovered how to camouflage. He hurried her to her nursery and played camouflage games, pretending to be unable to sense her when she flickered out of sight and exclaiming in surprise when she reappeared, until she exhausted herself and fell into a doze on his shoulder.

Such a precious gift, he thought, as he laid her in her cot. He did wish Marianne had not been present. She had radiated surprise, even shock, at his display, and it had certainly hastened the day when she would realize he was not what he seemed. Still, to have shared an honest moment with her was itself something to cherish. He could not regret it.

Kyza sighed and rolled over in her sleep. Smiling, he smoothed her blankets. He *could not* have failed to respond to her accomplishment. It was a significant one, and she had needed his approval more than he needed to hide his heart from Marianne. A thrill ran through him. Kyza would be a challenge, learning to camouflage so young—a mere five seasons!—but he could be nothing less than proud.

It was time to begin her training. Leaving his daughter asleep under the watchful eyes of her nurses, he set off to inform the family tutor, Proctor Storaas.

* * *

THE OLDEST TOLARI MARIANNE had ever seen joined her in the library the next day. White-haired, upright, and dignified, he greeted her with a smile full of wrinkles and a precision to his movements that reminded her of her grandfather. Unlike Gramps, he carried his thin frame with an air of gentle sadness. Kyza ran to tug on his dark indigo robe.

"'Raas!" she squealed. "'Raas! 'Raas!"

He picked her up and gave her a warm hug, then set her back down and turned to Marianne.

"I am Storaas," he said, in English—which surprised Marianne not at all.

He took a wooden box from a shoulder bag he'd brought with him. Kyza's attention riveted on the box as he set it on a table, and she climbed onto a chair to see what it contained. He opened it to reveal stacks of square, wooden tiles the size of Kyza's palms and as thick as one of her fingers. Each tile had a symbol from the Tolari syllabary burned into it.

"You have an unusual name," Marianne said.

"Indeed." He smiled and stacked a few tiles in front of Kyza, naming them as he did. "It comes from another time and another place."

"You're not Suralian?"

The question brought a chuckle from him. He stacked a few more tiles for Kyza, naming them as well. Some had tooth marks. "Yes, I am Suralian. I have taught several generations of Suralia's rulers."

Kyza giggled and scattered the tiles across the table.

"My activities with Kyza will resemble play," he continued. "I will also teach her games of camouflage."

Marianne frowned. "From what I've seen, camouflage exhausts her."

"Yes, of course. She is hardly more than an infant."

"But if she—"

"Have no concern, proctor," he interrupted. "Continue with your teaching. For now, I will occupy her when she grows restive or bored."

"I see." She leaned against the table and helped Kyza gather up the tiles she'd scattered, glancing at the old man. If he'd taught Suralia's rulers for generations, he must have taught the Sural. She tried to imagine the Sural as a boy or as a young man, happy and outgoing perhaps, before he became the somber man she knew. The thought struck her that she preferred the Sural distant and emotionless—as he hadn't been the day before, when Kyza had camouflaged for him. That said something about herself she wasn't sure she liked.

Storaas laid a gentle hand, gnarled and papery, on her shoulder. Quiet reassurance spread through her. She blinked and peered first at the hand, then at his face.

He removed the hand from her shoulder with an unreadable look. "Forgive me, proctor," he said with an apologetic bow. "I did not mean to intrude."

* * *

"Forgive me, high one," Storaas told the Sural. "She is bewitching. I forgot myself. An old man's mistake."

The Sural sat at his desk in the open study off the audience room. The old proctor had come to him of his own accord and admitted he'd laid a hand on Marianne's shoulder against the Sural's explicit orders that no one, *no one,* touched the human proctor.

You need the Jorann's blessing, old friend, the Sural thought. *You are too old to grow careless.*

Aloud, he asked, "What did you sense in her?"

"A deep pain, high one," the old man said. "She carries a profound wound. I have never seen the like."

The Sural tapped his fingertips together in front of him. "Tell me more."

"She does not fear me. I get a sense that I remind her of someone who loved her, perhaps a father figure of some kind, but I have not studied human family relationships well enough to say."

"Excellent," he murmured. "Is that all?"

"No, high one."

"And?"

"And she fears you."

The Sural shook his head and allowed himself to look grieved.

In an amused tone, the old man continued, "But she does find you —attractive."

The Sural raised an eyebrow. He had never sensed any indication Marianne felt attracted to anyone, much less to himself, but Storaas was renowned for his unusual sensitivity and ability to read others. If he sensed it, it was there.

"She fears you because of it," the old man finished.

He sat back. He had sensed anxiety in abundance, but never fear. Had a fear he did not sense been the reason he had so far failed to gain her trust?

"That makes no sense," he said. "Are you certain?"

"Nothing is *certain*, high one. Perhaps fear is too strong a word. Anxiety may be a better one. But yes, I am confident of my abilities."

"Astonishing." He had sensed her anxiety many times, always leading down into the deeper pain she hid. "Did you sense what it is she hides?"

Storaas spread his hands. "I cannot say more without further study. I am no apothecary, and ignorance of human psychology limits what I can tell you with any certainty. And I do not expect the humans to share their psychological information with us soon."

The Sural began tapping his fingertips together again. He had no honorable method to gain access to the humans' data archives. Unless... in his role as leader of the ruling caste, he had jurisdiction over Tolari space—and everything in it. He sent a summons.

Storaas stirred.

"Speak," said the Sural.

"Do not approach her, high one. Let her come to you."

"Explain."

"I cannot explain," he said, spreading his hands again in apology. "I knew it as soon as I touched her. You must let her come to you. If you pursue her, you will frighten her."

The Sural pondered. He could do worse than to trust the old man's advice. "Very well," he said. "I will wait."

"It will be a long wait."

"I am a patient man." He paused. "Proctor, when suitable opportunities present themselves, read her and report to me."

"Yes, high one."

A man in the dark brown robes of the science caste entered the room and stood waiting for the Sural to speak.

"I want you to determine if you can scan and copy the human ship's data archives without being detected," the Sural told him.

"I am not confident it can be done. I can defeat their protections, but not without alerting them."

"Look into it further. I want access to their medical information."

CHAPTER 7

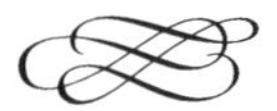

Marianne stood at a window in the family library, five standard years into her assignment—her second autumn on Tolar. The trees, bushes, and groundcover had turned yellow late in the season, preparing for the long winter. Kyza had become a little girl, and she held her father if not captive to her every whim, at least subject to them. Marianne herself found it difficult to deny the child anything. Only Storaas resisted her manipulations. The old proctor had tutored the children of too many Suralian rulers—no one could connive him into anything, not even a talented, beautiful, and charming child.

Storaas had directed a guard to search for Kyza when she burst out of hiding with a piercing shriek and flung herself at Marianne, clinging to one of her legs.

"Kyza, *NO*!" the old tutor boomed in deep, authoritative tones, gesturing to the guard, who sprinted out of the room. Marianne's stomach twisted in panic for no definable reason, and she reached down to pat the girl's head. "No!" Storaas barked, to Marianne this time.

Marianne jerked the hand back and looked up. "Why? What's wrong?"

"This is a matter in which you cannot become involved." His voice dropped to a low and intense pitch. "Do not move. Do not attempt to comfort her."

The Sural burst into view in the doorway, striding toward them. He dropped to his knees on the floor matting and pried his daughter from Marianne's leg. Once he had broken Kyza's hold, Marianne's stomach stopped twisting. Kyza flung her arms around her father's neck.

"Fafee, I am alone! All alone!" she cried into his robes.

"*Nuun*," he murmured, his eyes closing. "I am here now."

"Come, proctor," Storaas said in a low voice. "We must leave them." He took an arm and pulled her along with him out into the corridor, giving Kyza a wide berth. Marianne looked back at father and daughter. The Sural held Kyza in a gentle hug, eyes closed, but Marianne's skin still prickled from the wild panic in the air.

The Sural's face drained of expression and became serene. He was handsome enough to make a woman's heart ache. Why hadn't she noticed it before? Her own heart tightened, and she squashed the thought altogether. *That* was unprofessional.

* * *

KYZA'S EMOTIONS surged as she beat her senses against the Sural. With gentle ease, he caught her and wrapped his own senses around hers, holding her fast. The world faded, leaving only his small daughter, clinging to him and drawing on his strength with a tenacity and fierceness that swelled his heart with pride. *So strong*. And she was *his* child—*his* continuation—*his* legacy. Instinct sent his senses questing outward, seeking adults close enough to interfere and try to take her from him, and found two guards. He turned toward the nearest and scowled.

* * *

STORAAS GUIDED the human tutor to safety in the corridor, relieved that bonding with his daughter occupied too much of the Sural's attention for him to notice the woman's flash of desire—Tolar's captivated leader needed no further encouragement. As he led the object of his ruler's infatuation away, two guards flew out the door of the library, where the Sural remained with his daughter. Storaas chuckled.

"What was that all about?" the human proctor asked, turning toward him.

"Let us walk in the garden," he said, ignoring the question and heading out a nearby exit.

"All right." She followed him into the morning sunshine, and he sensed annoyance rising in her. Her voice rang with it as she added, "You Tolari, you have a lot more going on under the surface than you let me see."

He released her arm and picked an autumn flower from the groundcover, holding it close to his face and taking a deep breath of its sweet fragrance. "A pity you cannot smell this. It is quite lovely."

Her annoyance gave way to curiosity. "Is that an allegory?" she asked.

"Human senses are quite dull compared to ours," he continued, hoping she might make the conceptual leap from comparing physical senses to other, less obvious, ones.

A thoughtful look crossed her face. Then she shivered. It was a brisk autumn morning—which, he remembered, must seem quite cold to her. He turned to her and smiled.

"Come, child." He colored his voice with paternal affection. "I forget you consider this weather cold. Take my arm."

She let him take her hand. He tucked it into his elbow as they continued down the wandering path. Focusing on her, he angled toward a gazebo and strolled at a slow pace as he sorted through the many and varied emotions flowing through her. Gentle and harmless, with a bit of temper, he thought, touching around the edges of the buried pain. *She tries to hide this even from herself.* He probed into it. Violation and fear of death wove through a tight ball of anguish. He had never seen anything like it.

"Had you friends on Earth?" he asked. "Do you miss them?" Her emotions swirled into a complex mixture of surprise, longing, and a touch of homesickness. No intimate feelings rose—she was not entwined with anyone on her home planet.

She nodded. "Why do you ask?"

"The Sural would not have you be unhappy."

The mention of the Sural sent a cascade of unsettled emotion through her, attraction warring with anxiety. The girl clamped down on herself, not even aware of what she did. He rubbed his chin with his free hand and glanced at her. The time the Sural had spent with her had had a deep effect. If she were Tolari, she would have long since shared her blanket with him—but intimacy terrified this child, with a deep and reflexive terror. He guided her into a gazebo and assisted her to a seat, taking the one opposite her.

She radiated gratitude and stopped shivering. The gazebo, though open, was warm.

"I remind you of someone," he said.

She smiled and nodded. "Gramps," she replied. "My grandfather—my mother's father. He worked as an... account-keeper—very bookish, like you."

Storaas returned the smile. "You are your mother's heir, then?"

"I suppose you could say that," she answered. "I was an only child."

"An only child?"

"My parents had no other children," she explained. "I was the only one."

"Ah, I see. A human two-parent family."

"Yes, exactly."

"Why then did they not have two children," he asked, "to give themselves an heir for each?"

She pulled her smile sideways. "We don't think of it that way. Humans just have children—however many they decide to have. Some people don't have any, other people have a lot, or any number in between. It's up to them."

"How peculiar. Should Kyza pass her trials and become the Sural's heir, he will not have another child."

Marianne laughed. "How would you know how many children he'll have?"

"It is our law. He can have but one heir."

She sobered. "Truly? What happens if she dies before he does?"

"He would be permitted another child. It is not only his right, but also his duty. Suralia must continue."

"What about you, do you have an heir?"

He fell silent for a moment. "No," he replied, focusing on her. "And I am too old for that now," he added. "Do you plan no child for yourself?"

"No." Her response snapped out almost before he finished speaking. As if she realized she'd revealed something of her anxiety by her quick answer, her expression turned rueful. "I'm in the 'some people who don't have any' category."

"You are young," he said. "You may change your mind."

Her voice went flat. "No I won't. And anyway, by the time I leave Tolar, I'll be too old to have children."

"It would be a shame for your gift of language to die with you. Perhaps the Sural would allow another human on the planet for a short time, to father a child for you."

"*No,*" she exclaimed.

Anxiety—close to panic—burst out of her. Her desire to avoid intimacy ran deep, and he had triggered a stronger reaction than he intended. Storaas spread his hands, apologetic.

"Forgive me. I did not at first realize you cannot bear a child. Can your medical science not correct this?"

Marianne fell silent, eyes wide. The anxiety turned to surprise.

He smiled. "You would like to know how I could know that."

"Yes, actually." She closed her slack jaws with a soft click and swallowed.

"Among my people, I am renowned for my ability to read others."

"To re—"

"You are familiar with our science of observation?"

Marianne nodded, and he sensed her surprise settling into comprehension. She could not truly understand—not yet—but he let her think what she would. She resembled a flutter with broken legs—able to fly, unable to land, pained and frightened by the very trees which should give her rest. Yet to be so gentle, even with all the pain she harbored, was remarkable, and he could understand the Sural's attraction. He wondered what could have given her a wound so grave. Whoever harmed her was unforgivable, he decided, to wound such a beautiful flower.

"Come," he said. "Let us return to the keep. Your time is your own for a few days. Kyza will be unavailable."

* * *

MARIANNE SPENT the remainder of the day reading in her quarters and studying in the library. It surprised her when neither Kyza nor the Sural appeared for the evening meal. They continued to absent themselves the following day, so she began to join Storaas at a lower table to take her meals. He welcomed her company.

"Proctor," she asked during the evening meal of the second day, "what's happening?"

He paused a moment before answering. "Kyza has reached a critical point in her development. The Sural must—restructure—his parental bond with her. Their relationship will then remain stable until she comes of age." He paused again, then added, "The process requires three or four days."

"Ah." Marianne nodded. Storaas smiled at her, but was otherwise unreadable, and she got the feeling she'd amused him. She grinned. "No, I don't understand. What do you mean?"

He gave her a Tolari stare before answering. She'd grown used to them, but they could still unsettle her. "Our children are bonded to us, for emotional stability. To the mother from birth, then to the father—if the child is his heir—from a little later in childhood. Kyza has reached the age of second bonding. Her first bond with the Sural dissolved, and she panicked when she felt alone. For several days, she will seek comfort and strength from the Sural, in the same manner you witnessed today. It takes place in seclusion, because while she draws on his strength, his instinct will be to protect her should another adult approach—with violence, if necessary. When their parental bond has re-formed, they will resume their normal activities." He fell silent and regarded her with another stare.

"Wait—she's been bonded to the Sural all this time rather than to her mother?"

"It is unusual, but it does occur." He bowed and left the refectory before she could voice the next question on her mind: Who was Kyza's mother?

Such a strange people. If she could have found woman friends among them, maybe then she'd understand them better, but perhaps Tolari women didn't have the same need she did. She couldn't talk to anyone on the ship other than Addie and Laura, though she would have liked to get to know that young lieutenant she met on Tau Ceti station. They might have become friends.

Adeline didn't seem inclined to tease her during the next morning's chat, much to Marianne's relief. "So you haven't seen either the Sural or his daughter since the day before yesterday?" she asked.

"Not a sign," Marianne answered. "They don't even come to the refectory for meals. Storaas said the Sural needed to 'restructure his parental bond' with his daughter. She will seek reassurance from him for several days, or something like that, and while she does that, he'll protect her from any adult who comes near. Storaas wasn't clear."

"Interesting," Adeline said, taking notes.

"The room felt charged with emotion when the proctor dragged me out," Marianne added. "The Sural just knelt there on the floor with his eyes closed, holding her, but there was something else going on."

"What kind of something?"

"I'm not sure, to be honest. When I asked Storaas about it, he picked a flower and made a comment that human senses are dull. I think he was being allegorical, trying to tell me something was going on with them that he could see but I couldn't. I think—" Marianne thought back to the unfocused panic. "When Kyza grabbed onto me, I felt panic. Now I wonder if it was really hers."

Adeline chewed on a lip, digesting that. "That would suggest empathic projection."

"That's what I think."

"If that's the case, it's the first time we've ever run into any evidence of it. Most people think telepathy and empathy are impossible *within* a species, much less *across* species."

"Most people think parallel evolution is impossible, yet here it is, staring us in the face."

"Good point," Adeline said, almost under her breath. She sighed and looked up. "Well, I have to go get some work done for Smitty. Keep up the good work, Marianne."

"Talk to you tomorrow."

* * *

TWO DAYS LATER, Marianne wandered alone through the library, thinking about the Tolari and what she had learned of them in the five years she had lived on their planet. She'd shared little of her current train of thought with Adeline, and regretted what she had.

As she browsed the books of art prints, looking for something to occupy her eyes while she thought, the Sural joined her. He seemed the same as he ever did, calm and impassive, which surprised her, though she couldn't say why. Perhaps she had expected him to be somehow changed by this *parental bonding* thing. Shaking herself out of her thoughts, she shot him a smile. The smile he returned carried real warmth, but then he seemed to look into her.

"Speak your thoughts," he said.

"I've done a lot of thinking about you the past few days," she said. "You Tolari, I mean."

He motioned toward a table and took the chair across from her, lacing his fingers together on the table in front of him.

"You do a good job of hiding things from me," she continued. "You carry on as if you're all a bunch of cold, heartless monsters, but I've been here for five standard years. Every now and then, something happens—or something slips—and over time it's added up."

The Sural's enigmatic smile appeared. She ignored the deliberate attempt at distraction.

"It's more than just coming to believe you Tolari have a vivid emotional life," she went on. "But the last straw came when this whole parental bonding thing started a few days ago and Kyza grabbed my leg. I felt panic. But it wasn't *my* panic, I'm sure of it. I'm *sure* of it. And Storaas ordered me not to touch her when she clung to me. What could that accomplish? Why would anyone order me not to offer comfort to a distressed child?"

The Sural steepled his fingers under his chin.

"I'll tell you what I think. I think you're all empaths. Honest to God, for-real empaths, the kind our scientists say can't exist, and you don't want every race in the Orion Arm to know about it. That's got to be why you don't want contact with other races—I bet we step all over your empathic toes. But it leads me to wonder why you wanted to have anything to do with humanity, whether or not you look like us, because we're a bunch of chatterboxes who couldn't keep this sort of thing secret if your lives depended on it, and they just might. My government uses information, people, resources, anything, like weapons. If they decide to start using you, they'll just start using you, the way they use me. Why did you let us in? Why am I here?"

"I do not fear your government," he said, his voice mild. His eyes didn't stray from hers, and he was very still.

"You should!" she exclaimed. "You don't even have air travel, much less space travel. Earth Fleet ships could bombard you from above!"

He smiled and shook his head. "We are not as primitive as we seem. I would never permit an attack on my planet."

His words brought her up short. "Eh?"

"I would never permit an attack on my planet," he repeated.

"And just how would you manage that?" She waved a hand around her. "Look at this. You live in an archaic stone fortress. Forgive me if I give offense, but you haven't even split the atom, if you know what an atom is. We did that six *hundred* standard years ago."

He chuckled and stood. "Come with me," he said.

He led her to the stronghold entrance. To one side of the great doors, he pressed a panel which looked no different than the others. With a stony grating, the wall opened, revealing a large, open room. An ovoid crystal pod, perhaps four meters long and three meters high, hovered over one of two empty shafts in the middle of the floor. The Sural touched its side, and the crystal melted away to form an oval doorway. He motioned for her to enter it.

"What is this?" she asked, eyes wide, as she stepped in.

"A transport pod," he replied, following her. At another touch, the doorway melted over as if it had never been, and a small panel extended up from the floor in front of him. "It is alive and dimly sentient. When I touch it, it knows what I want it to do." He placed his hand on the panel, and the pod dropped.

Marianne uttered a little screech and grabbed onto the Sural's arm. He looked down at her, his impassiveness gone and amusement lighting his eyes.

"You are quite safe," he said.

She swallowed and let go. Something flashed in his eyes—regret?—but then it disappeared, and his usual impassive expression slipped into place. A moment later, reassurance filled her, as it had when Storaas had lain a hand on her shoulder, except... no one touched her now. She glanced up at the Sural. He studied the control panel.

The pod came to rest at the shaft's base. A long tunnel opened before them, bright as day, but she could see no source for the light.

"We have an extensive network of these tunnels beneath the surface of every province," the Sural told her. "It is how we travel."

"You don't need air travel."

He shook his head. "No. We have control over Tolar's weather, but even so, the skies are too perilous. In the days when we traveled by air, too many of us died in treacherous air conditions. This way is as swift and much safer."

The pod leaped forward into the tunnel before them. They sped along for a time, until they burst into open ocean.

"Ohhhhh," Marianne sighed, looking all around.

The Sural's mouth twitched, and he aimed for a school of small sea creatures, bursting through them with an open smile. Marianne laughed. Then she realized, as the pod swooped and dove, she didn't feel the rolling or the accelerations.

"Transport pods possess inertial dampening," he said.

"How did you know I was wondering about that?" she asked.

"I am very good at reading others."

"Like Storaas?"

"He is more proficient than I," the Sural admitted, eyeing her. "More proficient than most, in truth. He is a noted sensitive."

Marianne shook her head. If the Sural really was an empath, at least he wasn't the most sensitive of them. As he guided the pod into deeper water he peered around as if searching for something.

"What are you looking for?" she asked.

"The hevalra migrate through the waters off Suralia during the autumn," he answered, and then pointed with his free hand. "Look. There. A hevalrin. The largest creature on Tolar."

She looked. A shadow loomed in the distance, and he aimed the pod for it. As they drew closer, she realized it was enormous—a vast marine creature larger than a terrestrial blue whale, with three sets of fins and a long tail. *Six limbs. Like the flutters.* The hevalrin seemed to notice the pod.

Marianne gasped. "It's coming toward us!"

"Have no fear," the Sural said. "She means us no harm."

"She?"

He nodded, and the pod stopped. The creature approached until it hung in the water in front of them like a wall.

"Greetings, old friend," the Sural murmured as the hevalrin gave the pod a gentle bump. He put a hand on the wall where the creature contacted it, and his hand sank through the crystal until he touched its skin. Then he put his other hand on Marianne's shoulder and closed his eyes. "Just feel," he said.

Marianne drew a sharp breath. She could *feel* the hevalrin, calm and deep and ancient. It bumped its feelings against her, playful as a puppy. The Sural smiled, his eyes still closed.

"She likes you," he said. "Touch her."

"But I'm not an empath."

"She is." He took a hand and guided it onto the crystal. Then he pushed, and her hand sank in as if through half-set gelatin, until she reached the frigid water and the hevalrin's rough, warm skin. Her sense of the great creature grew clear, a direct connection rather than feeling the ancient leviathan through the Sural. To her surprise and wonder, the world faded, the universe contracted to only herself, the Sural, and the hevalrin. She felt as if a large, stately old dog, full of affection and calm strength, licked her mind. She tried to return the warmth, and the creature's entire body shivered, rocking the pod. Delight surged through the connection.

A distant call echoed. With a brief flash of reluctance, the hevalrin broke the contact and backed away. Flicking her six fins, she rocketed toward the surface and breached, taking in a fresh supply of air. Another flick, and she headed into the deep. As they pulled their hands back into the pod, Marianne noticed her hand bore little trace of moisture. The Sural had a fond smile as he watched the enormous marine animal disappear into the depths.

"You know her?" she asked, as he put his hand back on the controls.

"Oh yes," he replied, his eyes still distant, gazing into the deep. Then he turned a brief smile on her. "She is a great matriarch of her kind. I have known her since I was a boy." He retreated behind his usual impassiveness and fell silent.

Marianne let the quiet stretch as they returned to the stronghold, but when the library door closed behind them, she spoke.

"I can see why you don't fear my government," she said. "Did your people invent those pods?"

"Yes," the Sural replied, nodding. "What will you tell your admiral?"

"I don't know." She knitted her eyebrows. "I don't know how to feel about this. I love my world—but I don't have any illusions about my government. They're rapacious, expansionist, and greedy. I thought I needed to protect you from them. I thought yours was a beautiful, primitive, pastoral world. But now I'm wondering if I need to protect my world from you."

"Your people have nothing to fear from me unless you make yourselves my enemies. My people wish to pursue their own arts in peace."

"If I tell the admiral what I saw today, my government will either panic, or they'll try to weasel your secrets from you any way they can.

Or maybe both. They already use me to get information from you. It will get a hundred times worse."

He smiled. Then he grew serious. "I do not wish to see your spirit clouded from deceiving your friends," he said. "Have a care what you do if you decide to take that path."

"Do I have any choice?"

"You have always a choice." He steepled his fingers under his chin. "What you do freely is of great value to us. What you do under compulsion is of no worth."

"That's why you wanted me to say I was staying of my own volition, my first day here."

He nodded. "Even so. I would prefer to see you retain the clear spirit my people value, but it is your choice. You can see there is no need for you to protect us, so you may tell the admiral whatever you like. He cannot harm us. None of the space-faring races you know can harm us."

"What if he calls me back to the ship?"

"Do you wish to leave?"

She shook her head. "Not yet."

"Then you need not go. You may stay as long as you like."

"Do I really have that choice?"

"Of course. You are under my protection."

Marianne chewed on her lower lip for a moment. "Why do you put such strict limits on the human technology you allow on Tolar?"

"It interferes with our own."

Marianne's eyebrows flew up.

"Perhaps the best descriptive phrase for human technology is, 'it leaks,'" the Sural added. "Phase platforms more so than most of your devices."

Marianne laughed. The Sural gave a one-shouldered Tolari shrug and smiled. "Have you more questions?"

"Why aren't you out there," she pointed upward, "in the stars?"

He rose from his chair and paced, hands clasped behind his back. "When our civilization was young, we went to the stars," he began. "Thousands of years ago."

"*Thousands?*" she gasped. "In *Tolari* years?"

"Your people still killed each other with weapons made of bronze," the Sural continued. "Perhaps fifty-five hundreds of standard years. We found this arm of the galaxy then much as you see it now: an assorted collection of dissimilar races, all vying for what they saw as a limited quantity of resources, all protective of *their space*. We thought to trade, to exchange knowledge and culture, to learn about other races and civilizations. The peoples out there," he waved at the ceiling, "had more interest in gaining an advantage from us or over us. We threaded our way through the petty rivalries for a time, then wearied of it and returned to our own world.

"On occasion, a leader of the ruling caste will conceive the idea of sending out ships to renew old alliances in the sector, but it has been many hundreds of our years since that last occurred, and now the possibility no longer exists. None of the space-faring races of your Trade Alliance have known us to leave our planet. The races we once knew have all moved on, or died out, or annihilated themselves, or gone back to their homeworlds and turned inward, as we have. We are content here, on our own world, developing our art, our science, our culture."

"Then why let humanity make contact?" Marianne asked. "Why am I here?"

"Because I can end such contact any time I decide. Allowing a relationship with Earth was not an irreversible decision. And it was good to see how our human cousins fared, that they had risen above their barbaric nature and become an interstellar civilization."

Marianne blinked. "Cousins? What do you mean, *cousins*?"

"We are related, you and I. Is it not obvious?"

"Well—no, not entirely. There's the little matter of your ability to disappear into thin air."

He smiled. "I cannot share anything regarding that with you. I can only say we are related. Your government has not yet obtained a tissue sample from one of us—but when they do, they will discover this for themselves. A Tolari and a human could produce fertile offspring, so long as the mother was Tolari."

"Why must the mother be Tolari?" she asked, frowning.

"Otherwise, the child would die long before birth."

"But—"

He shrugged a shoulder. "If you like, I will allow you to 'obtain' a Tolari tissue sample to phase up to your ship. That would create quite a distraction, I should think." He flashed a crooked smile. "It will give you time to consider."

"I bet they'd be excited enough not to ask *me* too many questions," she said.

The Sural nodded, a thoughtful expression on his face. "Proctor," he added, "you will find the guards in your quarters have learned English. Consider choosing another language to speak when you wish the admiral to believe you conceal something from me."

She blanched a little, thinking about some of the things Adeline said. "You've been spying on me!" she exclaimed.

"You have been spying on me." His voice was mild. "How do your people put it? *That makes us even.*" The saying seemed to amuse him. "All the same, it is not espionage to observe what happens in my own stronghold—or, as Tolar's ruler, what comes into Tolari space."

"How much of what I say on the comms gets to you?" she asked, biting her lip and holding her breath.

"Everything you say is reported to me, and I receive a copy of every report you send to your admiral."

She buried her face in both hands and groaned, too embarrassed even to be angry. He chuckled. "You must think I'm a fool," she said into her palms. "I feel like seven different kinds of an idiot."

The Sural stopped pacing and half-sat on the table next to her. "Do you feel I have betrayed you?"

"I should," she said, peering at him through her fingers. Anger eluded her, but she should be furious.

"No, you should not. I pledged my life to protect you. To that end, I must know as much as possible. Your people have not left behind all their more treacherous habits, and as for mine—there are those among the provincial rulers with more ambition than is good for them. They sometimes forget they cannot harm me."

"Old age and treachery defeat youth and beauty," she quoted in English.

He laughed, nodding, eyes glinting.

"You adhere to your guarantee of my safety more than my own government does."

The Sural smiled.

On a whim, he let the warmth he felt show.

"Wait a minute," she said. "Why *are* you protecting me? I'm an enemy spy."

"You are hardly my enemy, proctor, and you are not an intelligence operative. You are my daughter's tutor, who is being shamefully used by her own people."

She eyed him. "You're an empath. Truly an empath."

"Yes," he answered, sensing a fearful suspicion growing in her. "What troubles you?"

"How much of what *I* feel can you—sense, or read, or whatever?"

He fell silent, thinking about it for a time, staring at her. She valued her privacy—a privacy she could not know was impossible to maintain on his planet. He spread his hands. "Physical contact is required to fully read another. I gave explicit orders when you arrived that no one was to touch you."

"Oh," she said, relief radiating from her. Then she blinked, and the relief turned back to suspicion. "Wait a minute. Storaas has, at least twice. The last time was just a few days ago. He took my hand under his arm as we walked in the garden." Her eyes went wide. "Was he *reading* me?"

The Sural raised an eyebrow. "Very likely," he answered, watching her. She flared, indignant, struggling to repress it. *Magnificent.*

"That's—that's—" she sputtered.

"Not against my orders," he finished.

"*What?*" Shock slackened her jaw.

He laced his fingers together over one thigh. "I told him to find a suitable opportunity to read you."

She opened her mouth and closed it again, the shock giving way to an anger she fought to control. The guards flickered into sight, watching her, alerted by the strength of her ire.

"Have a care, proctor," he said, gesturing the guards to stand down. They disappeared again.

She heaved a heavy sigh, deflating. He could sense her getting a grip on runaway emotions.

"I—" She sighed again and withdrew into herself, taking refuge in formality. "Forgive me, high one," she said in an even voice, setting her face and looking down at the table. She was soft and gentle again, but sadness drifted from her. "The familiarity with which we speak sometimes allows me to forget who and what you are." She fell silent, staring at her hands and taking ragged breaths.

He had hoped for a more positive response. He suppressed disappointment as she continued to gaze at her hands on the table, letting the silence lengthen. If he told her the truth, he risked an even stronger reaction.

"I asked him to read you because I know you hide something," he said.

Her head jerked up, and she flared with indignation again. "I'm not a spook!"

"I did not say you were."

She grumbled and shifted in her chair. Her gaze wandered to the windows. "I'm just a schoolteacher," she said. "I've never done anything else."

"Of that much, I am certain," he said, "but you hide something, all the same. Something which pains you."

She went still and looked up at him, her eyes huge and frightened. Startled, he extended a hand. "I will never harm you," he said. "Will you trust me to help you?"

For a moment, it seemed to him as if she might take his hand. Then her presence shattered into panic, and she stood in a rush, knocking her chair backward, staring at his hand as if he might strike her. She paced over to the windows, agitated, hugging herself. Confounded, he went still and remained leaning against the table, allowing her time to calm.

"It's personal," she said. "Nothing to do with you, or Kyza, or my sneaky government." She sat in a low chair near a window and drew her knees up under her chin. "You need not be concerned."

He pushed away from the table and took a chair near hers. It had everything to do with him, he thought, but pursuing it would only frighten her more. *What demon hurt you?* he wondered.

"Hey!" She straightened and swiveled to face him. "You put your hand on my shoulder in the transport pod!"

He spread his hands. "Forgive me," he said. "I could not resist the opportunity to see the hevalrin through the lens of your perceptions. Your wonder was delightful."

Marianne mumbled something, mollified. She leaned her jaw on one hand and winced.

He sensed pain. "What was that?" he asked, focusing on her.

"Nothing, just a toothache," she said. "I've had them before. It'll go away."

He made a motion. "You will see my apothecaries."

She started to protest. "High one, it's not—"

"You will see my apothecaries."

She sighed as a woman in a pale yellow robe entered the room and bowed to the Sural.

"The human proctor has a physical ailment," he told the woman. "You will examine her and determine what needs to be done for her."

"Yes, high one," the woman said. She bowed to Marianne. "Proctor, if you will honor me with your presence in my examination room?"

Marianne sighed again and quit her chair to follow the apothecary.

* * *

"I NEED to have my wisdom teeth aligned," Marianne told the admiral. "The Sural's apothecary said the toothaches are just going to keep getting worse until I do. The Tolari have advanced enough dentistry to do it, but they need anesthetics for it and they don't have any which will work on me. They need those and some basic physiological information, and they can do it."

"Most people get their alignment done at age twelve," the admiral said with ill humor. "Why didn't your parents have it done then?"

Marianne winced a little. "They had other worries at the time."

The admiral grunted. "All right, I think I can okay this on my own authority, but I want to check on a few things first to be sure. I'll get back to you tomorrow on it."

"That's more than soon enough, Admiral. It's not an emergency."

"Howard out."

* * *

MARIANNE FIDGETED with her hands as the Sural's head apothecary prepared her for the procedure. The apothecary, a serene and graying woman who went about her work with grace and a sure touch, shunned the dental instruments phased down from the ship in favor of her own arcane devices.

After making sure Marianne couldn't feel what she did, she prodded and pulled with various gadgets for what felt like a half hour. Marianne had no idea what the woman did. From cheekbones to chin she had no feeling, and she wasn't even sure when her mouth was open or shut unless her ears happened to wiggle. She closed her eyes and recited poetry to herself, trying to ignore the strange non-sensation, until the apothecary called her name to get her attention.

"We are finished, proctor," she said.

Marianne opened her eyes and tried to smile. The lower half of her face refused to work. She would have frowned, but she couldn't do that either. She knitted her eyebrows together.

"Forgive me, proctor, but your ship did not phase down an antidote for the anesthetic," the healer apologized. "It will be some time before sensation returns. Until it does, I suggest you drink with care and avoid eating. You will have some discomfort. When you need relief from it, have a servant summon me."

Marianne nodded. She sat up and bowed her gratitude rather than try to speak and embarrass herself. The apothecary accompanied her to the door of her quarters. She bowed her thanks again and headed to her sleeping mat for a nap.

The next morning, she could eat nothing for the pain in her face and had to make a meal of tea. As she sipped, its warmth soothed her aching jaws. Absorbed in her misery, she didn't notice the Sural until he took his usual place at the table. Kyza carried her food into the kitchen.

"Proctor," the Sural said. Something in his tone prompted her to meet his eyes. His brows creased together, and his mouth was a horizontal slash. "It is not only for your own sake you must see my apothecary." He nodded toward the kitchen. "Our children find pain in others difficult to tolerate. Kyza is avoiding you for it."

"Oh," she said.

He gestured. "You will go with my apothecary," he ordered as the yellow-robed woman entered the room.

She yielded, too miserable to argue. "Yes, high one," she said, getting up to follow her.

* * *

THE SURAL WORKED in his study, sorting through reports and composing proposals to his allies. A presence came into range and approached—Storaas, the one individual allowed unannounced into his private apartments. The old man stopped before the desk and waited.

"Speak," the Sural murmured, half his attention on a report.

"While Kyza bonded to you, I had opportunity to read Marianne."

He riveted his attention on the old tutor. He straightened and put his tablet aside, lacing his fingers together in front of him. "Tell me."

Storaas explained the wound he had seen. He could not identify the injury with any certainty, but the Sural had done some research into human crimes. He thought he might know.

"High one—the wound is deep," Storaas finished.

The Sural nodded and sat at the desk for a long time, tapping his thumbs together, thinking, his barriers shut. When he wished, he could make himself as unreadable as a stone wall, even to one as sensitive as Storaas. He stood and walked to the window to gaze out on his province. Sighing, he closed his eyes and opened his empathic barriers enough to let Storaas see what he felt.

"A human life is very short, high one," the old man said. "Very short indeed."

The Sural shook his head. "That could perhaps be remedied," he said, in an almost inaudible murmur, as he paced back to the desk. In a louder voice, he continued, "I have waited, Storaas. I have been patient. I have offered her nothing but kindness and understanding, but after ten seasons, she has not yet begun to trust me." He stood with his back to Storaas for a time, gripping the desk with whitened knuckles, then loosed his grip before he cracked the wood and turned to look at the ancient man who had once been his tutor.

"Do you have any advice, old friend?" he asked.

CHAPTER 8

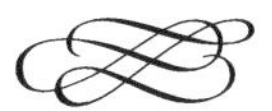

Marianne spent her fourth winter on Tolar working to expand Kyza's vocabulary, while the girl embarked on a rigorous physical conditioning program, learning to camouflage for longer and longer periods and sparring with the Sural's guards. Marianne often witnessed the camouflage exercises, since those took place daily in the library. The physical training was another matter. That took place elsewhere in the stronghold, and she heard about it from the Sural, who left out the details while allowing his pride to show. Kyza, he reported, took after him, with a real talent for physical combat and a drive for excellence at everything she did.

A month into winter—according to the *Alexander*'s calendar—Marianne asked to see Kyza's physical training. Her interest seemed to please Storaas, and he suggested she follow them that morning to the guard wing's lower level, an area of the stronghold she'd never explored.

A large arena occupied most of the lower level. Guards exercised and sparred in twos and threes, staying within mat-covered areas of various shapes and sizes, some clear and others filled with obstacles. At the far end of the huge room, a few children gathered around a sturdily-built Suralian who carried himself with an air of easy authority. Kyza headed toward them, Marianne and Storaas following in her wake.

"The head guard," Storaas murmured as they approached. "He teaches Kyza and a few of the guards' heirs. See—they are pairing off now."

The guard matched Kyza with a boy a little older and taller than she. The pairs of children spread out and circled each other.

"Begin," the head guard called.

What began, Marianne thought, resembled an acrobatic display. It bore no resemblance to the martial arts she had expected. The children spun, flipped, and somersaulted away from and toward each other.

"What are they trying to do?" she asked Storaas.

"A touch to the hands, face or neck ends the match," he answered.

"Just a touch?"

He nodded. "As guards, they will carry drugged needles on their fingertips. A touch imitates the needle's prick. The defeated child drops to the floor to acknowledge it."

"The Sural told me about the needles, but I didn't know high ones carried them as well." She cocked her head.

Storaas uttered a soft chuckle. "No, she will never carry the needles. She must first learn to fight as the guards do. Then she will learn to fight as a high one."

"And learn to kill." Marianne shuddered and turned her attention back to the children. The matches had not lasted long—a minute, perhaps two. As Marianne refocused on them, Kyza managed to touch her opponent's hand, and the boy dropped to the mat. She grinned and offered him a hand up.

"Very good, child," Storaas said.

Kyza turned to the old proctor with a grin, then looked up behind him. Her face brightened. "Father!" she called.

Marianne turned. The Sural, winter-idle and smiling, had wandered in. She assumed he came to observe his daughter's training. Kyza launched herself at him. His smile tilted as he dodged, eyes dancing. Marianne had never seen anyone move so fast, as he kept out of Kyza's way, his motions blurring as he spun or somersaulted. After giving her a good workout, he touched her face as he flipped over her head. Kyza dropped to the mat, breathing hard but grinning. The Sural chuckled and scooped her off the floor into a hug. His face shone with open approval.

"You improve, daughter," he said.

"I will best you yet!" she replied.

He chuckled again as he set her on the mats. "First you must best all the guards."

"I will, Father. You will see!"

He smiled and propelled her back toward the head guard with a pat between the shoulders, then headed for an open bathing area Marianne hadn't noticed. She glanced over again to see the Sural pulling off his clothing as he walked. Face heating, she turned away.

Oh my God. She glanced over her shoulder as he bathed. Hard muscle rippled as he rubbed soap over skin like cinnamon caramel. His body seemed to be as free of hair as his face, except— Her face grew hotter, and she turned back to face the children.

Beside her, Storaas chuckled.

"You're reading me." She could hear the aggrieved tone in her own voice.

"Forgive me, proctor, but you are broadcasting," he replied. "We do not have your human nudity taboos. If his form pleases you, you are free to admire it. He finds a woman's appreciation gratifying."

She blushed again and turned her back on Storaas to watch the children spar. The old man continued chuckling. She sighed, trying to quell a rising exasperation.

"If you will excuse me, proctor," she said through her teeth and walked away.

Back on the main floor, she strolled into the guest wing common room and dropped into a chair facing the windows, thinking about the Sural. His form pleased her, all right. She gave herself a mental kick and told herself he was her employer. Notions of anything more than casual friendship were a fantasy she could not allow herself to entertain, but the Sural didn't make that any easier. He'd always treated her with kindness, but during the past Tolari year, her fourth on Tolar, his behavior toward her had grown even kinder, and it made him so *damned* appealing. Professionalism, along with a conviction he couldn't think of her as anything more than a friend, kept her from making a fool of herself. She talked to herself, reciting the litany of reasons why only an idiot would look for more.

The litany calmed her enough to consider the Sural in a more even light. When the winter set in, he'd started to bring books from a personal collection of manuscripts and spent hours with her in the common room, poring over hand-written poetry and Tolari art prints in brilliant colors. She filled her reports to the ship with descriptions of ancient Tolari landscape art and literary genres. She had animated conversations with Laura about the landscapes. The admiral's wife was an avid patron of the arts, and the depth of her knowledge surprised Marianne.

Then the Sural had given her a critical introduction to Tolari music. The recordings he played for her were, without exception, a single instrument playing complex melodies. Marianne, whose musical taste ran to twenty-fourth century orchestral music, found it difficult to enjoy listening to Tolari music for extended periods, although she had begun to develop some liking for a wind instrument called the laerta.

Marianne pulled her thoughts back to the present and quit her chair to stand at the windows. Ice coated them, distorting the view of the landscape outside, where snow blanketed the garden, the plateau, and the glacier-strewn mountains beyond. She laid her forehead against the frigid window, hoping it would cool her agitation. Her breath steamed. She thought about ice, and snow, and glaciers.

Music filled the room, a Tolari laerta playing a melancholy air. She turned to see the Sural in the doorway, a small stack of books in his arms. He entered the room and took a seat.

"What did you think of my daughter's training?" he asked.

She sat in the next chair, the heat returning to her face. His eyes fixed on her blush. "She seems to—to be as talented as you've said," she stammered.

He nodded, lips twitching, then to her relief, changed the subject. "This," he waved a hand in the air, "is a recording of a performance Corvestal gave during my grandmother's time. He was a great musician with a wondrous gift. He played at the peak of his abilities when he came to give this concert. Years later, before he walked into the dark, he entrusted to me his laerta. It is an exquisite instrument. I hold it in trust for the next great player."

"Why did he go into the dark?" she asked.

"A landslide killed his bond-partner," he answered. "She was a geologist on a field investigation. Corvestal himself sustained injuries in the same accident. He would have recovered, but he would not live without his beloved. A great loss."

She winced. "Forgive me."

"It is a common response to a bond-partner's death."

They listened without speaking for a time, her face cooling.

"You know, we have an instrument with a sound similar to the laerta," Marianne said, breaking the quiet.

"Tell me."

"It's called an oboe. The musician blows into the instrument through a folded reed. It's quite lovely and difficult to play."

"Your people write music composed of many instruments playing at once," he said. "I have heard some samples. Quite interesting."

She smiled, then pulled her mouth to one side. "Central Command didn't allow me to keep my music collection on my library tablet, or I'd play some for you."

"A pity."

"I could try begging and pleading to get it back," she offered.

He smiled. "I am a patient man," he said. "I will hear this music, in time."

"Your lives are a lot longer than ours, aren't they?"

He nodded.

"How long?"

He shook his head. "For now, I cannot tell you that," he answered. "You will know, in time. Have patience."

"I'm a schoolteacher. I taught high schoolers—they're adolescents. I *had* to be patient, or I would have lost my mind."

He made an amused sound. "You are far too young to have true patience, proctor."

"And I suppose you're an old man?"

"That would depend upon whose definition you use. For a Tolari, I am not old at all. For a human?" He spread his hands. "I cannot tell you." She grumbled, and he chuckled. "Storaas—I can say he is truly old."

"And sad," Marianne added.

The Sural shot her a sharp look, then nodded. "Very astute," he said.

"No, I just catch him sometimes staring out the windows toward the west—toward where all the tea plantations are in the Kentar Valley—with the deepest, saddest look on his face," she explained. "Even *I* can tell, and I'm bad at reading others, even for a human."

One black eyebrow climbed his forehead. "I must persuade him," he murmured.

"What?"

The Sural studied Marianne, considering what to say. She glanced back, her curiosity showing on her face as well as in her emotional landscape, long since accustomed to and no longer perturbed by what she called 'Tolari stares.' "Storaas needs to visit the Jorann," he said, after a time. "I cannot persuade him."

"Who's he?"

"She."

"Who's she, then?"

"Our highest one."

Marianne straightened. "There's someone higher-ranked than you?" she asked, blinking.

He nodded, enjoying the empathic flare of her astonishment. "Highest rank and highest status. She guides the ruling caste, and can raise, lower, or change the rank or status of anyone at her whim, though she seldom interferes in our affairs. To be summoned into her presence is a high honor. Any of us can request to see her."

"So she's like a kind of pope."

The Sural cocked his head, gazing past her as he thought about it. "That would be a—loose—way to describe her role in our culture," he answered.

"Why does Storaas need to see her?"

He paused again. "She can heal what distresses him."

Marianne stopped. "I shouldn't ask, should I?"

"No, you should not," the Sural answered, smoothing his face into a gentle expression. "I would not answer if you did. He would know."

"High one—" she started.

"Yes, proctor?"

"You've become very candid with me of late."

He raised an eyebrow at her, letting one side of his mouth curve up. "Having an alien in my stronghold has advantages."

"Ah, I see," she said. "*Uneasy lies the head that wears a crown.* You can say things to me you can't tell anyone else."

"Indeed."

She fell silent for a time, listening to the music, allowing it to soothe away the last of the agitation she had radiated in the arena. The Sural extended his senses toward her, keeping a light contact, pleased she had relaxed in his presence. As her calm deepened, curiosity sparked through her.

"High one?" she asked.

"Yes, proctor?"

"Don't you have a name?"

He started and stared at her, pulling his senses back. Instinct howled at him to thrust her away. He gritted his teeth. He refused—*refused*—to be a slave to his instincts. Marianne began to shift in her chair and radiate feelings of awkwardness.

When he could trust himself to speak, he met her eyes, smiled, and explained. "When most Tolari rulers take power," he said, "the Jorann takes their names from them and bonds them to their people. From that day onward, we identify them as their provinces. I am the Sural of Suralia. I have pledged my honor and my life to every man, woman and child of my province. I cannot be identified apart from my people again, and to lose them would kill me."

"That's why you would walk into the dark if your province were destroyed?"

"I would die if I lost my people, whether I walked into the dark or not."

The Sural stared out the icy windows at the distorted view of the glaciers. He closed his eyes, seeing his people glowing like stars around him, then opened them and tapped his tablet. The music changed, the soft sound of a stringed instrument filling the room.

Marianne took a deep breath and sighed, closing her eyes as she listened, a gentle smile curving her lips. "Mm, that's nice," she murmured.

The Sural gazed at her, stomach clenched in longing, yearning for her to turn such a smile on him. He tore his eyes away from her face and pulled a book from the stack he had brought, sadness descending over him as he studied its cover.

Marianne seemed to sense his mood and opened her eyes. "Is that special?" she asked, pointing at the book with her chin.

He nodded. "My father's poetry."

"I didn't know your father was a poet," she said, straightening. An eager note entered her voice. "I'd love to hear something he wrote."

"You may find it disturbing."

"It's that dark?"

"No," he answered. "Not dark."

"Then I can't see the problem," she said.

The Sural raised an eyebrow and eyed her. *Perhaps.* He debated with himself. She seemed more receptive than usual. Storaas would advise him against doing anything to stir her. Still, the Sural had not ruled as long as he had without taking an occasional risk—and she *had* asked. "Lean back," he told her. "Close your eyes."

She did as he asked, settling herself back. He opened the book. By chance, it fell open to the last poem his father had ever written, a ballad poured out to the woman who had captured his heart, composed mere hours before he died. It was a raw first draft, intense and passionate—as all his father's poetry was intense and passionate. The wisdom of reading any poem his father wrote to Marianne seemed doubtful, much less that one. He pushed the misgivings aside and began to read aloud, finding a strange relief in the opportunity to give voice to his own feelings without the complication of Marianne discovering how he felt.

Marianne drew in a breath and blushed as the Sural began to read a deep and passionate poem about his father's love for a beautiful woman. With her eyes closed, she could almost imagine the Sural spoke the words to her, something so tender and so—so *personal*—haunted his voice. She let out the breath with a sigh and wondered if the Sural had inherited his father's passion. Could such an impassive man be so tender, such a powerful man be so gentle? Gentle... not like... she pushed away unbidden memories and concentrated on the idea of tender and gentle. She might be able to cope with that. Maybe.

The Sural sensed her emotions change with a rising heart. Marianne had allowed the poem to affect her. He sensed a stab of yearning pierce her—and then watched in helpless frustration as a powerful wave of panic swept away the yearning. He stopped speaking as Marianne bolted out from her seat and strode to the windows, pacing back and forth in agitation.

Of all the days he had to choose to read something like *that* to her, it had to be a day when she already struggled. Her hands fisted even while her insides quivered. She didn't need this, on top of that look at him in the arena—dear God, he was attractive. He was just a friend. She gave herself a fierce mental kick. *Just* a friend.

The Sural blinked and took the empathic blow in silence, his heart sinking. With slow and careful movements, he rose and moved not toward her, but to one side. Her emotions roiled, and he could not know what she might do if he came too near. The anger triggered by her panic had eclipsed her normal gentleness. What did she fear?

What Storaas had said came to mind. Did she fear he might hurt her? Despite his many assurances? He made a subtle hand gesture, a casual signal to the guards to remain camouflaged and silent. She seemed, for the moment, to have forgotten them. He leaned against the window, arms crossed over his chest, face schooled into warm gentleness.

"Who hurt you?" he asked.

She stopped pacing. "No one," she lied, her sharp look daring him to contradict her. She resumed the restless pacing. "You were right," she snapped before he could point out the lie. "I did find your father's poetry disturbing. Your *father* wrote that. How can you read it? It's like—it's like—gah!" She shuddered.

"Forgive me," he murmured, bending into a profound bow.

Marianne stopped pacing again, surprised at both the apology and the bow, and turned her back on him, not wanting him to see her face. She wanted to throw herself into his arms. She fought it down, surprised, telling herself how inappropriate that would be. *Get a grip, girl!* she told herself with another furious mental blow. Deep winter gripped the province, leaving the Sural with little to do. He was bored. He couldn't realize how a human would react to such a poem. How *she* would.

That had to be it—he just didn't realize. She tried to imagine the look on his face if she had acted on the urge to throw herself at him. Surprise, of course. Discomfort, very likely. Scorn? She didn't think she could face the possibility.

She tightened her arms around her ribcage and took a shaky breath. Then she let her arms fall to her sides and turned to face him.

He was gone.

* * *

THE SURAL CURSED, long and eloquently, as he shattered a training pell. The arena fell silent, the guards eyeing him as they moved away, their motions slow and deliberate. He expelled a breath and forced his muscles to relax. Alarming the guards solved nothing. Destroying their training equipment solved even less.

He could not have stopped Marianne's self-destructive spiral. He moved to an undamaged pell and landed a hard but controlled blow. If he had revealed how much of her pain and conflict he could sense, would she have turned to him?

He vaulted up and over and used his momentum to kick the top of the pell as if he were crushing the skull of the man—it had to have been a man—who had hurt her. *No.* Such a revelation would have humiliated her. He could not risk that. So instead, he had stood in silence while she rejected him.

Not a rejection. The pell shuddered at a spinning kick delivered with more force than he intended. How could she reject him when she saw only his friendship? He knew she valued that.

Storaas came into range. The Sural shut him out and continued pummeling the pell with hands and peds. Someone had informed the old man of his mood, or perhaps he had come upon Marianne, who must still be in turmoil, and deduced that his ruler had made a mistake. Whatever the case, he had no desire to discuss the matter.

Receiving no permission to speak, Storaas moved into his line of sight. The Sural ceased his attack on the pell and stared. The old proctor cradled a large bottle of spirits in one arm.

The Sural nodded. "My quarters."

* * *

THE WINTER FELT long to Marianne, fraught as it was. She greeted spring and the chance to escape outdoors with gratitude. The temperatures were still winter cold by her standards, but it had warmed enough to venture out to a gazebo to take some fresh air in the garden, where laborers had dug paths through the snow. She supposed some hidden technology maintained the strange warmth in the graceful pavilions.

Even she could see, unperceptive though she sometimes was, that the Sural had withdrawn from her after the incident with the poetry. He'd avoided her for several days, then resumed spending his free time with her, but for much of the winter, it just wasn't the same. Adeline had teased her without mercy, forwarding the ridiculous notion that he had acted like a spurned lover, not the hurt friend Marianne assumed. Marianne herself wasn't sure what had possessed her to turn on him. He had only read to her, even if the subject matter was rather—intimate. She missed the easy friendship which had seemed to blossom between them during the first part of winter.

The ease and friendship had begun to return during the last few tens of days—it amused her to find herself counting time in Tolari terms. The Sural started sharing manuscripts of short stories from a celebrated author of several hundred years earlier. The stories consisted of succinct and gripping accounts of everything from spiritual epiphanies to psychological studies. The insights she gained into Tolari thinking fascinated her, but the Sural often had to explain motivations the author assumed the reader would know. The only story with which the Sural himself found fault was one in which the protagonist walked into the dark.

"His description is not accurate," the Sural told her. They sat across from each other at a table in the family wing library. "It is a common belief, but it is not accurate."

"And you know this—how, exactly?" she asked.

"I have experienced it."

Marianne lifted her face from the manuscript to gape at him. "What?"

"I have walked into the dark."

"But—but—"

"I am not dead?"

She nodded.

He smiled at her. "We call it the great trial. Suralia's heirs must choose to walk into the dark to save their honor and their province, before they are considered worthy to rule. Only Suralia knows how to bring someone back from it. Other provinces—their people cannot have quite the same faith in their rulers the children of Suralia can have, because other rulers are not tested to the death as we are. My people *know* I will walk into the dark for them, because I have already done so."

She couldn't think of a single thing to say and just stared at him. *He's been dead?*

He chuckled. "When our heirs reach a certain point in their training, they must be subjected to the great trial," he continued. "They are never told they are being given the great trial until they have passed it. If they pass it."

"*If* they pass it?" Prickles went up her spine. "What happens if they fail?"

"They die."

Her eyes popped, and his lips twitched before he assumed a more serious expression.

"They can also fail if they are strong enough to return from the dark but not strong enough to recover from the shock without permanent damage to their empathic abilities. The shock is painful." He stared past her, his eyes growing distant. "Extremely painful."

"And you've done this?" she asked.

"My father would not have declared me his heir if I had not, nor would I rule now."

"How old were you?"

"Younger than is Kyza."

Marianne rocked back in her chair.

"I was unusually young," he added.

"So it will be soon, for Kyza?"

"Indeed, most likely in the coming year. She is pressing Storaas for challenges and passing them. I would have her slow her pace and be closer to five than to four when she faces the great trial, but she is strong-willed."

Marianne stifled a snort. The Sural eyed her, eyebrow raised. "You were even younger than she is now, and you call *her* strong-willed?"

He smiled with deliberate mystery. "I admit I was a challenge for my father."

"I just bet."

"Regardless of comparisons, my daughter is still headstrong."

"Your daughter has you in her thrall."

He laughed. "Yes," he said, smiling. "Even so."

Marianne sobered. "She'll pass the great trial, won't she?"

"She is strong," he answered, "but no one can say with any certainty."

Marianne bit her lip and gazed at the manuscript on the table.

"Tell me about this story," she said, changing the subject. "Why *does* the protagonist follow his friend into the dark?"

CHAPTER 9

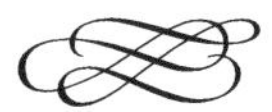

The midspring thaws brought green life back to Suralia, and buds appeared on the cora trees in the Sural's gardens, swelling as the days lengthened. Kyza made her way along one of the sparkling brooks dividing the garden. Storaas had given her leave from her studies to play in the gardens until the midday meal. She chose a rock and sat, splashing her peds in the water, basking in the spring sunlight. Tiny water creatures nibbled at her heels. She giggled and splashed at them.

Flutters winged past, alarmed and calling, shedding brilliant feathers in panic. Kyza camouflaged and dove into a hollow under a nearby cora tree's thick basal branches. The flutters knew her father and every member of the stronghold staff and would never have fled from them. If it were a guest, a guard would have flicked a signal that she was safe.

Where are the guards? She concentrated, opening her senses without extending them, and found no nearby guards. If this were a test, she thought, would they not be in their places? Test or not, she must not be found. An intruder—one of her father's enemies—would try to capture her, and if it were a test, the proctors would give her a heavy load of extra work for allowing them to find her. Careful, silent, she molded herself into a hollow under the branches and made herself one with the dead vegetation.

Time crawled past. Her hiding place lay too far into the gardens to hear the activity in the keep, but several times she heard the sounds of a search. Someone crept along the path—someone she did not recognize with her senses. Kyza slowed her breathing and her heart rate as Storaas had taught her. Whoever tried to find her, proctor or enemy, would track her by many different methods: the smell of her breath drifting from her hiding place, the thud of a panicked heartbeat, an oh-so-slight ripple in the air, a stray emotion. She breathed into the soft moss lining the hollow and concentrated, absorbed with becoming undetectable to any Tolari, even—especially—her own tutors. She could not hide from her father, or from Storaas, but if *they* sought her, she was in no danger.

She let her mind settle. She melted into the winter-killed vegetation under the cora tree, scattered with dead twigs and peaking with faint bits of spring life. Her thoughts lengthened, feeling the life in the soil as it woke from the long winter, becoming one with the flow of it. The searcher went past her hiding place without a pause.

Time passed, and still no signal came from a proctor or a guard. Running feet pounded by. Kyza concentrated on controlling her heart and breathing. The proctors had given her tests this long before, and she knew she could endure it. She had not eaten since the morning meal, and it began to occupy more of her attention to keep her stomach from complaining. The proctors must have timed the beginning of the trial to make hunger a part of the test. She would never admit it to any of her teachers, but she knew she did not have an adult's endurance. The stronghold guards could remain camouflaged and motionless all day, but she had only four years of life—her body would betray her, sooner or later.

More time crept by. The sounds of searching had ceased. She could feel the sun setting and the darkness flowing across the garden. She had remained hidden and motionless since before the midday meal, through the long afternoon. Now she focused all her concentration on the one imperative task of keeping her body from betraying her position under the tree. Her body cried for food, water, and the need to *move*. A rock pressed into one leg. Her left shoulder was at an awkward angle. Her side ached.

She did not move. The vital need to remain still and undetectable absorbed every thought, every bit of her awareness. Desperate, she sent her mind roving back to Storaas and his most recent lessons. She could hear his gentle voice in her memory.

"It is always possible—however unlikely it may be—that one of your father's enemies will find a way to defeat his defenses and take the stronghold. If that happens, you cannot allow them to capture you. Kyza, dear child, cherished daughter of Suralia—if the stronghold is taken, then you must walk into the dark. We must all go into the dark. You must find the strength and courage to go bravely."

There. She smelled it. *Smoke.* She sorted through the smell as it grew stronger. The smoke cloyed in her nostrils, sweet, as if fire feasted on incense and seasoned wood. Shock flooded her, almost breaking her concentration. *This is not a test. The stronghold is burning.*

Father! She did not dare reach out her senses to search for him. It would lead his enemies to her. If the stronghold burned, then he was dead or dishonored. *No!* she thought, he was *not* dishonored, her father would never allow himself to be captured. *He must be dead.* She felt along the bond she shared with him and found... nothing. Her struggle to remain concealed had absorbed so much of her attention she had failed to notice she was alone.

Her heart drowning in grief, her body screaming for release, she turned her mind into the dark, the quiet dark that, it surprised her to discover, dulled her body's discomfort. She almost cried out in relief as her pain and hunger and thirst faded into the welcoming night. *I will be strong for you, Father,* she thought. *You would have been proud of me.* She would not be taken alive.

* * *

"Kyza. Tell me." The Sural's voice was flat, emotionless.

Quiet filled the private study as the agitated ruler paced. Ancient effigies of even more ancient ancestors looked down from the ancient, fragrant paneling lining the walls. He stopped pacing the mat-covered floor before the desk and faced Storaas.

"She went into the dark, high one." He twitched his deep indigo robe, betraying his mixed feelings. He was proud of Kyza. Apprehensive of the Sural.

The Sural waved a hand. He was unreadable, his empathic barriers closed, but Storaas knew the man was in an agony of apprehension. "Will she live?"

Storaas bowed, arms spread, palms forward. He could not discern if the Sural was pleased or displeased with how advanced Kyza's training had been at such a young age, and the news was uncertain. He had had to deliver worse news when the apothecaries were not able to bring a potential heir back from the dark. It had become more difficult each time, and each successive death had devastated the Sural the more.

With Kyza, it would be much, much worse. It was not only that the Sural cherished her more than her predecessors. If she could not make a complete recovery, the Sural would have to command his daughter to walk back into the dark, because a weakened heir could not legally rule Suralia. Though the Sural had ordered him to administer the great trial, she should have had another year of life before facing it. For good or ill, her level of proficiency demanded it at this time. Kyza had been so delightful he could not resist teaching her everything she wanted to know, and he could not suppress pride that she was almost the youngest child of Suralia ever to come back from the dark.

The only one who had been younger, he thought, was her father, but he was a special case. Kyza, though brilliant, was not in the same category with the Sural. *He* was a grandchild of the Jorann.

The Sural's voice cracked through the air like a glacier calving. "Speak," he commanded, tearing apart the net of Storaas' thought.

"She lives, high one. Barely." Storaas twitched his robe again, a nervous habit he had never, in all his long years, succeeded in breaking.

"Will she recover?" The question was flat, toneless.

A hesitation. "That is not yet clear, high one. She is still near the edge of the dark, deep in shock. Your apothecaries need more time to determine if she has sustained permanent damage."

The Sural let out a breath. "I wish to see her," he said and strode from the room, slamming his already-closed barriers even tighter before entering the keep's main corridor.

Three other times, Storaas had come to him after administering the great trial to one of his potential heirs. His children. *His sons.* Each child had failed the test—dying from it, not strong enough to return from the descent into the dark. The Sural pushed away the memories. Kyza was the fourth to endure it and the first to survive. If she could not recover her full strength—he rejected the thought, refusing to dwell on the possibility that he would have to command her to go back into the dark. He clamped down on his feelings, but he could not control a stray hope that sent his heart soaring. *She survived!* He exulted in the knowledge as he made his way to his apothecary's quarters. *She must recover. She* will *recover.*

* * *

SMITHTON RUSSELL DROPPED into his chair and rubbed his temples with large hands. "She's near death? What kind of monster is that Sural?"

The adjutant standing on the other side of Smithton's desk, a fresh, clean-cut young man, shrugged. "They're an unemotional culture."

The ambassador scowled. "Don't pretend to teach me my job, pup," he snapped. "Learn to recognize a rhetorical question when you hear one."

Aurelio Johnson—odd name, he thought—paled under his dark skin. "Yes sir." The young man straightened his already straight posture and glued his eyes to a spot on the bulkhead behind the ambassador's head.

Smithton scowled again. "Don't go all military on me either."

"Yes sir. I mean, no sir. I mean—"

"I know what you mean. Out."

"Yes sir." He turned on his heel and left the room, relief clear on his face.

Smithton sighed as the door closed behind the young man. He leaned back in the chair, gazing out the viewport at the beautiful world below. He uncorked a bottle of brandy and poured himself a drink. "Harsh world, my foot," he muttered as he settled into the seat's cushions and sipped. "That planet is greener than Ireland."

"Are you sure about that?" came a woman's voice from behind him. "It looks a little too blue to me."

Smithton started and put down the drink. "Adeline!"

His wife moved around the chair and sat on the desk with an impudent grin. "If you don't want a conversation, don't think out loud."

"Stop sneaking around!"

"Oh Smitty, you know I can't help it," she chided. Her voice was bland.

Smithton grunted. His wife made barely a sound on stone floors with hard shoes. On a carpeted floor in slippers, she made about as much noise as a cat. He'd always thought her a natural for an intelligence operative, but she had maintained she had no interest in even learning self-defense, much less how to kill. She put a delicate hand on his large, blocky one. For the hundred thousandth time, he wondered what she saw in him.

"Tell me what's got you grunting and scowling." She peered into his face, scrunching her own into a parody of his expression.

"It's that adjutant of mine."

"No it's not," she said. Smithton started to speak but she shushed him with a finger. "Oh no, don't tell me. Yes, I'm sure you grumped at him for something he did. No, I'm not interested in what it was. He behaved like the Earth Fleet lieutenant he is, I'm sure, but it's not fair to fault him for behaving the way he's been trained to behave. You're scowling because something else has you lathered. What is it?"

Smithton glared up at his wife, then softened and took a sip of his brandy. "It's that damned Sural of theirs," he said, gesturing at the planet in the viewport.

"What's he done this time?"

"Damned near killed his daughter in one of their damnable tests. She might not live."

Adeline rocked back a little. "Ouch."

"Eight years we've been waiting since she was born, another eighteen years before she's old enough to be their ambassador, and they risk it all in one of their damned trials!" He cursed the Tolari custom that a ruler's ambassador must be his heir and quit the chair to take up a brooding stance at the viewport, staring out at the planet below.

Adeline picked up his drink and handed it to him, then slipped her arms about his waist. "Too bad we can't offer to send down a medical team."

He glared at her. "'Course not," he grated. "Sometimes I forget these people aren't human. They look so much like us—unless that's camouflage too."

"Oh Smitty," she said. "I'm sorry. I'll put her on my prayer list."

"Damned girl should already be on your damned prayer list. Or maybe the damned little alien shouldn't be on any proper prayer list."

"Smithton!"

He turned and gave her an unrepentant smirk.

"You're impossible!" Adeline accused.

"No, just highly improbable," he retorted.

Despite himself, her silver laughter brought a smile to his face.

* * *

A PURPLE DAWN filtered through the dark, wooden blinds in the head apothecary's quarters. The Sural, sitting on the edge of the examination bed on which Kyza lay, studied his daughter, looking for signs of returning consciousness. He had scarcely left her side for two days, rejecting the head apothecary's suggestions to get some sleep. She had given up trying to convince him to rest and instead had joined him, monitoring his daughter's condition.

During the night, he sensed Kyza begin to approach consciousness and refused to leave her for any reason. Now the dawn rewarded his long vigil. When the sun's first rays reached through the windows, Kyza stirred.

She almost could not stifle a cry and arched her back as agony slammed into her awareness, every nerve in her body on fire. She clamped her jaw and convulsed, a scream trying to escape her throat. Her eyes fluttered open, unseeing, as she fought to remain silent. She could not, would not, draw the enemy to her.

Somewhere in the distance, she heard her father's voice. "I am here, daughter." A gentle hand touched her forehead. He took one of her hands in his. "You are not alone. Take strength from me."

Father! She dug her nails into his hand and threw her head back so far the bones in her neck popped, gritting her teeth to stifle a cry as the pain increased. Desperate, she threw her senses at her father, beating against him. He caught her with practiced care and wrapped his own senses around hers, letting her cling to him and draw strength from him. His love surrounded and supported her, and her rebellious body began to relax. As she regained control, the pain receded enough for her surroundings to come into focus. The hard comfort of an examination bed, the smell of the apothecaries' potions biting her nostrils, and—her eyes slitted open.

"Father." Her voice was almost inaudible, even to her own ear. She sensed more than saw him sitting on the bed beside her. *How am I alive?* Memory sparked. "A test?"

"Yes, daughter."

Kyza tried to swallow. "I regret my... failure, Father," she whispered. "Forgive me."

"You did not fail, Kyza." Her father chuckled.

She twitched her brows together. "But I... live. I would be in... enemy hands. I... have failed."

"You were outstanding, daughter. The guards and proctors could not find you, and you chose death before capture."

Death. Capture. A test? She tried to make sense of it, but her thoughts muddled. "Father?"

"Death was the trial, Kyza. Do you think we would tell you that you must walk into the dark, if we did not know how to bring you back?"

"If you can—"

The Sural laid a finger on her lips. "Suralia knows the way. It is one of our secrets." He took a small cup from the apothecary. "Now, daughter, my apothecary has something for your pain. You will drink it."

"Father—"

"Do not disobey the Sural, Kyza. I know your tutors have taught you to refuse drugs, but you have passed this trial—and *one* of the rewards is relief from the pain it inflicts. Drink." He slid a hand under her head, lifting it, and held the cup to her lips until she drank its entire contents. "Good. Now, did that taste as bad as all her other medicinals?"

She could not laugh, but a faint smile curved her lips. The Sural nodded. "I suspected as much." Her eyes unfocused as the drug took effect. "I will leave you to your dreams," he said, stroking her hair. "Sleep now, daughter."

Warm muzziness closed in.

* * *

"WELL, THANK GOD FOR THAT." Ambassador Russell grumbled as he tossed Marianne's latest status report away from him onto his desk.

"Thank God for what, Smitty?" came Adeline's voice from the next room. Smithton scowled. Adeline often pretended to be deaf to what she didn't want to hear, but mention God and she was all ears. It was infuriating.

"The girl is going to live," he called.

Adeline, clad in a pink leotard and tights with a loose red sash tied around her waist, ran into the room and threw her arms around him. *Damn she's a fine-looking woman,* he thought, as his arms went around her.

"That's *wonder*ful!" she cried, giving him a sound kiss on the nose. That accomplished, she disentangled herself from him and jogged back into the next room. Twentieth century music began to play. The Beatles, he thought, but he didn't know the era well enough to be sure.

"What the hell are you doing in there, Addie?"

"Exercising! What do you think of the Rolling Stones?"

Rolling Stones, Beatles, it was all the same to him. He was past trying to figure out why she listened to six-hundred-year-old music rather than something more modern.

"Can't you do that in the ship's gym?" he growled.

"What, and have all those callow youths drooling over the wife of Earth's Ambassador to Tolar?" He could hear the capital letters. "Besides, they don't like classic music."

"Neither do I!" he bellowed.

"But I'm allowed to torture *you*." Glee filled her voice.

Smithton grunted and left to find a quieter place to work.

* * *

In her quarters in the guest wing, Marianne opened a bottle of essential oil of lavender and applied a single drop to the warmest part of her neck. It was one of her favorite scents. Adeline had had it phased down from the ship a few hours earlier with her vitamin and protein supplements. The Tolari could not comprehend why she mixed her body's odor with such scents. To them, it was a form of deceit, or at least they had thought so until they understood her sense of smell was quite dull compared to theirs. Most of the time, she complied with their preferences, but it had been a long, stressful day and she felt like indulging. She'd bathe in the morning and remove the scent, but for now, she breathed it in and sighed.

The guard by the door—a woman, since any guard assigned to her quarters was a woman—flickered into view. *I wish they wouldn't do that,* Marianne thought, a little startled. The guards in her quarters, as a general rule, remained camouflaged and silent. The lavender's scent must have been a little too strong for this one.

The guard, as observant as any Tolari, noted her reaction and bowed an apology. "Forgive me, proctor," she said in English. *More and more of them know English now,* Marianne thought. "I did not mean to startle you."

"Is there something you wished to say?" Marianne asked.

The guard started to shake her head, but her curiosity seemed to get the better of her. "That fluid, proctor, what is it?"

"Lavender oil. Lavender is a flower on my world, on Earth. This is an essential oil derived from the plant. It has medicinal properties as well as a pleasant scent. Do you like it?"

The guard spread her arms in apology, shaking her head. "Perhaps in a weaker concentration," she suggested. "Do you use it now for its medicinal properties?"

Marianne thought about it a moment. "I might be," she answered. "It can soothe anxieties, and I've been worried about Kyza."

"Worried?"

She sighed. The Tolari also could not comprehend human worry, or at least the guards didn't. They didn't worry about anything at all, that Marianne had ever detected. For the guard, as for every other Tolari in the stronghold, either Kyza survived her tests, or she didn't. Since she had survived, they were unconcerned. If she hadn't survived, they would have grieved, but it never occurred to them to anticipate grief before it happened.

"I have no answer for that, guard," she responded, "It is a human thing."

The guard nodded, bowed, and disappeared into the background.

Marianne settled back in her chair and picked up the tablet containing her personal library. She felt like reading a little Jane Austen. "Life in the fishbowl," she muttered. In Hungarian, so none of the invisible guards would understand.

* * *

Kyza opened her eyes on quiet darkness and lifted her head. Then she stirred her arms and legs, pushing herself up on her elbows. No pain. The apothecary's noxious-tasting potion had done its work. She sat up with care. An apothecary's aide watched her but did not speak or interfere. Weakness pulled at her limbs, but not so much that she could not stand—she thought. Scooting to the edge of the bed, she slid down until her peds touched the floor, then tilted forward as a wave of dizziness washed over her. She avoided falling by letting the momentum carry her to the window.

Clinging to the sill, she looked out into the night, panting, until the dizziness passed. Tolar's single large moon, half full, hung above the far mountains, beyond a mist-filled valley spotted with the tops of an occasional tree. Paperbark trees, she thought. She could not be sure on that point; her academic education had not yet progressed beyond giving her a fluent ability to read. She remembered Storaas mentioning that paperbark trees grew so tall they pierced the fog in the Kentar Valley. The peaks beyond were the High Fralentolar Mountains along Suralia's border with Detralar province. She knew they lay farther away than they looked.

Her legs a little steadier now, Kyza turned away from the window and navigated through the room to the keep's main corridor. Hunger gnawed at her. Perhaps the kitchen servants had left some food out—sometimes they did, to allow it to cool for the morning meal. She walked down the corridor with a prickling awareness of the camouflaged guards watching her. She could sense where they stood but ignored them. Training enabled her to cross the entire stronghold blindfolded without touching a single wall or piece of furniture or unseen guard, but—

Kyza stopped halfway down the hall when she encountered an unfamiliar smell. It alarmed her into camouflaging until she realized the new smell mingled with her human tutor's scent. Marianne must have anointed herself with one of those strange, scented oils she favored, one Kyza had not yet encountered. Satisfied, she dropped out of camouflage and moved on to continue her quest for food, calculating how long she had slept. More than two days had passed.

Moonlight streamed through the kitchens' large windows, illuminating trays of grain rolls set out to cool. Her mouth watering, she plucked one from its tray and bit into it, hunger driving her to devour the entire roll before slowing down. Still not satisfied, she grabbed another and chewed on it as she leaned back against the near wall, sliding down until she sat on the floor with her knees against her chest.

Eating at a more civilized pace, she finished half the second roll, thinking about the trial. If it had accomplished anything, it had removed any fear she had of the dark. Perhaps that had been its purpose? When she became the Suralia someday, she must have no fear of the dark and be willing to lay down her life for her people. The pain, though—she shivered and closed her eyes, leaning her head on her knees. If honor ever required her to walk into the dark, she would make certain she was too far from a Suralian apothecary to be brought back.

CHAPTER 10

Kyza woke, a half-eaten grain roll still in one hand, when one of the cooks approached her at dawn. Stumbling to her peds, she let the smiling head cook shoo her out of the way and into the refectory. Steaming carafes of tea stood on a table by the door, with a collection of mugs beside them. She poured some and went to her usual seat at the high table to finish off the roll. Her father walked in as she ate the last bite.

"Father!" she called out as his gaze fell on her. She slipped from the chair and started to run toward him, but stopped when her knees wobbled. With a few long strides, he crossed the space between them and swept her up into a warm hug.

"Will I get all better?" she asked, rubbing her forehead against his cheek.

"So say the apothecaries," he said as he set her back down, smiling. He radiated a pride that went straight through her, straightening her back, swelling her heart, and firming her resolve to be worthy of Suralia.

Servants began to appear with trays of food, readying the refectory for the morning meal. Satisfied with her father's answer to her question, she grabbed a piece of fruit from one of the trays and returned to her place at the high table.

"I have something to discuss with you, dear one," Father announced as he began to eat.

Dear one. The familiar salutation of a high one. Kyza focused her full attention on him, eyes wide.

He smiled, eyes twinkling. "You passed the great trial."

"The great trial?" Kyza exclaimed. "That was the great trial?"

"Even so."

"I thought I was supposed to be older."

"You pushed your training ahead of schedule," he said, disapproval lacing his tone, "by a year."

"Is that why Proctor Storaas always tells me to be patient?"

"One reason," he replied. "You must listen to him in the future. There is enthusiasm, and there is recklessness. You must have the one and not the other. It was almost your undoing. You came close to death."

"Forgive me, Father."

He gave her the smile he used when he wanted to reassure her. She grinned back at him. "It is past now, daughter. The apothecaries confirm you will make a full recovery. I do expect you to continue your physical conditioning, but from today, you will have no further trials, only practice—rigorous practice. You must see the Jorann, and then I will declare you the legal heir to Suralia."

Kyza bounced out of her chair and into Father's lap, hugging him tight. He gave her a squeeze and tapped her nose with a long, strong finger, his smile luminous with pride. Her heart wanted to fly.

"You begin your more academic studies today," he said. "You will spend as many long hours studying as you did in your physical training. Are you up to the task?" He quirked a smile. "I can replace you if you are not."

She giggled, then sobered. "I will make you proud of me, Father."

"You could not make me prouder—" He interrupted his reply. She winked out of sight and slipped from his lap to return to her chair.

"Marianne comes," he said, his attention fixed on one of the guards, a trace of disapproval in his presence. The guard had been in her line of sight and had not flickered—and he should have. She climbed into her chair and dropped her camouflage just before her human tutor appeared in the doorway.

Marianne was clad like a Tolari, in a robe of pale Suralia blue—the only color she could wear since she belonged to no caste. The clothing she had brought from Earth was not durable and had worn thin, so she had begun to wear Tolari robes more and more often. It pleased Father to see her in them, and sometimes Kyza thought he had forbidden the humans to phase down more human clothing for that very reason.

Marianne smiled at her as she chose morning foods safe for her to eat. She still smelled of the fragrance she had used during the previous evening, although it seemed she had tried to scrub the scent from her skin. Father gestured to a servant and gave a quiet order for the tutor's quarters to be disinfected and deodorized. Again.

Unaware of all this, Marianne took her usual seat across the high table, to Father's left—the place reserved for a bond-partner, if he had had one. It was funny to see a human sit there, unaware of what it meant. Kyza almost grinned, but he reached along their bond to help her suppress it.

"You are glad to see Kyza," Father said. In English.

Marianne nodded, recognizing the compliment the Sural gave by using her language rather than his own. "I'm always glad to see Kyza," she answered. "But you know I couldn't help being worried."

"Worry is counterproductive."

She shrugged and focused on the food.

The Sural continued to stare at her for a time. Then he broke into a crooked smile and continued, "Then you will wish to continue tutoring my heir."

Heir! Marianne thought. *The great trial!* When she'd heard Kyza had almost died, she thought it had to be. The Sural had maintained a forbidding silence while Kyza lay near death, so she hadn't dared to ask.

"So that *was* the great trial!" she exclaimed. She beamed a smile at Kyza. "You passed it!"

Kyza grinned around a mouthful of food.

"Even so," the Sural said. "As a consequence of Kyza's accomplishment, the Jorann has requested her presence. She has also requested," he paused for effect, "yours."

Marianne stopped chewing and met the Sural's gaze, eyes wide. The grain roll's spicy afterburn hit, and she snatched up her mug to gulp some tea. The Sural grinned and took a huge bite of his roll, eating with his usual hearty appetite. The man consumed vast amounts of food. She had no idea how he could stay so lean. He emitted a snort. He enjoyed this, Marianne thought. She glanced at Kyza. The child's face glowed.

She turned her attention back to her meal. There weren't many reasons why the Jorann would request someone's presence, and most involved a status change, whether up, down or sideways. The reason to send for Kyza was obvious, but Marianne wasn't Tolari—she had no family and no status to raise, lower or change. Unless—unless they had some ritual to give her status. She looked up at the Sural again. His smile turned enigmatic. She'd come to think he should patent that smile.

"Yes, we do have a way to give you status," he said. "It is necessary now. Kyza has become a member of the ruling caste, and we have no law to allow for an individual without status to tutor a high one."

"High one, of course I—"

He lifted a hand, and she stopped. "Do not consent before you give it thought. I will give you time to speak with your admiral."

"Of course—but... why?"

"You must become Tolari," he answered. "To have status, you must become a daughter of Suralia. Do you know what it means to become Suralian?"

Marianne searched her memory and shook her head. She couldn't remember hearing him say anything on the topic. "No, high one."

"As you are, you are nothing to my enemies," he replied. "They have no interest in harming you. If you become a daughter of Suralia, you will become a prize, something they might think they can use to dishonor me. They will try to capture you just as they would try to capture my daughter. And you are in far more danger from them—in truth—because you are untrained. A Tolari child could capture you."

Marianne gave a rueful smile. There were humans the Tolari would find difficult to sneak up on—spooks, intelligence operatives, what-have-you—but she wasn't one of them. She put down her food and met his eyes.

"Understand before you consent," the Sural went on, "I must require you, as I require every Suralian, to pledge your life to mine. Can you do that?"

She let out a breath. Pledged to the Sural, she would have to walk into the dark if he died in dishonor. She couldn't imagine how he would ever allow anyone or anything to sully his honor, but the pledge carried a serious obligation. She would have to commit suicide.

It's been two thousand years since the last time a ruler died in dishonor.

"There are... ways," she said. "I'm not trained or equipped for it, but we do have ways to kill ourselves even faster than a Tolari can."

The Sural nodded. "Good. Then I can give you permission to consent if it is what you decide."

Marianne blinked. It seemed circular that the Sural had to give permission for her to consent to something he had asked her to do. *Infinite loop, see loop, infinite.* She studied the grain roll in her hand. This was important to the Sural, she thought. Why?

"Marianne," he said. She jerked her head up—he seldom used her name. "Could you be content to spend the rest of your life here?"

"You mean—stay on Tolar after my assignment is complete?" she asked.

"Yes." His eyes were fixed on hers, but she couldn't interpret his expression.

"Never go home?" Her mind refused to absorb the idea.

"You will be Tolari," he said. "You will be a daughter of Suralia. My province will also be your home. Perhaps you will never want to leave, once you are one of us."

"What if I become Tolari and decide to leave anyway?"

"You would be free to leave. I will not coerce or compel you in this matter, proctor. Freedom gives value to your choice, and nothing else." He paused. "But I hope you will stay."

"And if I decide against becoming Tolari?" she asked. "Will you order me to leave Tolar?"

He gave her a small, patient smile. "No, proctor, I would not order you to leave Tolar, nor would I order you to leave Suralia. I have said this before. You are welcome to stay here, in my stronghold, as long as I hold it, as long as you like—until your natural death, if that is your wish. You could even travel anywhere you wish on Tolar. But I could not permit you to tutor Kyza."

"Meaning I would have no purpose here."

"Unfortunately. Would you be content here with no purpose to serve other than gathering information for your admiral up in the ship?" His mouth twitched.

Marianne laughed at the reference to her implicit role as an untrained spook for Central Command.

"No, I wouldn't—you're right." She sobered again, her mind drifting into thoughts of pledging her life to the Sural's. "I would have to go up to the ship—I'm sure I would require some sort of surgical implant."

He shook his head. "No."

That stopped her. "High one?"

"Having been given this choice, you may not even leave the stronghold until you give me your answer. If you leave, I cannot allow you to return." He met her eyes. "That is not the outcome I prefer."

"Will you allow a medical team to phase down, then?"

"No."

"But—"

"My apothecaries can perform any procedure you require, given the necessary equipment and information."

"I begin to see why you require me to consult with my people."

"Yes," the Sural replied. "Your admiral will want to think about this."

He will indeed, Marianne thought. *He will indeed.*

* * *

HER ADMIRAL DID *NOT* like what Marianne was telling him.

"What does he want with it?" he asked, in Danish, his mother's language. "Is the Sural just trying to weasel more information on human anatomy and physiology from us?"

Marianne understood Danish but didn't speak it well enough to reply. She shook her head. "I don't think that's the case, sir," she said. She spoke Hungarian. Admiral Howard didn't speak *or* understand Hungarian, but his computer provided an English translation of her words. "He can't allow me to leave the stronghold after giving me the opportunity to join his people."

"You know I can't send the Tolari such sensitive information without clearing it with Central Command first, especially not in advance of a full exchange of cultural and scientific information."

"I know that, sir, but this is too good an opportunity to pass up," she said. "Just think about what I could learn once I'm considered one of them. And I would still have no restrictions on what I could put in a written report."

She was right, of course. He suspected Central Command would give the go ahead, but he still couldn't authorize it on his own authority. He dropped back into English, which he knew the invisible listeners could understand. "I'll get back to you in a few days."

Marianne followed suit. "That's all I ask, sir," she answered in the same language. "Woolsey out."

The monitor went blank. The admiral got up and stared out the viewport at the planet below, considering ways to approach Central Command with the request. Five minutes later, he glanced at the wall clock. His secretary's duty shift ended soon. He punched the comms button on his desk.

"Yes sir?" came the secretary's voice.

"Get me Ambassador Russell and his wife."

* * *

"DAMN, John, we have a fantastic opportunity here," Smithton said. The admiral and the ambassador sipped whiskey by the viewport while their wives clattered and chattered in the kitchen. Delicious smells wafted into the admiral's sitting room.

"The Sural had to know from the beginning this would happen," the admiral said. "He had to know his daughter would become a high one and Marianne would then be ineligible to teach her."

"Not necessarily," Adeline called from the kitchen.

"That wife of yours—" the admiral started.

"—is useful to you," she finished, brushing flour off her hands as she walked toward them. "The Sural's daughter is already fluent in every language he wanted Marianne to teach her. That was his original purpose in allowing a human to live in the stronghold. At this point, she just needs to expand the girl's vocabulary until she comes of age. You know what I think?"

"No, but I suspect you're going to tell him anyway," her husband said.

Adeline poked Smithton in the ribs and continued, "I think he's attracted to her."

Admiral Howard laughed. "They're not even human. What would he see in her?"

"They might as well be human. You've seen the DNA analysis from that sample Marianne managed to get. They're kissing cousins to humanity. Marianne's naturally reserved manner and her looks—tell me you've *never* wanted to gaze into those amazing eyes of hers—those might just make her exotic and interesting to a Tolari. If only he hadn't requested a female tutor for his daughter!"

"They're cold and calculating bastards," Smithton grumbled.

"Calculating, sure, but cold? We don't know that either. That's just the face they show us."

"Addie has a point, Smit," the admiral said. "Some of their customs don't make sense if they have as little emotion as they let us see."

A loud crash and a yelp came from the kitchen. "Exactly!" Adeline cried, hurrying back to rejoin Laura.

"How do you explain the way the high ones let their children die in their damned tests?" Smithton called after her.

"Ask me later—the vegetables need my undivided attention right now."

Smithton grunted and took another sip of his drink.

* * *

"So you see," Adeline finished, "as in some of our own Asian cultures, they reserve emotion for the privacy of the family. And if you never anticipate grief, which they don't, you're going to be a lot more sanguine about everything. Think about it—if she's a member of the family, they could drop their guard around her. She could learn so much more about their intimate family relationships!"

Smithton had to admit she had a point. "So you think he's inventing ways to keep her around because he wants to bed her?"

His wife shrugged. "We don't know enough about their culture to speculate if they would allow one of their high ones to have an intimate relationship with an outsider, much less an alien outsider, so that particular activity may not even be a part of his plans. But it does look like he wants to keep her around, and if she has *status* in his household, she'll have access to a lot more information than she's had up to now. You can't pass that up."

"Marianne was also clear it puts her life in danger, Addie," the admiral pointed out.

Adeline's face clouded a little. "I know. That's the fly in the ointment."

"No, that's not the fly in the ointment, Addie," Smithton said, "the suicide switch is."

Her eyebrows flew up her forehead, and her fork clattered onto her plate. "Suicide switch? What?"

The admiral cut in. "The Sural requires her to be willing to die for him, as he does every other member of his household," he said. "That means she has to be wired. The Sural won't allow her to leave the stronghold to get it done up here on the ship, nor will he allow us to phase a medical team down to the planet to do it there. He's asked us to send his apothecaries the necessary equipment and information for them to do it. Suicide wire technology is classified at the highest levels, and even if their medical technology were up to the task, we haven't released the required level of human anatomical information to them either. That's why I can't okay this on my own authority."

"Oh. My. God." Adeline's voice was little more than a breath.

"I know how you feel about things like that," Smithton said, taking her hand.

Laura spoke up. "What if she wasn't wired? What if we use simpler technology which is just as effective and doesn't require specialized equipment or detailed physical information?"

"What did you have in mind?" the admiral asked.

"You know how I like to watch old movies—"

"You and my wife," Smithton grumbled. "You're both stuck in the twentieth century, the pair of you."

The admiral began to hum an ancient song about a submarine. Smithton glared.

"Some old spook movies had secret operatives with a false tooth filled with cyanide, an early version of the suicide switch," Laura continued. "Cyanide is pretty crude—we can come up with something better than that—but the principle would be the same. Or maybe two false teeth that have to be broken at the same time, each containing a harmless substance which only turns deadly when mixed with the other. But you get the idea. You wouldn't even need to send them any information—the Tolari already know how to fix human teeth because Marianne had that problem with her wisdom teeth a few years back."

Adeline roused herself from her shock. "It's still unethical."

"But it's not *as* unethical, is it?" Laura asked.

Adeline shot the admiral's wife a blank stare. Then she picked the napkin from her lap and put it beside her plate. "I'm not hungry anymore," she said, and got up to leave.

Smithton let her go.

* * *

"MARIANNE, YOU CAN'T DO THIS," Addie said as Smithton walked into their quarters later. She glanced up. He shook his head at her and continued on to the bedroom, yawning and untying his cravat as he walked. He seemed to doubt she could say anything to sway Marianne Woolsey once she had made up her mind. She turned her attention back to the monitor.

"Addie, I have to," Marianne replied.

"No, you don't! You told me yourself, you wouldn't have to leave. You don't even have to stop talking to Kyza. You could still learn so much for us in the coming years before Kyza comes of age."

"I doubt I will ever have to use the suicide switch, or the poison tooth, or whatever it is the medical team comes up with. The Sural is the most honorable man I've ever met and the most powerful Tolari on the planet. He won't be dishonored unless he's captured, and he would die before he allowed that to happen. And have you *seen* the strength of his defenses? Suralia hasn't even been attacked in a couple of generations. *Tolari* generations, which I think are probably twice as long as ours."

"Just being willing—"

"It isn't the same thing," Marianne interrupted.

"It's unethical."

"In the opinion of some, yes, but it's legal on two of the Six Planets."

"Marianne!"

"I promise I'll consider what you've said. Will that help?"

Adeline slumped back in her chair, feeling glum. "It's the best I'm going to get, isn't it," she said.

"I'm afraid so."

Adeline sighed, then sat up straighter. "There's something else you need to know."

"What's that?"

"We think the Sural wants you to stay because he's attracted to you," she said, putting on a professional face. "If you *do* just find him attractive—if you don't find the idea of intimacy with an alien repulsive—it would be helpful if you could—well—let him court you."

Adeline put her head in one hand for a moment, and then looked up at the monitor again. "I know I've teased you about him for years, but I'm serious this time. If he's interested in you, give him a chance."

Marianne went still, eyes wide and mouth agape, and then she burst into laughter. "Addie, it's been *eight years*. Don't you think if the Sural were attracted to me, he would have said or done something by now?"

"You tell me, you're the one down there living with him. But no, I don't think so, not necessarily. They're a long-lived race, and we're sure the Sural's a lot older than he looks. He could be eighty or ninety, even a hundred standard years old. He might consider four of their years too short an acquaintance before a first date. And it's not as if you've encouraged him. I love you like the sister I never had, Marianne, but you're blind when it comes to men. You wouldn't believe he was courting you until he went down on one knee with a ring."

"Oh Addie, you're making this up as you go along, just to yank my chain. And if he's really *that* old, he's way, way, way too old for me. I'm only thirty-four. Or is it thirty-five now? What's the date today, anyway—I keep losing track."

Adeline sighed. "You're thirty-five. But Marianne—just remember this one thing: nothing is more important than doing the next right thing. Just focus on doing the next right thing."

"I promise I'll try."

"That's all I ask."

* * *

SMITHTON HELD his wife and stroked her hair. She'd come to bed broody and silent. "It'll be all right, Addie."

She shook her head. "I argued the admiral into an unethical course of action. If Marianne takes her own life, some of the blame will be on *me*."

"No, darling, you didn't argue John into anything, and Marianne is a grown woman. She's responsible for her own decisions."

"I didn't help!" she exclaimed. "What am I going to do?"

"You can try to argue the admiral out of it. The inimitable Adeline Russell can argue anyone into or out of anything, remember? Sell ice cubes to Eskimos, all that. You should have been a traveling salesman."

Despite herself, she laughed a little, then fell quiet again and whispered, “I couldn’t talk Marianne out of it.”

“Hmpf,” Smithton grumbled. “No one can talk *that* woman out of anything. She’s practically a sociopath.”

“Smitty! You can’t be ser—oh, I see. You’re trying to argue *me* out of my mood.”

“Is it working?” he asked, making his face as blank and innocent as he could.

Adeline pulled the pillow out from under her head and clobbered him with it.

CHAPTER 11

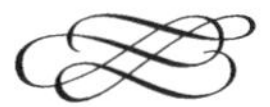

Marianne entered the open study off the stronghold's audience room. Several days had passed since the admiral forwarded her request to Central Command, and she had an answer for the Sural. He motioned her toward a chair without looking up, engrossed in reading a report. She settled into the chair he'd indicated and studied her hands.

A few minutes later, she looked up as he stood and rounded his desk. He sat on its edge in front of her, a gentle smile playing across his lips.

He already knows.

What Addie had said about his feelings crossed her mind. She dismissed it. *He's pleased, that's all,* she thought. *Courting a peasant like me! What a bizarre idea. But if even I can tell he's happy, the whole stronghold has to know.*

"It is not a secret," he said in Hungarian, his smile broadening.

She laughed. "That took you longer than usual," she said, wondering if the computers on the *Alexander* could translate Yup'ik. It had become a game with the Sural to see how long she could use a human language in her communications with the ship before he learned it. He already knew French, Hindi, German, and Mandarin. At this rate, she would run out of languages before Kyza came of age.

"When do your apothecaries phase down the implants?" he asked in his own language.

"In a few hours," she answered. "The drug is a controlled substance. They can't synthesize a sufficient quantity of it all at once. The computer won't let them."

He nodded. "A wise precaution."

Marianne studied the Sural, trying to read him. *Maybe they'll teach me how they do that, once I'm one of them.*

"We might," he said.

She laughed. "How do you *do* that?"

"Humans are easy to read." He smiled.

She shook her head and sighed, pushing down feelings of inferiority. "I don't have your empathy. I can't read you, and I don't know how to mask myself."

He raised an eyebrow. "No one can read me unless I allow it," he said, "but as soon as your doctors phase down the drugs, my apothecaries will insert the implants. And then—" He stopped.

"And then?"

"Then you will visit the Jorann and enter a new world. Our world." He pushed away from the desk and waited for her to get to her feet. "Come. Walk with me."

She fell into step with him as he walked out into the gardens. Flutters chattered and sang in the cora trees, their plumage flashing in the sunlight, and flowers bloomed in the bluish-green ferny groundcover she still called grass. Mid-spring on Tolar was beautiful, if colder than her idea of spring. They wandered along a sparkling brook. The Sural broke his silence as he stopped by a large rock next to a tree near the stream.

"This is where Kyza walked into the dark," he said. "Under this cora tree. This is where she proved herself a worthy heir to Suralia." He reached up and picked a twig.

Marianne could almost feel the pride he radiated. *Am I reading him?*

"Yes," he replied, looking down at her with a lopsided smile. "I am broadcasting loudly enough for even you to read me." She blinked. "I want to give you a taste of what is to come. But tell me—before you go before the Jorann and become one of us—tell me if you can be content to make Tolar your home. Tell me you will not miss your homeworld enough to make you unhappy. Can you tell me that?"

She mulled it over. She couldn't give him a quick, glib answer, but how could she know what she would feel in the future? "I've been content here these past eight years," she answered. "Four years," she amended, trying to think of time in Tolari terms.

"You evade my question."

She bowed in apology. "Forgive me, high one, but I don't think I can answer your question. I can say I'm content here now, and I'm content to remain here for now. I don't know what the future will bring."

"A wise answer."

"A satisfactory answer?"

"Yes, proctor. Quite sufficient." He turned and continued down the path. She followed. "If I told you why I wish you to stay on Tolar, would you be required to tell your admiral?"

"Yes, if he asked. And he probably would."

"And if I told you after you are one of us, and I commanded you to say nothing of it to anyone?"

"Then I wouldn't tell him."

"Ah," he said. "Then I shall not tell you—until then." He stopped broadcasting and closed his emotional barriers. It surprised her to feel it.

"I understand, high one," she said, bowing. "I'm at your service."

The Sural stopped and turned. "I know that, proctor," he said, his voice devoid of expression. He headed back into the keep.

* * *

ADELINE STOOD with Smitty in the ship's infirmary when the *Alexander*'s chief medical officer phased two implants, each with a clear, bold label, down to the planet.

"I hope you know what you're doing, Smitty," she said.

"Of course I don't," he grumped at her. "Diplomacy is an art, not a science."

"*That* wasn't diplomacy," she snapped, pointing at the empty phase platform. She sighed, shoulders slumping a little, and turned to the ship's physician, who still stood next to the phase platform, making notes. "So what exactly were those drugs and what are they going to do to her?"

He looked up. "The one contained an overdose of a sedative, the other held its antidote. They'll be inserted inside each side of her jaw.

The sedative causes painless death in about four minutes—we were careful to choose a drug that would be short and sweet, but not too short. As long as the antidote is administered within three minutes, she'll survive with no permanent aftereffects."

Adeline shuddered. *It's too late now,* she thought. "At least it's not a suicide switch," she muttered under her breath.

"What was that?" the doctor asked.

"Nothing."

* * *

MARIANNE GROANED and opened her eyes. A troupe of spiky little fire demons danced inside the entire lower half of her face. A warm, gentle hand took one of hers. Calm strength flowed from it. Then a voice spoke over her head.

"Give her relief for the pain," the Sural said. "Humans are not like us."

She tried to speak. "N-n—"

A finger touched her lips. "Trust me," he said in English. She tried to nod and gasped from the pain. The Sural bent over her, slipping a strong hand beneath her head, touching a cup to her lips. "Drink."

She tried. When she opened her lips, fire blazed through her jaws, and the liquid tasted the way floor polish smelled. She gasped, making a face and spluttering into the cup. The Sural chuckled.

"Drink," he repeated. He held it to her lips until she managed to swallow the entire contents, and then lowered her head. Her thoughts went muzzy.

What did I just drink? she wondered. *I hope it's not poisonous to humans—*

* * *

WHEN MARIANNE WOKE AGAIN, a pink and orange dawn painted the eastern sky and tinted the walls of her sleeping room. Quiet surrounded her, and warmth had replaced the pain. *I know doctors who would pay good money for a drug like that,* she thought. She raised both hands to her face, running her fingers under her jaws, finding the implants nestled where the apothecaries had said they would be.

Something fell from the blankets as she pushed herself to a sitting position. She picked it up.

The twig the Sural had picked from the cora tree lay in her hand, half the thickness of her little finger. Swelling buds covered it. *A budding branch,* she thought. To the Sural's people, the budding branch was a symbol of renewal. It was also the symbol of hope: hope for new life, hope for better things to come, hope for joy and hope for gentle rain and growing things. Some Suralian poets used it as a symbol for blossoming love.

She ran a finger along the twig, wondering why he had left it. *I'll bet it's a symbol of my new status,* she decided, as the door to her sleeping room opened. The Sural and Kyza stepped in, both wearing layers of heavy brocade robes in shades of Suralia blue, followed by a female servant. The servant carried a tray of food and a steaming carafe.

The Sural's eyes fell on the budding twig in her hands, and he smiled that infuriating, enigmatic smile. "How do you feel?" he asked.

She licked dry lips before trying to speak. "No pain," she replied, her voice a little rough. She cleared her throat.

"Good," he said. "The servant will help you to dress. You must eat, and then it is time for you and Kyza to see the Jorann."

"I thought that wasn't until tomorrow."

Kyza grinned. "It *is* tomorrow," she chirped.

Marianne rubbed her face with both hands. "I slept so long?"

"The drug we gave you is known to have that effect," the Sural said. Marianne started to protest, but he raised a hand to stop her. "We knew it would not harm you. My apothecaries know more of your physiology than the admiral thinks, after studying you for eight of your years."

She blinked, thinking about the admiral, about the ship, about the humorless spooks at Central Command Security. "Well," she said with a grin twitching the corners of her mouth upward, "don't tell *him* that."

Kyza giggled. The Sural turned toward the door. "You will find the robes you must wear in your closet," he said as he left. "The servant will show you how to wear them."

Marianne snatched bites of food while she dressed. It took some time, but the servant managed to get her into the correct pieces of clothing in the correct order. The lightest weight, darkest-colored robes lay next to her skin; the lighter-colored, heavy brocade robes covered them, the shades of Suralia blue ranging from dark to pale. Something warm and soft lined the three inner layers. Kyza gave her a visual inspection after the black-robed woman left and nodded approval.

"You will need them," the girl explained. "It is cold down there."

"Down where?"

"In the ice cave where the Jorann lives."

"I see."

"No, you do not—but you will!" Kyza grinned and scampered off. Marianne blinked at her. She hadn't seen Kyza display so much emotion the four Tolari years she'd lived on the planet as the girl had in the past three days. Four days, she corrected herself. She'd lost a day to the vile potion the Sural had made her drink.

They're already letting me in.

Moving like a mummy swathed in the five layers of heavy robes, she went into the hallway and found the Sural waiting. Her heart skipped a beat. In the flickering torchlight, wearing the Suralia brocade, he dominated the primitive-looking, banner-lined corridor like a New Chin emperor.

His mahogany eyes flashed. "Follow me," he commanded, setting off toward the family quarters at a brisk pace. At the end of the corridor in the family wing, a short hall split off to the right and ended at a winding staircase leading down. She looked into the stairwell. Lights spotted the wall as far as she could see. The Sural started to descend. Marianne hesitated.

"It is a long way to the bottom," Kyza said. "Are you strong enough? Father can carry you if you are not."

Marianne flinched at the thought of being carried down a bottomless staircase by Tolar's sovereign ruler. It would be like hiring a king to be her chauffeur. She couldn't imagine how she'd ever explain it to the admiral, and if Addie ever found out, she wouldn't stop teasing her until the heat death of the universe.

"I'll be fine," she said, hoping it was true. Setting her jaw, she followed the Sural down the stairs.

With the Sural leading and Kyza bringing up the rear, they descended the long stairwell. It seemed like forever, though Marianne thought a half hour was closer to accurate. The stairs ended at a wide, chiseled tunnel which continued for perhaps a kilometer, then came to another staircase, this one leading up. She hesitated, her legs shaking.

"Marianne," the Sural said.

She looked up.

"You are no burden." He smiled and swept her into his arms to carry her up the staircase. Marianne looked over his shoulder at Kyza, who gave a one-shouldered Tolari shrug and grinned. The Sural carried her without effort.

Marianne leaned into him and tried to keep a grip on herself. He glanced at her with an impassive expression and adjusted his hold. She'd never been this close to him before, and it provoked sensations she didn't welcome. He radiated body heat, and she could smell his skin—it was a little like almonds. Spicy. Male. Her stomach clenched. If the Tolari released pheromones to attract each other, she could make a fool of herself.

She felt attracted all right. Her arms ached to return his embrace. Giving herself a vicious mental kick, she held her arms rigid and concentrated on counting the steps of the broad spiral staircase, hoping he concerned himself too much with climbing them to give any thought to reading her.

The staircase they climbed was much shorter than the stairs down from the keep. That helped. She wasn't sure how much longer she could keep a lid on herself with the Sural's arms warm around her. She found herself wondering if his lips were as warm as his arms and gave herself another mental kick. She'd never wanted to kiss anyone before; she couldn't start now with her employer. Her *aristocratic* employer. For good measure, she bludgeoned herself again.

When the staircase opened up into a grand cavern, the Sural let her down onto her own feet. She took a quick step away from him, shivering. The Sural and Kyza looked relaxed and comfortable, but they belonged to this world, cold as it was. They stood silent and still, facing the cavern's center. She imitated their example.

As the minutes ticked past, Marianne became aware of a figure sitting motionless on the ice in the middle of the cavern—the most wizened, old white-haired Tolari she had ever seen, in a sleeveless robe of icy white that might have been a shade of pale blue.

This must be the Jorann, she thought. She blinked. *Her skin is* pale?

"Do you bring guards or weapons or implements of destruction into my home?" the Jorann challenged in a strong voice belying her age.

"No, highest," the Sural replied. His voice resounded with a sincerity even Marianne could hear.

"Come, children."

The Sural led them forward. The Jorann motioned them to sit on thick fuzzy white blankets covering the ice before the dais. When they had seated themselves, she spoke again.

"I greet you, children." Her face wrinkled into a fond smile.

"You honor us, highest," answered the Sural.

The Jorann turned her attention on Marianne. "You are not one of my children."

Marianne looked up into the old crone's face and gasped at the blue eyes gazing back at her. The Jorann broke into a merry laugh.

"You are human?" Marianne blurted.

"It is more accurate to say that I was *once* human."

"What—" Marianne stopped herself.

The old woman cackled with glee. "Oh ho, you have learned good manners from my grandson!" In the corner of Marianne's eye, the Sural bent his head to acknowledge the compliment. "I can see why he wants to take you into the family. Brains as well as beauty."

Marianne swiveled to look at the Sural. He raised an eyebrow in reply.

"You realize that you are quite a beauty by our standards?" the Jorann continued. "Breathtaking. No wonder he is besotted. But never mind that. I have summoned you and Kyza here to give you my blessing."

The Jorann gave Marianne no time to digest her comments. She pushed herself off the dais and hobbled over to a rock on which sat a crystal box, taking from it a number of small whitish cubes, the shape and half the size of sugar cubes. She turned to Kyza and placed one in her hand.

"You are Kyza," she said. "Daughter and heir of Suralia. I give you rank and status second to the Sural."

"You honor me, highest," Kyza said, sitting up straighter, her face wreathed in a huge smile. Her eyes shone.

The Sural cast an indulgent smile at his daughter. The Jorann shuffled toward him and placed a cube in his hand.

"Grandson," she said. "I greet you, Suralia."

He gazed up at her, the expression on his face resembling something akin to worship. "You honor me, highest," he murmured.

The Jorann's eyes glinted, and her lips twitched. "The seal on your heart has broken, grandson."

"Yes, highest."

She shook with dry chuckles and moved in front of Marianne. Marianne held up both hands to accept the cube the Jorann offered. She flicked a glance at the Sural. Both eyebrows climbed his forehead.

"You are Marianne," the Jorann said. Marianne's attention snapped back to the old woman. "Today you are a daughter of Suralia. You belong to us."

The Jorann nodded to the Sural, and both he and Kyza put the cubes in their mouths. Marianne reached for her scanner, which she had slipped up a sleeve before leaving the stronghold.

"You will not need that, child," the Jorann said.

"But highest—"

"You must obey me in this. If you scan my blessing, its molecular structure will change, and it will not then do what I need it to do for you. If you scan it, it *will* poison you. If you do not, it will make you one of us."

Marianne looked at the Sural. "Trust us," he said. Marianne took a deep breath, looked up at the Jorann, and nodded.

"Put the cube in your mouth and let it melt on your tongue," she said.

"Yes, highest." Marianne put the tiny white cube in her mouth.

The world went away.

* * *

THE SURAL CAUGHT Marianne as she slumped against him. The Jorann's blessing sent her sinking into unconsciousness so deep her presence dimmed from his senses, despite the physical contact. Shifting sideways, he cradled her head in one arm and supported her upper body with the other.

"Heir to Suralia," the Jorann said, "you will find blankets against the wall. Bring one."

Pride flashed through his daughter at the title. She jumped up and scampered off. He glanced at the Jorann and met eyes which seemed to penetrate his soul.

"Your senses are bruised," she said.

He lowered his gaze to Marianne. So deep in unconsciousness, her face had relaxed into a serene beauty that filled his heart with longing.

"She fought herself and struck me. I shielded Kyza from the blows." The old one snorted. He let his lips curve. "She has no awareness of how little privacy she has. The stairs did not seem an appropriate place to educate her."

"That will change when she wakes."

Kyza returned and tried to throw a blanket over Marianne, managing only to drape her... *feet,* while the rest of the cover lay alongside her. Still supporting her head, he let her slip down until she lay in his lap, which freed an arm to assist his daughter.

Expressionless and unreadable, the Jorann sat silent as he and Kyza smoothed the blanket over Marianne. When she lay covered, he raised his eyes once more to the revered ancient. Her hands curled in her lap, a sliver of white showing between her fingers.

"Will you take your blessing?" he asked.

She lifted an eyebrow, eyes sparkling. "Do you worry over me, Suralia?"

He bit back a response. The Jorann was a powerful empath; she could read his concern even with his barriers shut. The idea she would walk into the dark during his rule appalled him, but he could not read her to know if she intended to allow her long life to end. He could do nothing if she did.

"No, grandson." Her face softened into a gentle smile. "I have yet to lose interest in life." She placed the cube on her tongue.

Relief washed through him. His heart easing, he gazed down at the women he held. She used her people's separation of person and profession as a barricade against him. While carrying her up the steps, he had sensed every nuance of her struggle with her own desire, had felt the fear provoking her to quell it with painful emotional blows.

He would need all his experience and insight to help her adjust to the revelations she faced when she awakened.

CHAPTER 12

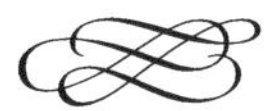

Marianne floated into consciousness, a strange energy thrumming from head to toe. Three presences glowed around her, two of them blank and unreadable, one eager and fidgeting. A quarter day had passed. *How do I know all that?* Her head lay in a warm lap, and a musky, male scent drifted over her from the Sural.

Wait—what?

"The blessing makes you one of us." Kyza's voice rang with a world of meaning—a child's pride in her own knowledge. "It is not just a ritual that says, 'Now we say that you are one of us.' It *makes* you one of us."

Marianne opened blurry eyes.

"Welcome to our world, child," said a young woman with white hair cascading around her in long, intricate braids. Marianne's head lay in her lap. As her vision focused, she recognized the young woman's eyes. They had looked out of the ancient Jorann's face.

"The blessing gives youth to the old," the Sural said.

"This is—"

"The Jorann," he answered. "Yes."

"What did that stuff do to me?" she asked, probing her face with her fingers.

"Your appearance is little changed," he said, "but you are changing, becoming one of us."

"I am *becoming* Tolari?" she gasped. "What? How?"

"I did tell you, did I not, that you would become Tolari?"

"I did *not* think you meant it literally!" Marianne's hands flew to her jaws. "Then why...?"

"You are new," he answered, "and you are only beginning to become Tolari. When your ability to walk into the dark has developed, my apothecaries will remove the implants."

"It will take some time, child," said the Jorann, "before you are fully one of us. Five or six seasons, perhaps as much as two years. The process will accelerate as it progresses, but the beginning is quite slow."

"Who *are* you?" she asked.

"She is the first Tolari," Kyza answered, voice still ringing with pride.

"But Tolari civilization has existed for thousands of years!" Marianne exclaimed, sitting up. The world spun around her. She groaned and fell back.

"Yes it has, dear one," said the Sural.

She gasped. *This woman is thousands of years old.*

"I have a lot to learn," she said, sitting up with more care.

"Yes, dear one." The Sural smiled. "You have."

Her thoughts whirled at the idea that the Tolari possessed a fountain of youth. "The admiral must *never* find out!"

The Jorann's golden laughter filled the cavern. "He will not, child."

"But what will happen the next time I talk to the ship? I cannot go audio-only. They would suspect right away that something was wrong."

"The humans should not be able to see any visible change in you," she answered. "Your face has not changed beyond a slight thickening of the skin on your forehead—more to the point, your hair and eye color have not and will not change, though they cannot be passed on to any children you might bear."

Marianne winced. She covered it by getting to her feet.

"Other physical changes will happen slowly or not be readily visible at all, such as your feet changing to peds. It will take one or two of our years after you become fully Tolari before you will be able to camouflage."

The Sural added, "You should be able to eat any of our foods by the time we return to my stronghold. That will be the first noticeable change."

"I encourage you to try all our foods now, child," said the Jorann. "You will find that even the ones you know will taste different."

Marianne nodded, the flood of sensation overwhelming. She shoved at it, trying to create a quiet space to breathe.

The Jorann chuckled. "Go now, child. Let my grandson take you back to his stronghold. You need familiar surroundings to settle your mind, and he can tell you what you want and need to know along the way." She started to turn away, then turned back. "You still do not realize?" She uttered a soft snort. "Receiving the blessing from my hand makes you a member of the ruling caste. My grandson has already realized this. You are his equal in status now, though your rank?" She shrugged a shoulder. "We will decide that after some time has passed. Know this—I do not want you harmed, by anyone, in any way. My children *will* respect that, even my grandson's enemies. Go now, daughter of Suralia." She turned away again.

Dumbfounded, Marianne stared at the Jorann's retreating figure. Kyza pulled at her hand to follow the Sural as he headed in the opposite direction, toward the stairs.

"H-high one?" she whispered.

"Walk with me," the Sural called back, inflecting it as a request to an equal.

She hurried after him. Kyza camouflaged and dashed ahead, playing. The Sural gave Marianne a warm smile. She sensed more than saw the warmth. *And the humans think him cold,* she thought. *If only they knew.*

His smile became enigmatic.

She dropped into English. "Will I always be easy to read?" she asked.

He laughed. "Perhaps not to others, dear one," he said, taking her hand. "To me? Always."

She gave him a rueful smile and changed the subject. "I should be angry."

"For what reason?"

"For not telling me this would change me physically."

"I did tell you."

"You *knew* I didn't understand!"

"It was necessary."

"But—"

"Can you say, in truth, you did not wish to be one of us?" he asked.

Marianne brooded. "No," she answered. "But I wish it had been a more conscious decision. *My* decision."

He shrugged an apology.

She sighed, lips pressed together. It was the best she would get from him. Tolari! *Dear God, he can be an arrogant bastage.* Heaving another sigh, she said, "She called you her grandson."

"I am many times her grandson," he replied. "The title as she uses it is symbolic. I am one of the few born among us with heightened abilities. No one can see me when I do not want to be seen, touch me when I do not want to be touched, or sense me when I do not want to be sensed. I can be a very dangerous man, and it is not just my training that makes me so. That is why *I* rule Tolar and not another of the provincial rulers. They could not stop me if I wanted to kill the ruler of every province on Tolar and take their lands and peoples for my own, and they know this. Ones like me are called the Jorann's grandchildren. Only seven others have been born into the ruling caste since our civilization's beginning. I am the eighth."

Marianne's skin prickled. *An invisible assassin.*

"Do not fear me, dear one," he said. "I am dangerous to my enemies, not to those I protect. And I have enemies only because certain of the ruling caste have more ambition than is good for them. Despite the stability the Jorann's grandchildren bring, they would rid themselves of my rule if they could."

"So... the Jorann is protecting me?"

His face lit as he nodded. "No one will dare touch you now, not my allies, not my enemies. Any provincial ruler who tried to harm you would earn her wrath."

"What does *that* mean?"

He hesitated. "It means... she turns her back on such a one."

The air gusted out of her, hard. "You are a powerful man, high one."

"Dear one."

"Huh?"

"Ruling caste address each other as *dear one*."

She flushed, fiddling with the cuffs of her sleeves and wincing. "Oh. Then—you are a powerful man, dear one," she said, pushing the awkward, far too intimate words through her lips.

"As long as I do not lose your favor," he said in a low voice, squeezing her fingers. She looked down. He still held her hand. She blushed, and his dark eyes glinted with the delight her blushes seemed to inspire in most Tolari.

She took a shaky breath, but didn't pull her hand away. The pressure of his fingers increased again, and her breathing hitched. Did he *want* to hold her hand? "What did she mean, she could see why you are besotted?"

He stopped and raised her hand to his lips. In the Jorann's ice cave, he had seemed—blank, walled off, unreadable. Now, his presence came alive with emotion, powerful, almost shattering in its intensity. Love and longing flowed from within him and washed over her. She pulled away and put both hands to her face, trying to hide the blood rushing to her cheeks. *Oh my God,* she thought. *Is that him? Was Addie right?*

Her stomach sank. If she could sense so much of him, he must have long ago sensed the inappropriate feelings she struggled to keep under control. She stared up at him, eyes wide. Her throat tried to close, but she had to know.

"The ambassador's wife told me you—you were trying to court me," she said.

"I am," he replied, his voice almost a whisper. "I have been. For quite a long time."

She couldn't breathe. "But that can't be true."

He pried the hands from her face and held them close to his heart with both of his. The contact brought his feelings into sharp focus again. Love. Tenderness. Longing. *Oh my God,* she thought again. *This can't be happening.*

"Tell me why."

"I'm just a teacher." Her voice dropped to a hoarse whisper. "My ancestors are all farmers. I'm a nobody. You're the sovereign ruler of a *planet*."

His face crinkled into a bemused smile. "Such distinctions mean nothing to us," he said, mirth coloring his voice. He touched her reddened face with his fingertips. "What matters to me is who you are, not what you are."

Marianne found her mouth dry. A concerned look replaced the delight on his face. Her mind raced, trying to absorb it all. It couldn't be possible. *He—he* loves *me. How—why—?* Fear stabbed her as the implications flashed before her mind's eye. He sensed it.

"I have never harmed you," he said, cupping her face with both hands and stroking her cheek with a thumb. "And I never will. Why do you fear me? Why do you fight yourself?"

"I don't—" she stammered. A voice rose above the confusion in her head. *You're a professional,* it said. *Act like it.* "I don't love—"

He locked eyes with her. She looked down, her voice silenced and the lie stuck in her throat.

"I can sense your feelings, dear one," he said. He folded his arms around her.

She trembled. He was so warm, the comfort he offered so… tantalizing. She let her arms slip around him, sighed, and sank into his embrace. Joy, fierce joy, burst from him, and his hold tightened.

Memory intruded of another taut pair of arms. She stiffened.

"Do not panic," he told her. "I will not hurt you, and I will not allow anyone else to hurt you."

She buried her face in his robes, her throat constricting, her knees turning to water.

"No one is hurting you," he said. "And no one can while I live."

Gulping air, Marianne struggled to calm herself. Breath by breath, the panic diminished. Grief for her came from the Sural, and longing for him pierced her heart, creating a trail of warmth straight down to where she didn't want to feel it. He lifted her chin to make her meet his eyes. Her stomach quivered.

"I will never harm you," he said.

Marianne nodded, biting back tears. The Sural stroked her hair. "I will never hurt you," he repeated.

She took a deep breath. "I—I don't know why I get so afraid," she said, her voice trembling.

"You have been hurt." The hand under her chin shifted to cup her face. His mahogany eyes searched hers, but he didn't probe. She thought. "Who hurt you? Will you tell me?"

She shook her head and looked down. "I can't talk about it," she whispered.

Disappointment flashed through him. He took a step back and offered an arm. "Walk with me," he said. "We cannot delay our return to my stronghold any longer."

She hesitated, then took his arm. The Sural touched her with a delicate probe, letting a little comfort flow into her as they walked. The turmoil within her began to ease.

When they came in range of the first guard—close to the top of the long flight of steps to the keep—he closed his empathic barriers with an almost audible snap. An instant later, Kyza stopped playing and became the sober child Marianne had always known.

Marianne did her best to imitate them but failed. Still, she reasoned, she could be expected to be in considerable confusion from her visit with the Jorann, which everyone in the stronghold knew she had just experienced. She hoped she didn't give away anything she shouldn't.

At the top of the stairs, her jaws itched and her lungs burned, but she had expected worse so soon after a medical procedure. The strange energy she'd awakened with still buzzed through her body, giving her a new strength, but she knew herself weaker than the Tolari around her. And they were *everywhere* around her. Guards lined the corridor, guards she always knew had to be there, but she had never known where or how many. Now they glowed like beacons.

The Sural led her to a door in the family wing. "Your quarters have been moved here, dear one," he said. The reaction to his words rippled through the guards. The news of just how high the Jorann had raised her status would be all over Suralia by nightfall—which was not far off. Through the window at the end of the hall, sunset painted the sky shades of red and purple. "Kyza's apartments are next to yours. The servants moved your belongings exactly as they were in your old quarters."

Marianne nodded, giving him a shaky smile, a little surprised. Then she decided she should have expected it. It was no longer appropriate to keep her in guest quarters. He opened the door for her and she peered into her new sitting room. It looked identical. She started to walk in, but he stopped her.

"No time for that now," he said. "Follow me."

"Yes, dear one," she replied, feeling an even stronger ripple of reaction run through the guards. She wondered what they thought.

He led the way to the audience room near the entrance of the keep. Dozens of representatives of the Sural's allies—provincial heirs, regents, or trusted chief advisors—and numerous representatives of the city and the surrounding regions of Suralia stood scattered through the huge room. As they entered, the guards along the walls flickered into sight.

The Sural left Marianne and Kyza at the door. “Stay here until I call you,” he said, walking ahead into the room with long, ground-eating strides. When he reached the dais, he lowered himself to sit on his heels in its center. The guards disappeared from view, and the guests sat.

The Sural spoke. “Kyza,” he called in a strong voice, “Today you are legal heir to Suralia. Come forward, dear one.”

As Kyza reached the Sural’s dais, one guest stood; a figure in a pale tan robe with embroidery from collar to waist. *The Detral.* Marianne had never seen him before, but the Sural had mentioned him many times as a friend and ally. His province lay on Suralia’s western border.

The ruler of Detralar held out both arms. “Who stands witness that Kyza has passed the great trial of Suralia?” he called.

Storaas stood from among a group of the Sural’s advisors.

“I stand witness,” he said. “I am the Sural’s family tutor. I administered the trial.”

The Sural’s head apothecary rose next to him. “I stand witness,” she said. “I am the Sural’s head apothecary. I witnessed her return from the dark.”

The Sural stood and gazed at his daughter. “Who receives your obedience?” he asked.

“Accept my obedience, Father,” Kyza said. “I pledge my life to your life. I will walk into the dark for your honor.”

He smiled and held out a hand. She climbed the steps onto the dais to take the hand and stand beside him.

“Hear me and stand witness that Kyza pledges her life and her honor to the Sural. Her life belongs to mine. I will defend her with my honor, my life, and my people. She is the legal heir to Suralia.”

Kyza looked up at her father, her eyes shining, then moved to the heir’s place behind and to his right and sat on her heels.

“Marianne, daughter of Suralia,” the Sural called. “Come forward, dear one.”

Marianne felt the Sural’s words hit the guests like cattle prods. *That will be all over the* planet *by nightfall,* she thought. She walked forward and stopped at the foot of the dais.

“Who receives your obedience?”

"Accept my obedience, dear one," she answered, repeating Kyza's words. "I pledge my life to your life. I will walk into the dark for your honor."

He looked out over the guests. "Hear me and stand witness that Marianne Woolsey pledges her life and her honor to the Sural. Her life belongs to mine. I will defend her with my honor, my life, and my people. She is a daughter of Suralia.

"Hear me," he continued. "The Jorann has given Marianne her protection."

The Sural stepped to the edge of the dais and held out a hand to Marianne. She took it and let him pull her up by his side. Loud conversation broke out as every man, woman, and child in the room crowded around. Music filled the room. Servants appeared carrying trays of food and drink, which emptied before they reached her. Thirsty, Marianne stepped down from the dais and searched for a drink, overwhelmed by the uncharacteristic revelry, wondering how she ever could have thought these people were cold. Her people. *My people.*

CHAPTER 13

The audience room emptied late in the night, the guests leaving to return to their own homes or to take guest rooms within the Sural's keep. The Sural stepped down from the dais, on which he had spent the entire evening, with a satisfied air. Marianne, on the other hand, was tired, giddy, and inebriated. At first, she hadn't realized the drinks were alcoholic. After the first few, she knew but drank them anyway.

"You could have the decency to be tired, even if you're too stubborn to let yourself *look* tired," she said in English.

He laughed. "What tells you that I am fatigued?"

She tittered. "A little birdie told me," she whispered.

He lifted both eyebrows.

"It's an old saying people on my planet used when they wanted to reveal they knew a secret but didn't want anyone to know who told it to them. *A little birdie told me.*"

"Ah," he said. "A colorful people, those people of old Earth." He led her from the audience room and into the corridor.

"I am not ashamed of them!" she said, tripping a little. "Oops!" She giggled. "I think I'm drunk."

The Sural put out an arm to steady her. "Yes, dear one, you are," he said.

She clung to his arm as he led her down the corridor to the family wing. The hard muscle of his forearm flexed under her hand, and her body, every inch of her skin, ignited with sensation. She wasn't sure if she should attribute it to the alcohol or her newly-acquired Tolari senses, but whatever the cause, she liked it.

He stopped at her door and gestured the guards out of range. She leaned with her back against the door and faced him. "Are you coming in?" she asked. Her voice came out husky and low.

He took her hands and brought them to his lips, shaking his head with obvious effort, eyes full of regret. "No, dear one."

Marianne gaped at him, confusion adding to the fog in her head. "But I thought you—"

"I had hoped we would take joy in one another this night," he said, tracing the line of her jaw with a finger. "Nothing would give me greater happiness, if I knew that you would not regret it in the more... sober... light of morning." He stopped. "But you would."

Her new empathic senses registered regret in his voice and pain in his heart. She drew a breath. "No I—"

"Yes, you would, and you know that."

She pouted a moment, and then had an idea. "Do Tolari know how to kiss?"

The finger stopped tracing. He cupped her face in both hands. "Yes," he murmured. "But we find that touching the empathic nerves in our foreheads is more—intense."

"I've never been kissed," she breathed. "I want to be kissed."

"I prefer your forehead." His head lowered toward hers, his gaze fixed on her mouth. Their faces were nearly touching.

Her heart tried to stop. In a moment, she would find out if his lips were as warm as—

They both heard the sound—a sliding sort of click. The Sural's face whipped toward it. Then he abruptly stood sideways between her and whatever had produced the soft noise. Startled, she swiveled her head in time to see an arrow, slick and wet, flying toward them. A split-second later, he stumbled against her as it hit him, penetrating his left side.

He uttered only a grunt, but his pain ripped through her and tore a scream from her throat. She wrapped her arms around him, one hand encountering sticky warmth below the arrow. An eerie silence fell over the scene. *The guards need to use their ears.* She surprised herself with the dispassionate thought. The Sural released a loud breath and slipped to the floor. She slid down with him, cushioning his descent.

"It was aimed at your heart," he gasped. "But I am—much taller than you."

Kyza flew out of her room. "FATHER!" she cried, dropping to the floor next to him, clinging to his arm.

"Kyza." His voice was a rasp. "Leave. You are in danger here."

The girl set her jaw. "I will not leave you to die!"

"It doesn't look fatal," Marianne whispered.

Pain shuttered his face. "It is poisoned," he replied in a grim voice.

Marianne gasped in horror, unable to see through the sudden flood of tears. Her arms tightened around him, despite the pain lancing through her from the contact, and through the blur she saw red. His blood stained her hands, his robes, even Kyza's sleeves where she clung to him. She fixated on the blood. She had not seen so much since... a horrible night more than twenty years earlier. On that night, the blood had been her own.

The Sural looked up at her, as if he knew the old horrors had arisen from her memory. Sweat broke out on his face, and his breathing grew more ragged. "If I do not survive," he said, "I want you to know—" He drew a gasping, painful breath and took her hand, pressing it to his heart.

Love wrapped around her like a warm blanket. Passion erupted deep within her. Wonder and delight not her own washed through her.

"Oh my God," she whispered, hardly able to breathe.

"If you accept my heart," he said, "call me *beloved*." He took another painful breath. "I would come back from the dark to bond with you."

Apothecaries arrived and began to treat the Sural just as a scuffle broke out down the corridor. The sound of the struggle drew closer. Two blue-robed Suralian guards rounded the hallway's curve, frog-marching a man in pale tan who struggled and cursed between them. Soft white embroidery covered the top half of his robe, and a long scratch marked one cheek.

Kyza went still and deadly calm, face devoid of emotion. She rose to place herself between the Detral and her father. "Why?" she demanded, using a superior's tone to a subordinate.

He spat in Marianne's direction. "It is not possible for *that* to gain the Jorann's favor. Your father dishonors himself by playing at something." He fixed his eyes on Marianne as she sat on the floor, the stricken Sural lying across her. "Status higher than mine? Impossible! You will die, *odalli*. I will be vindicated, and then I will kill you."

Odalli, Marianne thought. Alien. He'd hung back during the celebration, she remembered, spending time with most of the guests—but not her.

Kyza fixed the Detral with a frightening stare. She no longer seemed like a child. "You have condemned your people to death," she said.

"We will see."

"Yes, we will," she replied. "But *you* will not. You are *weak*," she hissed, full of a child's contempt for an adult who had failed at what she herself could do. "Captured, drugged, *dishonored*." She spat the words. She turned her attention to the guards. "Take him to the interrogators. Take his secrets."

They glanced at the Sural. He nodded, and then added in a strained voice, "Close our borders—search the stronghold and the surrounding area." He took a breath, grimacing. "Find the Detral's son and take him alive—he is too young to evade you long." He stifled a cry, his face a mask of pain, as an apothecary pulled the arrow free and took tissue samples from the wound. An aide ran off with both arrow and samples.

The Sural touched her cheek with his fingertips, and then went limp in her arms.

"No!" she cried.

"He lives, high one," someone said. "He has lost consciousness, but he lives."

Two apothecaries maneuvered the Sural onto a litter and ordered their aides to carry him into his quarters. Kyza followed the guards dragging the Detral.

Marianne, left alone in the emptying corridor, sat where she had cradled the Sural, trying to rub the blood from her hands. The ceremonial robes she wore were ruined. She sensed the guards watching her with sympathy as they returned to their places. Leaning her head back against the doorpost, she closed her eyes and flogged herself for what had happened. *If only I hadn't been so scared, down in the tunnel,* she thought. *If only I'd been more willing. He would have been in my room, not in the corridor taking an arrow for me.* She banged her head against the doorpost with enough force to hurt. *He's said so many times he'll never hurt me. Why didn't I listen? Why can't I get over my fear?*

Rousing herself, she staggered to her feet and went into her quarters. Everything from her old quarters lay in the same position in the new. Even the cora twig lay where she had left it, on the blankets at the foot of the sleeping mat. She picked it up and caught a whiff of the Sural's scent on it. The smell of him covered it. He must have spent time rubbing it with his fingers, and... across his face. She dropped onto the mat with the twig clutched to her breast, breathing in the scent covering the buds. Despite her distress, exhaustion and inebriation carried her into sleep.

* * *

SMITHTON GAZED out the viewport in the admiral's ready room, watching the planet revolve. While they had expected assassination attempts, neither he nor the admiral had expected one to come so soon, or from such an unforeseen quarter. An ally.

John shook his head. "The news from Marianne is pretty grim," he said. "The toxin was Tolari, tailored to kill a human but capable of killing one of their own, in sufficient quantity. They don't have an antidote for it, and it'll take time to come up with one. They may not have the time. The Sural survived the night, but he's in a bad way."

Smithton swore. Then he muttered, "Almost would have been better if it had hit Marianne."

"She'd have been dead in seconds if it had," John said. "That arrow was aimed for her heart."

He growled, as much to himself as for his friend's benefit. "What else do we know?"

"Not enough. Marianne doesn't know much of what's coming from the Detral's interrogation, the Sural's too sick to be communicating with her—if he's even conscious enough to be overseeing it—and his daughter is too young, even by Tolari standards. Marianne thinks the stronghold guard must be conducting it. Her theory, based on what little she's heard, is that the Detral was making a play for power, thinking if he could prove the Sural was dishonored, he could rule the planet himself. He didn't bargain on getting caught, or on the Sural risking his own life to save Marianne's."

Smithton started to pace in front of the admiral's desk, tapping his lips with a fingertip. "Why would the Sural, the most powerful leader on Tolar, throw himself in front of an arrow to save an alien?" he grumbled.

"I'd do it to save Laura," the admiral shot back. He returned to his desk. "I think that your wife was right about the Sural."

Smithton stopped tapping. "More's the pity," he replied.

John scoffed. "You don't mean that. And you don't want to impugn your wife's keen powers of observation."

Smithton grunted. "Compared to the Tolari, my wife is blind."

"As are we all, my friend." He leaned back in his desk chair and steepled his fingers in front of him. "You know, Smitty, it doesn't add up."

"What doesn't add up?" Smithton took a chair across the desk.

"Marianne said the Sural seemed dead certain that their religious leader's protection would keep her safe. Yet, within hours, his closest ally tries to assassinate her, claiming he doesn't believe in it and that the Sural played some dishonorable game. Why kill Marianne? Why want her dead?"

"Maybe the better question is, what would her death accomplish?" Smithton said.

His friend pondered that. He lifted a finger. "One: if the Sural is in love with her, it would make him seriously angry. Two," he lifted another finger, "if he's anything like me, he would want to track down anyone who had anything to do with it. Think about it. The Detral had to have thought he could get away with it. He was so surprised to be caught that the Sural's guards were able to drug him before he could commit suicide. Who stood to gain from it if the Detral had gotten away with it?"

"We may never figure this out, John—there's too much we don't know. Maybe there's history between the Detral and the Sural, bad blood we can't know about."

"Marianne said the Detral was his strongest ally."

Smithton shrugged. "Those people are cold bastards—living, breathing icicles. They could be capable of being staunch allies to someone they hate and deadly opponents to someone they love. We just don't know enough. We need Marianne to keep her ears open, get us more information."

The admiral nodded. "I'll talk to her."

* * *

Marianne found Kyza at a desk in the family wing library, absorbed in a thick tome of Tolari history. *Even at a time like this, they continue their routines,* she thought. She corrected herself. *We* continue our routines. Kyza looked up at her as she approached the desk.

"How are you, dear one?" Marianne asked, pulling over a chair to sit.

Kyza put down the book and sprang from her seat to throw her arms around Marianne's neck, burying her face in a shoulder. "I am glad that you are no longer human," she exclaimed, her voice muffled by Marianne's robe. "We do not ever have to send you away no matter what happens."

Marianne wrapped her arms around Kyza, leaning her cheek against Kyza's inky black hair. The girl needed comfort. *She's so little, but it's easy to forget how young she is,* she thought, *especially when she holds herself together like she did last night.* "I won't leave," she said, stroking Kyza's hair. "Your father wasn't ever going to send me away, whether I became Tolari or not."

A servant flickered into sight, bowing deference and apology. "Forgive this interruption, high ones," he said. "The head apothecary requests the honor of the Marann's presence in the Sural's quarters."

The Marann? Marianne thought. Kyza lifted her face, wide-eyed.

"Of course."

Kyza slipped down from her lap and went back to the book. Marianne rose and followed the servant to the ornately-carved—and well-guarded—door of the Sural's private apartment. It opened for her.

She caught her breath as she walked into the sitting room. The furniture lined the walls, creating an open space. The Sural, unconscious and almost grey under his coppery skin, lay on a raised bed in the center, clothed only in the loose trousers Tolari wore under their robes. To her surprise, despite the sophistication she'd seen of Tolari medical science, drains led from the open wound in his side. Apothecaries moved round him. An aide stood near his head, using a pipette to drip slow drops of fluid into his mouth.

Marianne's stomach twisted. *They told me he was in danger,* she thought. *They didn't tell me it was this bad.* The Sural's head apothecary approached her, hands spread in respect. Marianne nodded, not taking her eyes off the Sural.

"High one," the apothecary acknowledged. "You honor me to come at my request."

"Is there anything I can do for the Sural?" she asked.

"May I speak with you in another room?"

"Of course."

The apothecary headed through the door to the Sural's private study. Marianne followed, using a gesture she'd learned from the Sural to motion the guards from the room. One flickered in protest—she thought for a moment, and then nodded consent for the guards to stay. Their reluctance to leave her unguarded after the attempt on her life warmed her, and she reasoned that the Sural would have few secrets from his private guards.

"What is this about?" Marianne asked.

"May I speak frankly?"

"Of course," she answered, a nervous smile coming to her lips.

"The Sural declared his heir. Do you know us well enough yet to realize what that means for him—personally?"

"Forgive me, but I don't. Will you explain?"

"Before Kyza passed the great trial, he lived for the good of Suralia and of the entire planet. Once he declared Kyza his heir, our law permitted him to live for other things."

Marianne stared at her slippers, already regretting that she had allowed the guards to remain.

"One of the things he chose to live for—is you."

Did everyone know how he felt except *me?* she thought. "But I—" She stopped herself.

"I am his head apothecary, high one. It is necessary for me to know everything about him, including his emotional state. He tells me everything."

The blood ran from Marianne's face. This woman must know... She quelled an urge to flee.

"He knows that Suralia will go on and be led by his daughter should he fall," the apothecary continued. "He needs something more than his duty to Suralia now. You can give him that."

She's almost as bad as those scheming politicians up on the ship, she thought. *Everyone is conspiring to throw me at him.* She checked herself, remembering the moment in the hall when he opened his heart to her. But—

"High one," the healer said, "I implore you. If you want him to live —give him your heart. It is obvious his heart is already yours."

Before Marianne could protest, a commotion arose in the next room. Alarm spread in ripples. The apothecary ran out, Marianne close on her heels. The Sural had stopped breathing. One apothecary placed a mask over his face to breathe for him. Another positioned a device on his chest to stimulate his heart.

This is it, Marianne thought, making her way to his side, trying to stay out of the way of the busy apothecaries. *I'm losing him, before I ever even had him.* She blinked away tears, trying to imagine what life in the stronghold would be like without his presence. A sense of loss pierced her. She didn't want to lose him. Not now, not knowing how he felt about her. Impossible, she thought, almost by reflex. The sovereign ruler of a planet... and an Iowa farm girl. It was impossible. Wasn't it?

Whatever it takes. She reached out to take the Sural's right hand in both of hers. The head apothecary noticed and gave her a grateful nod.

"Don't leave me," she whispered to him in English. "I need you." In Tolari, she added, "*Beloved.*"

A long, frightening minute passed as the apothecaries continued to work on him.

She felt the atmosphere in the room change.

"He breathes," said an apothecary across the bed, near his head.

"He is stabilizing," said a voice behind her, pregnant with relief.

She slumped, letting out a breath she didn't know she'd held. A chair touched the backs of her calves, and she dropped into it, grateful for the kindness. She brought the Sural's hand to her face and pressed a cheek against it, shaking. A single day before, she'd believed he could never be more than a friend. It turned her world upside down to find him in love with her. Now, to save his life, she had made a commitment to what amounted to marriage, and she didn't know if she could follow through with what *that* entailed. She buried her face in the blankets and wept.

"Bring the high one some tea," the head apothecary ordered. "She will be here for some time."

* * *

DARK QUIET FILLED the room when Marianne woke. A gentle finger traced the line of her jaw, and warmth and love wrapped her senses. Sighing, she opened her eyes to meet the Sural's gaze in the gray light of evening.

"Beloved." His whisper was hoarse.

Tears filled her eyes, and she buried her face in the blankets again, crying in relief. He rested a hand on her hair.

"You heard me," she whispered. She felt rather than saw him give an almost imperceptible nod. "You came back from the dark for me."

"Yes." His voice was almost inaudible.

"It's all my fault!"

A weak smile touched his lips as he shook his head. "When my strength returns, I shall show you how mistaken you are."

She almost laughed. Men, she thought, were all the same no matter where you went.

"Marianne," he whispered again. The use of her name caught her attention. "Tell me what happened to you. Tell me why you fear your own—" She placed a finger on his lips to stop him, glancing at the aide who monitored him from the other side of the room. Alarm pulsed through her, but the aide hadn't seemed to have heard.

"Shh," she shushed him.

He breathed a ragged sigh. "I should have told you sooner. It has stopped your panic to know of my feelings."

She shook her head and took one hand in both of hers. "No, it wasn't that," she said. "You were dying. Your apothecary—she told me the only way to save you was—to give you my heart. Did everyone in the stronghold know?"

His face softened. "It was not difficult for them to see," he rasped. "I could not maintain a proper distance from you."

"I must have been the one person in Suralia who didn't figure it out," she said, almost whispering. "I thought you couldn't—it was unprofessional to let myself think—So I'd think about you, and then I'd have to think about what would happen if I ever let my feelings show. I thought you would pity or scorn me, and it scared me out of my mind." Her voice hollowed as she continued, "And now I still don't know if I can be more than just a friend to you, not even after—making such a huge commitment."

"Beloved, it is enough to touch your hand."

She pressed his hand to her cheek. "It's so strange to take your hand and know how you feel. You knew how I felt all along, didn't you?"

"It would have frightened you to know this."

She nodded. "Probably." She sighed and took a small cup from a nearby table. "Your apothecary told me to give you this when you woke."

The Sural made a face. "Another of her vile potions," he croaked, taking it from her.

"Drink up!" Marianne told him.

The Sural drank it and handed the cup back to her. "Not as bad as some of her mixtures," he said, his voice a little clearer. His eyes glazed. "But very... strong..." He sighed into sleep.

* * *

"THEY MOVED me to the family wing," Marianne said. "There are even more guards here."

Adeline laughed. "What did you expect?"

Marianne shrugged.

Adeline laughed again. "So tell me about that petty little religious leader, the Jorann."

"They don't have a religion," Marianne replied.

"Then what was all that ritual about?"

"It was about family."

"Family?"

"You can't have status on Tolar unless you belong to a family—and I couldn't continue teaching Kyza without status. It was more like a legal adoption. I had to be a member of the Sural's family. So—the Jorann had to do it, the one person on the planet whose rank and status are higher than his."

"You said she's like a legend on Tolar. The First Tolari. The Highest One. The one they would never think to disobey, much less harm—while the rest of them plot and scheme against each other like medieval barons."

Marianne's head on the monitor tilted sideways. "There has to be someone at the very top."

"And we all thought that was the Sural, but he's not sacrosanct. Why did she like you so much? Why is she protecting you?"

Marianne shrugged. "I really don't know."

Adeline paused the recording and looked over at the admiral. He nodded. "She's hiding something," he said.

Adeline sat on the edge of the desk. "I agree. There's been a sea change in her communications with us. She's less open, more calculating."

"Maybe it wasn't such a grand idea to let her do this," Smithton said. "Looks like she's taking her new loyalty to the Sural too seriously, if you ask me."

"He didn't ask you," Adeline replied in an officious voice, then grinned. "But you're right. She is."

"The question is, does her loyalty to Earth still mean more to her," the admiral said. "You know how the Chairman reacts to divided loyalties. Do we pull her out?"

"The Sural would never forgive us for it if we did," Adeline replied.

The admiral shrugged. "It's easy enough to invent a family emergency. Surely even the Sural would understand that."

"And surely the Sural would never allow her to set foot on Tolar again, family emergency or no family emergency."

"Damn," said Smithton. "She's right, John—it was one of that damned Sural's damned conditions for letting us send a teacher down there in the first place. After gaining their trust, she couldn't leave, because outside of their protection she could be tampered with by enemies."

The admiral went to the viewport and looked out at Tolar. "So—we can't trust her, and we can't pull her out to debrief her."

"That's about the size of it," Adeline replied.

"Play it out, John," Smithton said, "see where it goes."

The admiral growled. "Looks like I don't have any real choice."

CHAPTER 14

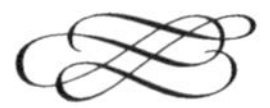

The Sural sat under a cora tree in the gardens. Three days had passed since the Detral's attack, and though the poison had slowed his recovery, he wanted out of his quarters. His apothecaries had given their consent to a walk in the garden, as long as he rested more than he walked. Now he basked in the afternoon sun, his heir laughing and playing in the brook nearby, the woman who had captured his heart sitting at his side. He was content.

He reached for her hand. She gave him an almost shy smile and blushed, a hint of fear and apprehension coloring her presence.

"I will never hurt you," he whispered.

She dipped her head, and her eyes fell on his wounded side. "I'm so sorry that happened. If I'd only—"

"No. I was able to survive. You would not have."

"Why did the Detral do it?"

He shook his head. "He is unbalanced and intolerant. He deduced my feelings for you."

"Apparently, I was the only one who didn't," she said, her voice dry.

He smiled, then grew serious. "He is sensitive enough to have heard the truth in my voice when I declared you. Yet he believed I attempted to deceive him."

"Enough to try to assassinate me? I didn't know Tolari used bow and arrow."

"It is a game of skill, nothing more. We do not use them to kill each other. For the Detral to attempt it is unthinkable. My guards thought nothing of it when he arrived with a bow, supposing him intent on testing his skill against mine, as he has done many times. He concealed his intentions well."

"It would be easy to assassinate a ruler with a distance weapon," Marianne murmured.

"It would be—unspeakable. Dishonorable. What he did—" He shuddered. "It is not unprecedented, but a provincial ruler has never attempted it."

"I thought he was your friend." Her forehead wrinkled, and she leaked confusion.

"He was a good friend and a strong ally for many years."

Marianne shook her head. How the Detral committed an atrocity, against a friend, seemed to defy her understanding. "The admiral doesn't understand why more Tolari rulers don't use archery to gain an advantage over each other."

He shuddered again. "To kill an unsuspecting individual from a distance is forbidden. Combat is only honorable if the intended target has an opportunity to defend himself."

"*This* target is glad you defended her, but I wish it hadn't almost cost you your life."

He smiled and squeezed her hand. "What do your friends on the ship think now?"

"They're relieved you're alive," Marianne replied. "But they seem to know I'm hiding something, especially Adeline, the ambassador's wife. She's a sharp one."

The Sural let his smile tilt. "Perhaps she would have been a better choice to be here," he teased.

Marianne cocked her head. "She's loyal to Earth to her very core," she replied, as if she thought it had been a serious statement. "And I think she used to be an intelligence operative. Who knows, it might be Central Command's way to keep an eye on Ambassador Russell. Maybe she never stopped being a spook." Her eyes widened as she said it.

"Now you begin to think like a member of the ruling caste." He allowed himself an open grin.

"Is she a spook?" Her face became wary, and he sensed uncertainty in her—she wasn't sure she wanted to know.

"I am certain of it. She is more than she appears to be. Much more than her ambassador thinks her to be."

"Humans have a saying: love is blind." A sigh gusted from her lips. "I'm not learning fast enough. I'm even giving myself away to humans."

He laid a hand on one shoulder. "Have no concern, beloved. She is unlikely to guess the true nature of the Jorann or of your transformation."

"No, I don't suppose she can." She lifted a hand halfway to her face and froze.

"What troubles you?"

"They'll discover everything if they pull me out."

He went cold. Fixing his eyes on hers, he straightened, suppressing a flinch as his wound spasmed. "Tell me."

"Before I left Tau Ceti station to come here, they put a locater chip in my brain," she said. "It's tiny, easy to insert, and impossible to remove. Central Command puts them in anyone who sets foot on a nonhuman world as a safety protocol. They can lock onto my chip and phase me out if something should happen that they think threatens my safety."

"Why did you not tell me of this?" He considered anger and discarded it.

She spread her hands in apology. "It's been eight years. It was a short little procedure in the middle of an eventful day. The layover on Tau Ceti station lasted all of maybe thirty minutes. I'd forgotten it until just now."

"It must be removed."

"That's impossible," she said. "Especially not after all this time. It's worked its way into my brainstem, and it's booby-trapped."

"We shall see." He started to get up. She helped him to stand and dusted bits of vegetation from his robes. "Beloved—"

She glanced up at him, expectation in her eyes.

"Trust me."

She nodded, but doubt still colored her presence. *Will she never trust me?* he thought. Withdrawing back into himself, he leaned on her as they made their way back into the keep.

* * *

Marianne blinked and raised her eyebrows when they entered the apothecaries' quarters. The Sural only twitched his lips. Several guards lay injured on the examination beds—apparent victims of the games they played to keep their reflexes sharp. Medicinal smells filled the air, and aides and nurses clogged the room, carrying medical scanners and other arcane equipment. The head apothecary was mixing one of her infamous potions and couldn't interrupt her work. The Sural went into her private study to wait. Marianne followed, sensing a guard even there.

"Must they be *everywhere*?" she complained.

The Sural chuckled. "I have seldom known a day without them."

"And I never knew a day *with* them until I came here. There's no privacy in this place."

"Ah." He sighed. "Is that what holds you back?" It was more of a statement than a question.

"Well... maybe, partly. Mostly. Well... yes."

"You saw what happened when I sent the guards out of range for you."

She flinched. "This is personal."

"The guards would give their lives for you, beloved," he said. "What have you to hide from them? They love you—why would they hurt you?"

"You tell me," she challenged, just as the apothecary walked in.

The healer bent in a respectful bow and took her seat behind the desk, waiting for the Sural to speak.

"How much will the physiological transformation occurring in the Marann's brain increase the risk of a medical procedure performed on it?" he asked.

Marianne made a mental note to ask the Sural about that title.

"It would not be wise to tamper until the transformation is complete, high one," the apothecary answered.

"How long?"

"Perhaps a year, perhaps more. Very little of her brain is Tolari at present, but the rate of change should accelerate over time."

"We may not have a single season."

Marianne added, "We may not have ten days."

The apothecary's brows furled, and she radiated concern. "What does this regard?"

"Central Command had a locater chip implanted on my brainstem while I was on Tau Ceti station, on my way here from Earth," Marianne answered. "It's tiny and easy to insert, but it's rigged to destroy my brainstem if it's tampered with. And as long as it remains, the humans can phase me off the planet whenever they decide to."

She digested this. "I see your concern," she said. She paused to think, then pulled her medical tablet from a pocket and studied it. The Sural allowed her time. "I think it can be done, high ones, but not without risk."

The Sural straightened. "Tell me."

"Accelerate her transformation."

Marianne blinked several times, taken aback. "You can do that?"

"No," the apothecary answered. "I cannot. The Jorann must do it."

The Sural gave a slow nod. "What are the risks?"

"It will be painful," she answered, "extremely painful. Pain can kill a human, and at present the Marann remains largely human. I cannot predict what it would do to her."

"Can the pain be controlled?"

She stared past them as she thought about it. "Possibly. It might be more practical to keep her unconscious until her brain has completed the change. Seven, perhaps eight days, if the Jorann consents. At that point, I can repair anything they did to her. However—if she is phased off the planet during the process, she could die."

The Sural pulled out his tablet and busied himself.

"What are you doing?" Marianne asked.

"Disabling the phase platform on the *Alexander*," he murmured. "I am uncertain how long it will take them to acquire a replacement, but it will gain us time."

"You can do that? From your *tablet*?" She gaped.

He turned to her with a crooked grin. "It is your decision, beloved."

She took a deep breath and ignored the sinking feeling in her midsection. "When do we start?"

* * *

THE JOURNEY to the Jorann's cavern took much longer than Marianne's first trip—an entire afternoon, since the Sural refused to stay behind and required frequent rests. The head apothecary seemed displeased with him, but kept it to herself, for the most part. Her medical authority extended over him only so far.

"What did you tell the ambassador's wife?" the Sural asked as he limped along.

Marianne blushed, and he radiated delight. She could not understand what Tolari found so enthralling about a blush. "I told her we were taking a romantic vacation and would be out of communication for ten days or so."

He chuckled. "Did she believe you?"

"Maybe not. Spending time in an ice cave isn't Adeline's idea of a romantic getaway. It's not mine either, for that matter, but I didn't tell her that. She wished me joy, and I blushed a lot. I might have pulled it off."

He drew a deep breath and released it. "We cannot rely on having enough time."

Marianne shuddered. She didn't want to think about what was coming.

"You called me the Marann," she said, to change the subject. "The guards and servants have called me that since I returned from my first visit to the Jorann. Does it *mean* something?"

"Your name is close to an Old Tolari word." He turned a smile on her. "In that language, *Jorann* means 'First One.' *Marann* means 'Second One.' The servants could not resist beginning to call you that amongst themselves, and it spread. Do you not find it appropriate?"

She stared at her hands. "I don't want to lose my name the way Tolari high ones do."

"Beloved, you *are* a Tolari high one," he said, "but you do not rule a province. There is no reason for the Jorann to take away your name."

They reached the stairs leading up to the ice cave. "You will rest, high one," the apothecary ordered.

The Sural nodded and sat on the staircase with a groan. "Willingly, apothecary."

Marianne bit her lip to keep from laughing as the apothecary forced the most powerful man on the planet to sit on a staircase for a full twenty minutes before allowing him to continue. She repeated the performance twice more before they reached the top.

"Why do Tolari rulers lose their names?" Marianne asked during their last stop on the stairs. "What purpose does it serve?"

"The Jorann took my name from me when she bonded me to my people." He put a hand to his chest. "I can feel them—I can see them, like stars shining on the surface of the province. I am Suralia. If I had a name, I could not be Suralia." He smiled up at her. "Beloved, I do not even wish to be anything else."

"So that time I asked you what your name was—"

"You asked him his name?" the apothecary interrupted, her eyes huge.

"Well—yes."

"And you did not banish her?" she asked the Sural.

The blood ran out of Marianne's face, and her voice came out thin and high-pitched. "Is there anything else I should be careful not to say?"

The Sural took her hands. "I will never harm you or send you away, beloved," he said. "Have no fear of me." He shot a vexed look at the apothecary.

"Forgive me, high one," the healer murmured, and turned to Marianne. "High one—it is not clear to us why the ruling bond affects our leaders the way it does. If you ask a bonded ruler his name, he will perceive it as a threat. It is extraordinary that the Sural did nothing."

"She could not have known." He grated the words. "I refuse to be ruled by my instincts."

"Is there anything else like that I need to know?" Marianne persisted.

The Sural shook his head. "I think you already know not to approach an adult in the grip of a bonding child," he said. "That is the truly dangerous instinct we all have."

"Is that why Storaas pulled me away when Kyza's first bond with you dissolved?"

"Yes. Storaas knows better than anyone how dangerous I can be."

"High ones, we should finish our journey," the apothecary said.

As he stood, supported by the healer, he shut his empathic barriers and disappeared from her senses. Marianne blinked. It had not taken long to become accustomed to his presence, and its absence unsettled her. He smiled down at her and reached for a hand. As their fingers twined, she sensed a faint echo of him.

The Jorann seemed to expect them when they reached the cavern. Without issuing her challenge, she pointed to the blankets at the foot of the dais. The Sural let go of Marianne's hand and limped forward, the apothecary hovering to one side.

The healer's words echoed through Marianne's head. *It will be painful, extremely painful.* She forced her feet to move forward until she stood at the Sural's side, looking up at the Jorann.

Looking *up*. Though shorter than the Sural, the woman towered over her, blonde braids and intricate knots cascading around her shoulders to the floor. Marianne's jaw loosened. Either she had colored her hair, or her blessing did impossible things. And if the color was natural, it raised questions about her origins. She had said she was once human. Had she been born on Earth? Why was she not, like her children, black-haired and caramel-skinned?

"I see you have a problem," the Jorann said.

He bowed with difficulty. "Yes, highest."

"You are injured, grandson. Sit. All of you sit." Marianne and the apothecary helped the Sural down onto the thick white blankets. The Jorann settled back on the edge of her dais. "The Detral defied my orders in his actions against the Marann. I want him brought to me."

"Yes, highest."

"And as for the request your apothecary makes of me... Grandson, do you understand what you ask?"

The Sural nodded. "We cannot allow the humans to remove Marianne Woolsey from Tolar."

"No, we cannot," the Jorann agreed, "but this is no light thing you ask, with no small amount of risk. Do you see no way to delay them?"

"I lack even human skill to mask what I feel," Marianne said. "It is one of the reasons they chose me for this. And one of the humans on the ship is a skilled observer—a spy, even, in the Sural's opinion. I cannot fool her."

The Jorann nodded, her face grim. "You are quite sure that you are willing to go through this?"

Marianne swallowed hard and nodded. The Jorann bent into a slight bow.

"It will take a great deal of my blessing to accelerate your transformation to the extent required," the Jorann said. "As it happens, I have a great deal with me—all that would have gone to Detralar this season."

Marianne shuddered.

"The entire people of Detralar will soon step into the dark. So many of my children. It has not happened in a thousand years. Such a waste, this game my rulers play."

"Highest," Marianne said, "why do you punish his people for his crime?"

She grunted. "Where did your manners go?" She motioned Marianne to lie down in the blankets. She complied without hesitation, and the apothecary piled more blankets over her.

"At least you are obedient," the Jorann said. "Very well then. Before we begin, my grandson will tell you part of the answer."

The Sural's face went grim. "He is dishonored, and all of Detralar is pledged to his life."

"Yes, but—"

"Every man, woman, and child above the age of four in Detralar has sworn their lives to his," the Jorann continued. "But their Detral is dishonored and will soon be dead. Tell me, child, have you learned enough of our ways to know what my children do when they are dishonored?"

"They—die," she whispered.

"Yes, child. They go into the dark. I do not choose this fate for them. They choose it themselves, and it would be cruel to send them my blessing to live in dishonor. Almost all will choose the dark. Those who do not will try to flee and die when they find no haven in other provinces. Those who are related to the Detral by blood—he has fathered many children—will feel it most keenly. It compounds the tragedy. Soon, there will be no Detrali left on Tolar."

Marianne squinted. "The Detral has—"

"He can have only one heir," the Sural said, emphasizing the last word, "but any woman in the province can request him to father hers. According to his own boasts, the Detral never declined such requests, even when the genetic analysis was poor. He fathered hundreds of children." His lips compressed until lines formed at the corners of his mouth.

She snorted. "He must have been busy at night."

The Sural laughed. "In a manner of speaking. Every adult has the right to an heir, but the Detral was... excessive in his devotion to that duty, perhaps."

"Beloved—" She stopped, uncertain how to ask the question on her mind.

"Yes," the Sural said, "I receive such requests."

"Do you—"

"On occasion. I am... more discriminating... than the Detral. I refuse requests if the genetic analysis is not favorable enough."

"How many children do you have?"

"Aside from Kyza, I have fathered thirty-six. There will be a thirty-seventh before high summer."

"Thirty-seven!" Marianne exclaimed.

"They are scattered all over Suralia," he added, eyeing her. He raised an eyebrow. "This makes you uncomfortable."

"The human customs I grew up with are—different."

"Humans would call our way promiscuous. Yet they dissolve relationships with wanton frequency, while we bond for life."

"If I—if we—will you—"

"Tradition demands that I lead by example."

"But—"

"You cannot think me an undesirable candidate to father a woman's heir?"

"No!" she exclaimed, then said, in a low voice, "I just hoped you would be more—well—unavailable..." She trailed off.

"It is my duty to consider any daughter of Suralia's request which meets my standards," he said. "Did I not, resentment would soon fester." He took her hand. "The liaison lasts only for the short period of time required to give the woman a child. Quite often, it is no more than a single encounter."

She took a deep breath and stared at the cavern's ice-coated ceiling, high above. Tolari ways came out of six thousand years of tradition. She could hardly expect them to change just because *she* didn't like it.

But I love him. She sighed and glanced at the Jorann. She sat motionless with her eyes fixed on Marianne, one corner of her mouth lifted and eyes glinting. Feeling naked beneath that gaze, Marianne flicked her eyes back to the Sural.

"Do I know any of your other children?" she asked.

"Yes," he answered. "My first. I fathered my apothecary."

"Your apothecary!" she blurted. "But she—" The woman smiled—the Sural's own enigmatic smile.

"Who better to care for my health than an apothecary I fathered?" he asked.

"You must continue this discussion at another time," the Jorann interrupted. She knelt on the blankets and handed Marianne a cube. "Take this."

Marianne settled herself, letting it dissolve on her tongue. It had no particular taste, and she didn't fall unconscious as she had the first time. The Jorann reached over her, offering some to the Sural. With raised eyebrows, he extended both hands to take them.

"Consume two," she said. "They will accelerate your wound's healing. Give one to your apothecary. She saved your life, and I approve of the way she handled you on the stairs. Her status should reflect her ability."

Marianne snorted with mirth and almost choked. The Sural shot her a rueful smile and handed a cube to the apothecary, who took it with reverence.

"You honor me," she whispered, placing it on her tongue.

The Sural consumed the two cubes and swayed. The healer turned her scanner on him, studying the readout on a tablet. She looked back at the Jorann with gratitude and relief plain on her face.

The Jorann grunted and shifted her attention back to Marianne. "Open," she said, dropping another cube in Marianne's mouth.

The apothecary opened her bag and fished out a piece of equipment the size and shape of the top half of a small apple. She set about adjusting it and, satisfied, placed it on the blanket beside Marianne.

"Again," the Jorann commanded, and dropped another cube in Marianne's mouth.

"How do you feel?" the apothecary asked, running a scanner over Marianne's head.

"Strange." Marianne's voice sounded distant and distracted to her own ear. "The world is rippling."

The Jorann nodded. "Open." She dropped another cube in Marianne's mouth.

As the youthful but ancient Tolari continued to feed her, Marianne began to think the apothecary had been mistaken about the pain. Then the world jerked and began to spin, turning into a whirlpool of razor-sharp knives, slashing at her. She screamed.

The apothecary placed her device on Marianne's forehead and turned it on.

Marianne slipped into blackness.

* * *

UP ON THE SHIP, John Howard faced an Adeline whose only sign of anger was her flaring nostrils.

"You *should* have the authority to open Marianne's psychological profile and personal history file," she said.

"Be that as it may," he said, "I don't. I'll kick your request up the chain of command. It's all I can do. I'll probably have an answer for you in a week or so. Maybe by then the phase platform will be repaired."

He could do nothing Adeline wanted, and she couldn't *not* know that. Scuttlebutt all over the ship concerned the phase platform and the possible causes of its malfunction. A phase coil had melted for no apparent reason, damaging it and rendering it unusable. Engineering had sent for a new unit, but until it arrived, he couldn't extract the schoolteacher without creating an interstellar incident.

Adeline chewed on her lower lip, nodding. "Let me know as soon as you hear anything."

"You'll be the first to know," he said, watching her retreating back. *Even before I do, I bet,* he thought, with a slight headshake. He couldn't warn her husband without risking his own life. *Smitty has no idea.*

* * *

MARIANNE SWAM back into consciousness and opened her eyes, shivering in the cold of the Jorann's cave.

"Is it done?" she gasped.

The apothecary shook her head. Her hair was still gray, but the lines on her face were gone. "No, high one. Forgive me, but I had to wake you. You were in peril, close to the dark. But you need not remain awake long. I will reset the device shortly."

The bones in Marianne's neck popped as she nodded. "I understand," she whispered. "How long has it been?"

The ticking time sense in her head told her the answer before the healer spoke it.

"Four days."

The Sural maneuvered her head and shoulders into his lap, and the healer pressed a steaming mug into her hands.

"Drink this," she said. "It will replenish you."

"Beloved," the Sural murmured, pushing her upper body a little straighter so she could drink.

She gave him a weak smile. "You look better," she whispered. She sipped at the mug, which proved to contain a savory broth.

"The Jorann's blessing healed me," he said with a warm smile. "I am well and strong again."

Her stomach lurched at the thought of what that meant for her when they returned to the stronghold, but she didn't have the strength to be afraid. "Tell me about—how it is for Tolari women, to have an heir."

His brows tried to meet his hairline. "Are you certain you wish to hear about that now?" he asked.

She nodded, settling back against him, drinking the broth. He folded his arms around her.

"Very well," he said. "Our customs and laws are different for women than they are for men. There are biological and developmental realities to take into account—you have a much greater physical and emotional investment in the child's early years. Women spend most of two seasons carrying the child during gestation and have a bond with the infant before it is born. None are required to bear more than their own heir, although many do—they must, or our population would fall by half every generation.

"We have special laws with respect to the ruling caste," he continued. "High ones are forbidden to request an heir from a Tolari who does not yet have an heir. A woman carrying the potential heir of a member of the ruling caste must live in his stronghold until her bond to the child dissolves between the ages of six and ten seasons."

"So Kyza's mother—"

"Would have lived in the stronghold until Kyza had ten seasons of age, yes. It is ever the way with daughters. They need the woman who mothered them longer than sons do. Our sons bond to us when they have five or six seasons."

"Do I know her?"

"No. She died shortly after giving birth. Kyza herself nearly died, refusing to bond to me at first. Infants by instinct seek the mother they knew before birth and will seldom be comforted by another."

"So that's why she was bonded to you instead of her mother."

"Even so."

Marianne shook her head and set aside the now-empty mug. The Sural eased her from his lap onto the blankets.

"Forgive me, beloved," she said. "I had no idea."

The apothecary replaced the device on her forehead and pressed a button.

CHAPTER 15

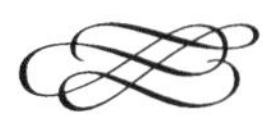

Marianne swam back to the light and opened her eyes. The Sural knelt beside her, one of her hands in both of his.

"Welcome back, child," said the Jorann. "It is done."

"How long—" she whispered, but again, she knew the answer.

"Another three days have passed," the apothecary replied, handing her a mug of the replenishing broth.

"You have little time, children," said the Jorann. "Go now."

* * *

MARIANNE TRIED to walk back to the stronghold. Her knees wobbled and threatened to give out before reaching the stairs, even leaning most of her weight on the Sural. Ignoring her protests, he picked her up and carried her.

Face heating, she swallowed her protests and sighed, leaning her head against his shoulder and letting an unaccustomed warmth creep through her. He smiled, and her hand twitched with an urge to run her fingertips down his cheek. She quelled the impulse. He had recovered his strength, and when she recovered hers, he would want to—

"You are a brave woman," he said.

She knitted her brows together and frowned. "Why do you say that?"

"You know you are weak, and yet you do the hard thing. You are afraid, and still you continue."

"Except—"

"Will you tell me what happened to give you such fear?" he asked. "There are no guards in this tunnel, and my apothecary follows at a respectful distance. No one else will hear."

She blew out a breath. She *did* want to tell him, but... She fought back the reflex to hide it. He would have to know, sooner or later. Better sooner, when the inevitable rejection would hurt less. She took another breath and began, in English.

"When I was twelve—Earth years—for humans, it's about that time most girls begin to become women. My parents let me walk to the summer fair without an adult for the first time. I went there with my best friend Susan, who lived next door. We spent the whole day at the fair, did all the normal things that kids do—ate too much greasy food, went on rides, played with the animals in the petting zoo, played games, gathered with friends. It got late and I wanted to go home, but Susan wanted to stay. So I said I'd be all right and left the fair without her.

"When I was walking through the old Ocheltree farm, a man I didn't recognize started following me. He wasn't one of the farmhands there. He was wearing dirty clothes, he had greasy blond hair, he was staring at me—a horrible, intense, icky stare. I got scared and ran into the cornfield to hide, but I couldn't get away from him. He chased me—I could run fast, I thought maybe I could get away. I tripped over a cornstalk that had fallen across the row." She stopped. Shaking a little, she took a breath and asked, "Beloved—do you understand what—what rape—is?"

The Sural nodded. His face was grim.

Marianne fell silent, courage failing her. She took several deep breaths to work up the nerve to say it. "He raped me," she admitted in a rush. "He tied me to the corn stalks with my own clothing, and he raped me. I don't know how many times, I lost count. Each time was worse, more... painful. He grunted like a pig. He yelled louder each time when he was—and the whole time he was ranting about how I'd better not get pregnant from it, he'd kill the baby if I got pregnant."

She drew a shaky breath, her eyes filling with angry tears. "I was only twelve," she sobbed, "It hurt so bad. I wasn't a woman yet, I hadn't even gotten my—" She swallowed. "At first light he stopped. He raved at me about how he had just gotten me pregnant, how he couldn't allow it to live, he had to kill it. He pulled out a barbecue skewer and said if he ever heard I got pregnant, he'd know it was his and he'd have to come back and do it again. Then he—he—" she squeezed her eyes shut, forcing the words, tears flowing, "he used the skewer on me..." She took a breath. "There was so much blood—"

The Sural pressed his cheek against her forehead, his eyes glistening.

"My parents had called the authorities when I didn't come home and people were out looking for me, but they hadn't searched the Ocheltree farm yet. Old Alec didn't like it when kids cut through his farm to get to the road, and my parents thought I probably wouldn't have done that. But I did. I nearly died. *Would* have died if Old Alec didn't get up early. He and one of the farmhands heard me scream when the greasy man started—when he was—" she forced the words out, "—mutilating—me." She stopped, trying to calm herself.

"Human medicine is pretty advanced. They were able to repair all the damage to—to me and make everything like nothing had ever happened, good as new. My parents did all the right things, put me in therapy, all that. The therapy was supposed to take the emotional impact out of it. But I had nightmares about the greasy man for years. He must have been insane, but they never caught him. I couldn't stand the idea of ever getting pregnant, couldn't stand the idea that the greasy man could come back and hurt me again. I believed him when he said he would come back. Maybe I still do, I don't know. When I was eighteen, I went to the clinic in town and made them sterilize me. They didn't want to—they said I was too young to make that kind of decision. But I was a legal adult and I insisted on my rights and I was willing to pay cash—I saved every bit of money I ever made, every summer job, every bit of allowance. I insisted they make it irreversible. I had to be safe. I kept at them until they gave in and did it for me.

"I never dated. I never even looked at boys. I never looked at girls either. I just didn't want to have any of... those feelings, ever. The greasy man raved about how he had to do what he was doing to me because he had *feelings*. He said I would get those feelings someday too, and then I'd *want* him to do that to me. I swore to myself I never would. I swore I'd never—ever—I would never let anyone be more than a friend.

"In junior high I spent all my time on schoolwork and track—all I wanted to do was run fast, really fast, so fast no one could ever catch me again. In high school I became fluent in Spanish in a month and everyone realized I had this huge talent, so after that, language was all I studied, all I thought about when I wasn't running. Life was comfortable in Casey. I had friends. I had a job. Then Central Command ripped me out of my life and sent me here—and there was you—and I didn't want to feel about you the way I was starting to feel about you. I didn't want to make a fool of myself, make you pity me... I'm a nobody, it wasn't possible you could notice me that way. But you were so—so kind to me—so gentle. That night the first winter I was here, when I had a nightmare and woke the whole stronghold—it was the nightmare about the greasy man. It was the first time I'd dreamed about him in years, but that time, in the dream I was looking for *you* rather than just trying to run away. I figured it was because I was starting to feel too much for you, so I shut it down and pushed thoughts of you out of my mind."

"I tried to comfort you that night," the Sural said. "You seemed to accept it at first, but then you panicked. It was your emotional blast that woke the stronghold, not your scream. It was very powerful. I knew something had hurt you. I could not imagine then what it was, but after a number of seasons, I did begin to suspect what it had to be."

She nodded, a strange peace filling her from the heart outward. "I want to be able to—to love someone with everything I am—love *you* that way—This past year you've been so wonderful to me—And I was horrible to you—But I can't let myself have those feelings, I just can't. I just can't."

He held her tighter.

"I will wait for you, beloved," he said. "I am a patient man, and our lifetime is long. However long it is, I will wait until you come to me. I will never hurt you."

Marianne sighed. "I will live a long, long time, won't I?"

"The blessing gives one hundred fifty of our years," he answered. What he sensed in her response troubled him. "This does not please you."

She shook her head. "No, living with my demons for that long isn't something I can look forward to. That's the only part about being Tolari I don't like."

"Trust me," he said. "Will you try to trust me?"

Marianne didn't answer. She was quiet, drained from reliving the horror she had related to him. "How long have you—" She stopped.

"When I showed you the flutter by the cora tree." He made his smile gentle. "You captured my heart with your smile."

"My first day here?"

"Yes, beloved."

She shook her head. "I never realized."

"I know."

"But now that you know I'm—" she took a breath, "—ruined," she finished in a whisper. "It's ugly." She forced the words out. "I'll understand if you don't want me—"

He stopped short, searching her eyes, his heart aching. "Hear me, beloved," he said. "I have known from your first day in my stronghold that you hid a deep pain. *You are not your pain.* It does not define you—it does not ruin you, or make you ugly, or do any of the things you fear. What defines you is that you give the better part of your nature to others though you are deeply wounded yourself. That takes courage, and strength of spirit, and beauty of heart. How can I not love you?"

More tears coursed down her face. He pressed a cheek against her forehead, grief for her pain making his own tears fall. He felt her struggling to hold down her feelings.

"You do not need to hold back, beloved," he whispered. "My heart is yours."

She threw her arms around his neck and burst into sobs.

Resisting an urge to make his way to Earth and kill the man who had hurt her, he carried her back to the keep as she wept herself almost to sleep in his arms.

* * *

MOONLIGHT WOKE MARIANNE, shining across her face late in the night. She sat up and stretched. The Sural's apothecary had insisted she eat a full meal and get some rest before the procedure, but she hadn't expected to wake before dawn. Rolling off her sleeping mat, she eased onto steadier legs and walked onto her veranda to gaze out over the dark, deserted garden.

The Sural had waited for her for so long. Eight years! And he never intruded, never let her know. It must have half killed him sometimes, to see her every day, to love her so much, to receive nothing in return. Always so gentle, always so kind, always so patient. And she'd rejected him at every turn. Adeline had been right—the Sural had acted like a spurned lover during deep winter.

Was it enough that she wanted to want him? She closed her eyes, remembering the long walk back from the Jorann's cave, his arms warm around her. A wave of longing to be in his arms again came over her, and she tried not to push it down. It would be different with him. It had to be. If in *eight years* he had never forced himself on her, she reasoned, he wouldn't start now. She had to try to trust him.

She could think of only one way to do that.

Mouth dry, heart in her throat, she left her rooms and crossed the short distance to the ornately-carved door of the Sural's private suite. As she approached, a guard opened it—the Sural must have left orders to admit her. It was a measure of his trust to allow her access to his privacy. It touched her despite her trepidation.

She searched the darkness in his sitting room. To the left she could make out the door to his private study, where his apothecary had begged her to give the Sural her heart. Beyond that, she thought, must be his sleeping room. Ahead, on the sitting room veranda, the Sural stood with his back to her, looking out into the night. The full moon shone on him from overhead as he gazed at the far mountains. She sighed and walked toward him, fighting the urge to bolt like a frightened rabbit.

He turned as she approached. She stopped just short of him and looked up. *Dear God, he's tall.* The air fled from her lungs, and everything inside her quivered.

"I'm here," she whispered. He folded his arms around her, and she slipped trembling arms around him. His entire being lit with joy that spilled over into her.

The Sural studied her upturned face. If he said or did the wrong thing, she would stop seeing him—and see the demon who hurt her instead—and flee. She buried her face in his robes, shaking with apprehension. He sensed her struggling to control it.

"You said—" she started. She took a breath and looked back up at him. "You said you would come back from the dark to bond with me."

He stroked her hair, almost overcome by the sensation of her arms around him. "Yes, beloved," he whispered.

"Tell me about bonding."

His breath caught. Had she come to him this night... to bond? "It is not easy to describe," he said, pausing to gather his thoughts. "When two Tolari find they cannot live without one another, each one shows the other everything that they are, and then—their hearts join. It is indescribable. Afterwards, there is always a part of the one in the other, each always has an awareness of the other."

"Have you ever done that?" she asked, avoiding his eyes.

He chuckled at the sparks of jealousy shooting through her. "No, the bond is for life. When one of a bonded pair dies, the other usually follows. Those few who choose to continue living can never bond again. They lose the capacity to do so."

Fear stabbed her again He waited while she took another deep breath and fought it down. When it subsided, she lifted her face. Moonlight caught her eyes, washing them silver.

"You are so beautiful," he whispered. "And so brave." He ran his lips across her forehead and sensed the shock of longing it sent through her. "I can no longer imagine my life without you in it."

He hesitated. She had spoken the words, called him *beloved*, but fear still ruled her heart. Yet—though she trembled, she had returned his embrace, had allowed the touch of his lips on her forehead to arouse her desire. He caught her eye.

"Will you bond with me?" he whispered.

He held his breath, awaiting her answer. He sensed her gather her courage, and then she pulled his head down to press her lips to his. Heart soaring, he buried a hand in her hair and lost himself to the soft touch of her mouth, all the years of longing transformed into joy. Parting her lips with his tongue, he tasted her, deepening the kiss as she responded, but shielding her from the desire she lit within him. The tiny sigh she uttered came close to shattering his hold on himself, and he tore his mouth away from hers, panting.

"What do I do?" she asked, breathless.

He pulled his scattered thoughts together. They should go to his sleeping mat and remove their robes, but that was almost certain to terrify her. Better to leave it until their hearts had begun to join, when he would be able, to some extent, to dilute her fear.

"Open your heart to me," he said, his voice low and ragged, "and look into mine."

He dropped his barriers.

Marianne drew a sharp breath. His radiance burst around her as she sank into him, and he was glorious. Strong, determined, caring... but parts of him were cold, calculating, and manipulative. A part of him stretched out over his province—his ruling bond. Near it lay a scar and a tight ball of grief connected to yet more griefs.

"My father," he murmured. "He died before our bond had faded. And... the sons I lost to the great trial."

"My heart grieves for your pain," she whispered, turning her empathic gaze away from the sadness, toward the more passionate side of him. Panic threatened to overwhelm her.

"Do not fear me," he said. "I am not enslaved to desire. I will not hurt you." He held her, his arms gentle, as she fought down the fear yet again. "Show yourself to me, beloved. I want to know you."

He wouldn't hurt her. He would *not* hurt her. Marianne forced herself to calm and relaxed the walls around her feelings. The Sural reached into her with his senses, gentle, tender, seeing everything... and didn't recoil. The fear, the pain, even the aching, pulsing part that she wished she didn't have—he took it all in and lit up with joy and wonder.

He loved her. He knew what had happened to her, and he could see what it had done to her, and he still loved her. Her heart burst from the cage she'd built around it and soared, the Sural's happiness soaring with it. Time seemed to stop as they shared the radiance. The Sural sought her mouth, and this time, she met his questing tongue with her own.

Like a bursting dam, something between them dissolved, and their hearts crashed together. Marianne and the Sural gasped. The radiance flared and filled the night. Euphoria, rapture, the *need* to be closer, to be inside each other, blazed through them, pounded in their loins. Marianne pressed into the Sural. He kissed a burning trail across the empathic nerves in her forehead.

"Take joy in me," he said, his voice a rasp.

"Yes," she whispered. She clung to him, her kisses hungry.

"You will never be alone again." He swept her up into his arms and carried her inside.

* * *

MARIANNE BASKED in the moonlit sleeping room of the Sural's apartments, every inch of her skin tingling. The Sural lay on his side next to her, propped on one elbow. With her eyes closed, she could see him glowing like a sun, *feel* his gaze on her face, the playfulness sparking through him, the joy lighting him, as if all of it were her own.

"I will never be able to hide from you again," he said, as he traced the line of her jaw with a finger. "You will always be able to close your eyes and know where I am."

"Fair's fair," she murmured in English. "I couldn't hide from you anyway." He gave a soft snort of amusement. She opened her eyes and smiled up at him, touching his face with her fingertips. "I never, ever dreamed it could be like that."

"Nor did I."

She stared at him, searching for words and not finding any.

"Yes, I have coupled many times," he said. "For pleasure, for lust, to father heirs, often when I was young and learning to control my heightened appetites. Never before with a woman who possessed my heart, never with the bond."

"But you've had so many—"

He smiled in the moonlight. "Beloved," he said, "before you, there was no one."

"And then you showed me a flutter."

"You were the most beautiful creature I had ever seen. And then," he added, twining his fingers with hers, "I held your hand with the hevalrin—do you remember I did not take my hand away? From that moment, my heart was yours."

A lump rose in Marianne's throat. "Beloved," she whispered. "I must have broken your heart so many times."

"I regret nothing."

* * *

IN THE MORNING, Marianne lay on a bed in what she thought of as the infirmary—a screened area in what would have been the sitting room of the head apothecaries' quarters. She trembled under the blanket covering her, though not from cold. The procedure to remove the locater chip from her brain would begin as soon as the head apothecary came out of her study. She took a deep breath, trying to calm herself. If she died—

The Sural approached, camouflaged, his barriers shut tight to prevent anyone else from sensing him. He appeared next to her.

"Beloved," he greeted her. Joy turned his dark eyes into pools of molten mahogany.

"Beloved," she said, taking his hand, her heart glowing. "What are you doing sneaking around?"

"My head apothecary would not approve of my presence here," he replied with a crooked grin. "I thought it best to give her no reason for further displeasure. But with bonding—this interruption is difficult. Normally we would remain secluded together until the bond is fully formed."

"Maybe we should have waited until after this procedure," she said.

He laid a gentle hand against her cheek. "But you came to me, after so long, and I could not imagine being with you any other way."

"If I don't wake up—"

"You will. My apothecary is the best in Suralia." He bent to press his forehead against hers. She gasped at the raw lust that pulsed through him. "When you wake, I will be here," he whispered, and disappeared.

The head apothecary rounded the screen. She stopped and frowned, then focused her attention on Marianne. "Are you ready, high one?" Other apothecaries and nurses came in behind her.

"Yes, apothecary."

The apothecary placed a now-familiar device on Marianne's forehead. "Let us begin," she said, then pressed a button. Marianne slipped away.

* * *

ADELINE POURED HER HUSBAND A DRINK—WHISKEY—WELL-AGED. "John got the authorization to pull Marianne out," she said, handing him the glass. She curled up next to him on the sofa in their sitting room. "They're almost finished repairing the phase platform."

Smithton grunted. "You just made my job a whole lot harder, Addie."

"That's what I'm here for." She gave him an apologetic smile.

He grunted again and knocked back the whiskey rather than sipping it. "Why are you doing this, Addie? First you talk John into it, then you try to talk Marianne out of it, now you're pushing to get her pulled off the mission altogether. What's in this for you?"

"Nothing, sweetheart—I'm just trying to follow my conscience," she answered, resting her head on his shoulder.

If Central Command is your conscience, he thought.

* * *

"LOCK ONTO HER SIGNAL," the admiral ordered the phase tech.

"Signal is acquired... an-n-nd... locked."

"Engage."

"Yes sir."

John Walter Howard walked over to the phase platform, prepared to face an angry schoolmarm—or perhaps a half-dead, unconscious one. The air over the platform shimmered.

No schoolmarm.

He looked down. There, on the platform, in what had to be a surgical tray, lay a tiny locater chip.

He swore and raced for the bridge.

* * *

MARIANNE STIRRED and opened her eyes. Her head throbbed. *This must be what a migraine feels like.* An apothecary she didn't recognize stood over her, but she could feel the Sural nearby.

"Do you desire something for pain?" the apothecary asked.

She rubbed her face. "No," she said. She didn't want to take a potion that would make her sleep again, not with her whole being yearning for the Sural. She could feel him aching for her. "It's just a bad headache."

"As you wish, high one."

"You got it out?"

"Yes, high one. Moments ago, the chip was phased away. We removed it with little time to spare."

Marianne's stomach quivered. That was too close. "Have there been any communications from the ship?" she asked the Sural.

"No," he answered, flickering into view. He nodded at the apothecary, who bowed and left. "I suspect they are spending their time composing an abject apology—which I do not plan to accept."

"They'll just keep sending it."

"Of course. And I may even relent. Someday." He shifted his shoulders, as if the robe irritated him. "But not today. I want every human on that ship replaced before I will accept an apology from Earth."

"All for one insignificant schoolteacher from Iowa?" she asked.

He smiled down at her and pulled her hand to his chest. She felt his heart flow into the bond between them. "Yes," he answered, fire lighting in his eyes. "All for one *beloved* schoolteacher from Iowa." She started to pull him down toward her.

"You may take the Marann back to your quarters, high one," the Sural's head apothecary said, entering the room to interrupt them. She nodded to Marianne, and then spoke to the Sural. "I am not pleased to see you initiated your bonding before the procedure. Her body is flooded with the bonding hormone—I had difficulty keeping her unconscious."

The Sural straightened and bowed an apology. The healer's face softened a little, but when she spoke, her voice was dry. "I do understand the circumstances. Joy of the bond, high ones. I would tell you to moderate yourselves for the sake of her recovery, but bonding pairs are renowned for their—single-mindedness." Her voice became even more dry. "Bonding is as effective a relief for pain as any I can provide."

The Sural laughed and slid his arms beneath Marianne to pick her up from the bed, blanket and all. She squeaked and giggled, holding the blanket up with one hand and clinging to his neck with the other as he strode out the door.

"Make sure she drinks sufficient fluids, high one," the apothecary called after them.

Back in his quarters, he lowered her onto the sleeping mat and tore off his robe and trousers. Sighing with relief, he lay on one side next to her. His skin looked irritated. She stroked a reddened area on his neck.

"An effect of the bonding hormone," he said. "Clothing chafes."

"Your poor skin. So what did she mean, bonding pairs are renowned for single-mindedness?"

"It requires three or four days to become fully bonded," he said.

"Three or four days of just—"

"—bonding," he finished. "It is best we remain here in my quarters."

"Oh my."

He chuckled. "In truth, the need is more emotional than physical. We will not sleep until our bond is mature. It is how we will know it is over—when we fall asleep."

Her stomach clenched.

"Beloved—do not fear. The compulsion is strong, but we are not enslaved to it. If you become afraid, we can guide the process." He gazed into her eyes and let his heart flow into her through the bond. His radiance burst into her awareness. "It is past time to bond again," he whispered. Her heart reached into him.

* * *

"I've changed my mind, Addie." Smithton called. He stood at a mirror in his bedroom, adjusting his cravat.

"About what, darling?" she asked from the sitting room.

"You wouldn't make a very good spook."

She joined him at the mirror. "Well then," she said, untying and retying his cravat for him, "it's a very good thing I'm not a spook." With a bright smile, she kissed his cheek before returning to the sitting room. Smithton watched her go.

"Yeah," he muttered in a low voice, reaching for his tailcoat and following her.

She made room for him on the divan.

"Marianne isn't answering her comms," he told her. "It's been four days since we phased up that chip." Adeline remained quiet. "We assume the Tolari knew we wanted to phase her off the planet and somehow got it out of her head. It's still operational—the failsafe hasn't been triggered. How they managed that, we don't know, because their neuroscience can't be much more advanced than trepanning, but it means there's a chance she's still alive. John's trying to get the go ahead to send down a shuttle to find out what's going on, but she could be a vegetable for all we know."

A signal beeped from Smithton's desk. He left the divan to answer it. "Russell here," he said.

"Sir," said a voice, "the Admiral wants to see you in his private office ASAP. He says Marianne Woolsey is on the comms."

* * *

ON THE MONITOR, Marianne was alive, herself, angry—and out of reach, for now. The admiral pressed his lips into a thin line. He should have ignored the Central Security mole and let matters play out. Adeline had created a disaster.

"The Sural requires Earth to leave Tolari space," Marianne said. "No one on board any Earth ship in the system is permitted to return. Ever. He will allow Earth to reinitiate contact in one Tolari year—*if* you leave now."

The admiral swore. "Damn it, Marianne, talk to him. Change his mind."

"You tried to abduct me."

"We thought we needed to pull you out."

"The Sural doesn't see it that way. As far as he's concerned, you tried to kidnap his wife."

"His *wife?*" Adeline blurted.

Marianne's eyes narrowed. "If you don't remove your ship from Tolari space now, it will be destroyed."

John scoffed.

"Admiral, I'm only going to say this once," Marianne said in her best schoolmarm tones. She leaned forward toward the monitor. *"Tolar is protected by technology more advanced than Earth's,"* she whispered. She leaned back and continued in a normal tone, "You can't win this. If you don't leave, you won't even see it coming."

She meant it. A deep cold settled into the pit of his stomach. "Very well," he said.

"Thank you, Admiral. You've just saved your crew's lives."

"Howard out."

The screen went blank. Admiral Howard left his office. Adeline followed him into the ready room, protesting.

"You're not going to take her seriously, are you?" she cried. "The Tolari still live in stone castles. We've never detected any evidence of—"

He turned and slammed a button on the ready room's conference table. "Security!" he barked. Two armed marines entered the ready room from the corridor side. "If Citizen Russell tries to follow me onto the bridge," he ordered, "throw her in the brig!"

He left her sputtering and strode onto the bridge of his flagship. "Ensign, plot a course for Tau Ceti station," he snapped.

"Yes sir."

"Comms, relay orders to the fleet to rendezvous at Epsilon Eridani."

"Yes sir."

"Tau Ceti laid in, sir."

"Engage."

End of Book One

APPENDIX

A RE-EDITED AND EXPANDED VERSION OF THE ORIGINAL FIRST CHAPTER FROM THE 1ST EDITION.

Marianne Woolsey never wanted to leave Earth. For that matter, she never wanted to leave her hometown of Casey, Iowa, where she taught young minds how to wrap their mouths around foreign languages that most of them would never speak again. On a cold day in early December, 2543, she leaned against her desk, staring down a classroom full of teenagers who didn't want to take a test.

She swiped the sigil on her tablet that would send the exam to their desks, as a knock came at the door. One of the school's social studies teachers stuck her head in, looked around, and entered the room, mouthing the word, "Sorry!" at Marianne.

"I'll be proctoring your test, class," she announced. "Something important has come up. Miss Woolsey has to leave."

The students murmured in mixed reaction as Marianne pulled her friend into the hallway, opening the door wide to watch for cheating.

"Susan, what's this about?" Marianne whispered.

Susan shrugged. "We don't know. There are three people here from Earth Fleet asking for you, and they aren't taking 'she's giving a test right now' for an answer."

"*What?*" Marianne exclaimed, her voice echoing down the hall. She glanced into her classroom to find eighteen pairs of eyes glued on her. She lowered her voice again. "There has to be some mistake. I don't know anybody in Earth Fleet."

"They're very insistent that they want to see *you*."

She sighed. "Look, I'll take care of this and be right back. Keep an eye on Jake, Mike, and Dave in the back right corner. They'll zip answers to each other if they think they can get away with it."

"Right." Susan nodded as she went back into the classroom.

Marianne strode down the hall toward the school office, her mind churning. Earth Fleet? Here? For *her*? It had to be some kind of mix-up. She didn't know anyone in Earth Fleet, and she wasn't sure if she even knew anyone who did. It couldn't be anything she'd done, because all she did was teach, spend time in computer chat rooms practicing languages, and bowl on Tuesday nights with several other women, all teachers from Reagan High. She spent holidays volunteering. Church on Sunday and the occasional Saturday with Susan at the big underground mall in Des Moines filled out her social calendar. Earth Fleet couldn't *possibly* have any interest in her.

She pulled open the door to the school office. Three officers stood in the student waiting area: a woman of medium height, a tall black man, and a younger, fair-skinned man who was almost as tall. As she walked in, they turned to look at her, their eyes going to hers. She smiled. Her eyes always drew attention. She was pretty enough, with even features, a trim figure, and wavy, light brown hair, but it was her eyes that caught people's notice. They were large, liquid, and a bright, startling shade of sky blue.

It was just as well. She would rather people noticed her eyes first.

"Citizen Woolsey?" asked the woman, extending a hand. She was a flaming redhead with sparkling green eyes and translucent skin. "I'm Clare Wilson, Captain, Third Fleet. This is Commander Scott Connelly," she indicated the tall black officer, "and Lieutenant Mark Hargrove," she finished, indicating the younger man.

"Pleased to meet you, but I'm sure there must be some mistake." Marianne shook the offered hands and glanced around the office. The secretaries were riveted on the scene, and the principal lounged in the doorway to his office. At least there were no students present to witness this.

"There's no mistake, Miss Woolsey," said the commander, in a voice that was soft, polite, and from the South. "If you'll come with us, we'll explain."

"Are you sure you have the right Marianne Woolsey?"

"Yes, ma'am," he answered, leading her by the shoulder back toward the door.

Marianne shrugged at her principal. "I sure this is some kind of mistake," she said. "I'll be back after I clear it up."

The commander opened the door and ushered her back out into the hall, shaking his head. "No ma'am, I expect you won't be back here today."

"Is the Marianne Woolsey you're looking for in some kind of trouble?"

He laughed. "No, ma'am."

"We'd appreciate it if you saved your questions until we have some privacy," Captain Wilson said.

Privacy. Of course. Marianne swallowed. "All right."

The captain put a light hand under her elbow, seeming happy to chat about neutral subjects while they walked down the hall to the school entrance. "Nice little town you have here."

"I like it."

"Ever dream of leaving? Of living someplace exotic and different?"

Marianne shook her head. "I was born here. I grew up here. I'm happy."

There was a large black utility vehicle with dark-tinted windows parked in front of the school entrance. *Classic,* Marianne thought. *Can this get any more stereotyped?*

She halted at the school's glass doors. "I need my coat and purse."

A finger tapped her shoulder from behind. She turned to find the young lieutenant holding her coat open with a big grin, her purse dangling from one muscular forearm. Marianne murmured a thank-you as she slipped her arms into her coat's sleeves, the blood running from her face. To get her things, he'd opened her locker. Which was locked. And required her thumbprint to open. Shoving that uncomfortable thought away, she buttoned her coat, flung her purse over her shoulder, and stepped out the door into the cold winter morning.

The vehicle was still warm. The captain took a place in the back with Marianne, while the commander sat shotgun in front. The lieutenant drove.

"What's this about?" Marianne asked. "Where are we going?"

"To the Earth Fleet offices in Des Moines," the captain answered. "And as to what this is about – I'll tell you that as soon as you sign this." She held up a large tablet. The title on the screen said, in bold letters, "Classified Information Nondisclosure Agreement."

"Um." She blinked, nonplussed.

Captain Wilson grinned and held out a stylus. "It's the only way to find out. Just realize that we'll know if your friend Susan drags it out of you."

Marianne shuddered, all the whispered stories she'd ever heard coming unbidden to mind. No one around Casey had ever ... disappeared ... but it was common knowledge the government knew everything about everybody, and that it was bad to get noticed by Central Command. Once that happened, all you could do was go along with whatever they wanted and hope you came out the other side alive. Otherwise, you vanished. Or one of your friends or family did. She gulped. "Do I have a choice?"

"Of course," the captain replied, smiling. Her smile was bright. Too bright.

The commander snorted but didn't say anything. Marianne looked from the captain to the commander and back. "Look, I can't be who you want." Unzipping her purse, she dug out her identification papers and held them up. "See for yourself."

The captain didn't take them. "Marianne Carter Woolsey, daughter of Thomas Larson Woolsey and Rose Tisdale Carter, born fifth of October, 2516, hospitalized thirteenth of August, 2529, for—"

"Yes!" Marianne broke in, her voice thin and high-pitched. "That's me!" She tucked her papers back in her purse, covering her alarm with a nervous laugh. "But I'm just a high school teacher. What on Earth could you possibly want with me?"

A slender finger tapped the highlighted signature line of the nondisclosure agreement.

She sighed and took the tablet and stylus. "All right, all right," she muttered, as she scribbled her name on the line.

The captain smiled again and settled into her seat as she accepted them back. "This is about the Tolari."

"That new race, the one whose leader wants a language tutor for his daughter?" Marianne blinked. "Oh my God, you want *me* for that?"

"Would that be such a bad thing?" The captain raised one perfect ginger eyebrow.

"It would be for me," Marianne said, frowning. "I'm happy here."

"Yes, so you said. Are you happy – or just comfortable?"

"Happy," she replied. A little too quickly, she realized. "I have a good job. I have friends. What's not to be happy about?"

"There's a lot to do and see in other places."

"I'm sure there is, but what could I do somewhere else that I can't do here? That I'm interested in, that is," she amended.

"Learn a completely new language. Learn about a completely new and fascinating culture. Live on a world where no human has ever lived before."

The linguist in Marianne perked. "A new language?"

"The Tolari speak a language all their own. Very difficult, I'm told. Do you think you'd be up to the challenge?"

"I'd have to take a look at it," Marianne hedged. "What would all this involve?"

The captain's lips twitched. "It's a very long-term assignment, you have to know that up front. The Tolari ruler – the Sural – wants six of our languages taught to his daughter—"

"Six?"

"—over a period of twenty-six years."

"Twenty-six *years*?" Marianne gaped until she remembered to close her mouth.

"Assuming you're selected."

"For twenty-six *years*?" She still had trouble not gaping. "Who all would be coming with me?"

"Just you."

"*Alone?* On an alien planet? For twenty-six years? Are you out of your minds?"

The three Earth Fleet officers burst out laughing. Captain Wilson's grin was broad. "It's not so bad as all that. They're technologically primitive, but they're a six thousand year old civilization. And there will be an Earth Fleet ship in orbit most of the time. We could pull you out if we needed to, and we wouldn't leave orbit if we thought there might be trouble."

"You sound like you've already chosen me."

"We haven't," said the captain. "But the job is probably yours if you pass the psych review."

"Is that why you're taking me to Des Moines?"

She nodded. "We have a battery of psychological tests we want you to take. Nothing painful, I assure you, unless your fingers get sore from typing. We pulled your medical records, so we already know you're in excellent health, but we'll give you a comprehensive scan, just to make sure nothing has changed. That's important, by the way, because we doubt the Tolari could treat you for anything serious. Their medical technology is based on potions made by apothecaries and who knows what else."

"Just how primitive are the Tolari?" Marianne asked.

"They're stuck in the Middle Ages, or thereabouts. The Sural lives in a massive stone fortress. The Terosha claim they managed to scrape a stone sample and dated his fortress back over six thousand years. From what we've seen, the Tolari don't have running water or plumbing. The researchers who discovered them deep-scanned the planet – there are one of those huge stone strongholds and a city of a few hundred thousand people in every province, but there's no evidence of weapons of any kind, anywhere on the planet, not even in the strongholds. They have lots of farms and orchards. There's evidence of mining. No fishing or boating. No land animals larger than a medium-sized dog."

Marianne frowned.

"Problem?" Captain Wilson asked.

"If they're that primitive, why are we bothering with them?"

The captain's lips quirked a tiny bit to one side. "That's classified."

"But—" Marianne blew a sigh out the side of her mouth and fell silent. Whether she liked it or not, the government was going to send her to another planet, away from Casey, away from her friends, and away from the comfortable life she'd built for herself.

If Central Command decided to send her to Tolar, she could do little about it. It was a horrifying thought.

"I worked hard to get where I am. There has to be someone else you can send who would *want* to go."

Captain Wilson gave her a small, sympathetic smile.

"What if I don't pass the psych tests? What if I'm – I don't know – wildly unsuitable?"

"Miss Woolsey," the commander broke in, "if we think you've skewed your test answers, we'll make the test results available to your school board."

Marianne's stomach dropped and took her breath with it. There would go her job. Her eyes darted to the captain's as an idea hit her.

"I've only been out of school three years. I can't possibly be qualified."

The captain's eyebrows flew up her forehead. "Qualified? You're more than qualified," she said. "You're fluent in *seventeen* languages, including the six that the Sural wants taught to his daughter, and you're trained to teach multiple languages. You're young – you'll only be fifty-three when you return, young enough to have a good career before you retire at ninety-five or a hundred. And we'll make sure you have a good career, Miss Woolsey. Central Command rewards loyal service well. You'll get any job you want, anywhere you want. You'll be wealthy, in addition – you'll get a good salary while you're on Tolar, deposited into an interest-bearing account. Twenty-six years' worth of wages, plus interest, makes for quite a tidy nest egg."

"But my house – it belonged to my parents. I can't just leave my house."

"We'll take care of your house."

Marianne sighed. "Why me? Why not someone with more experience?"

Lieutenant Hargrove, who had remained silent up to this point, spoke. "People with more experience tend to be attached. They have spouses, young children, people they don't want to leave, people who depend on them. Those who don't are often men, and the Sural specifically requested a woman to tutor his daughter."

"But there are thirty *billion* people across the Six Planets! Surely there's *someone*?"

"There is," the commander said. "There's you."

Marianne slumped. Twenty-six years? "How safe could I be, alone with aliens?"

Commander Connelly chuckled. "They don't look like aliens. You'll feel like you're living in a different human culture."

"But how *safe* will I be?" she pressed.

"The Sural guarantees the human tutor's safety," the captain said. "He expects whoever we send to learn Tolari etiquette, but he's also willing to give wide latitude for honest mistakes. And his own personal guard will have direct responsibility for his guest's safety."

Marianne's brows knitted. "Why does he have a personal guard if there are no weapons on Tolar?"

The commander chuckled again. "Our friends in the Terosha Federation say conflicts among the Tolari are rare, but they do fight among themselves," he answered. "There are about a hundred or so independent provinces, each led by a member of their ruling caste. They shift alliances now and then, but it's just the rulers and their guards that do any fighting. The rest of them are artists and scholars and farmers and such and stay out of it."

"You say they don't look like aliens?"

"The resemblance to us is uncanny. The Tolari aren't just humanoid. They look like they *are* human. They all have jet black hair and brown eyes and light brown skin, and they could pass for human on any street in the Six Planets."

"Not that the Tolari could *be* human," Captain Wilson added. "They're chameleons. They can disappear and reappear at will. Our xenobiologists can't figure out how they do it, much less how they do it with their clothes on. Nobody has been able to obtain either a tissue sample or a sample of their clothing for study."

Marianne nodded, her head spinning. She heaved a sigh and fell quiet until the vehicle reached Des Moines and pulled in front of an office building just outside of the city proper. Inside, the captain led her to a lab where an Earth Fleet officer in a medical uniform scanned her. After pronouncing her fit, he took her to a conference room and gave her a tablet with a battery of psychological tests programmed into it.

Completing the tests took her until late into the evening. None of the tests were timed, and she was free to get up to stretch any time she needed. There was a lounge where she could find refreshments. Lunch was take-out soup and sandwiches, and dinner was take-out Chinese. It was a long, grueling day, and Marianne was exhausted when the redheaded captain finally drove her back home to Casey.

As they neared the Casey exits, Marianne asked, "What do you think my chances are of getting the job?"

"Better than fifty-fifty," the captain answered. "I'll be the one calling you to let you know. Probably Sunday."

Marianne deflated, defeat choking her. "Can I at least finish out the school year?"

"Sorry, no." The captain pasted a pleasant look on her face. "We needed you there last week, and the Sural is displeased about the delay. He may be a primitive, but annoying a world leader is still bad politics. The most we can give you is three weeks. You have until Christmas."

Marianne balked at that. “But most of my students are going to college next fall, and the disruption would be bad for them if the school can’t find another Spanish teacher.”

“We can have your replacement lined up within days.”

“Oh.” A chill raced across her skin, raising gooseflesh. This just wasn’t getting any better.

The captain pulled up in front of Marianne’s house. “I’ll talk to you Sunday afternoon, either way, Miss Woolsey.”

“Thanks, Captain,” Marianne replied, feeling wooden. “I appreciate it.”

After the black utility vehicle drove away, she noticed her car sitting in the driveway. She halted, staring at it. Someone had to have driven it there from the Reagan High teachers’ parking lot.

No, this just wasn’t getting any better at all.

* * *

It got worse, as days passed and Marianne did what she could to get her house ready to stand empty during the coldest part of an Iowa winter. Earth Fleet lawyers showed up at irregular intervals with papers for her to sign, agreeing to the terms of her assignment, authorizing Central Command to deposit funds into a new account with a breathtaking interest rate, leasing her house to the government, and other details. It was scary how much they knew about her and what they could do without her consent, but what really surprised her was how well they intended to take care of her financially. The redheaded captain had not exaggerated when she said Marianne would be rich when she returned.

Her friend Susan, both excited and unhappy that Marianne couldn’t, and wouldn’t, breathe a word about anything, pestered her for information – what it was that Central Command wanted her to do, where they were sending her, how long she would be gone, and everything other detail she could think of. After hounding Marianne for a week, she gave up and agreed to take in Marianne’s 400-liter aquarium and six large, fancy goldfish.

Central Command gave her only three weeks to study Tolari language and culture, finish up at Reagan High, and say goodbye to all her friends in Casey. Christmas parties turned into farewell parties. She lied about everything and told all her friends, especially Susan, that she would call often to let them know how she was doing. She hoped Susan would forgive her, once she understood. Maybe, when she returned, the situation with the Tolari would no longer be classified, and she would be able to talk about her experiences with her friends.

If she still had any friends left after twenty-six years of silence.

With only a few days left before her departure, Susan dragged her off to go shopping in Des Moines on the last Saturday before Christmas. The mall was packed with shoppers. When they stopped for lunch in a food court, Marianne picked at a salad while her friend wolfed down a bacon double cheeseburger.

The idea of all that grease made Marianne's teeth itch.

"So," Susan said. "Are you coming to the Christmas Eve party Tuesday?"

Marianne waffled. "Do you know how early I have to get up Wednesday morning?"

"Come on, you'll have eighteen hours to sleep on the way to Tau Ceti."

"Sixteen."

Susan rolled her eyes. "Are you coming?"

"Who's going to be there?"

"The usual. Yes, the men will flirt. You'll deal with it, you always do."

Marianne tapped the fingers of one hand on the table and shoved lettuce around her plate with a fork. "All right, I'll come. But if anybody asks, I'll say you threatened to blow up my goldfish if I didn't."

"Great! I'll tell Brenda."

READ THE NEXT BOOK

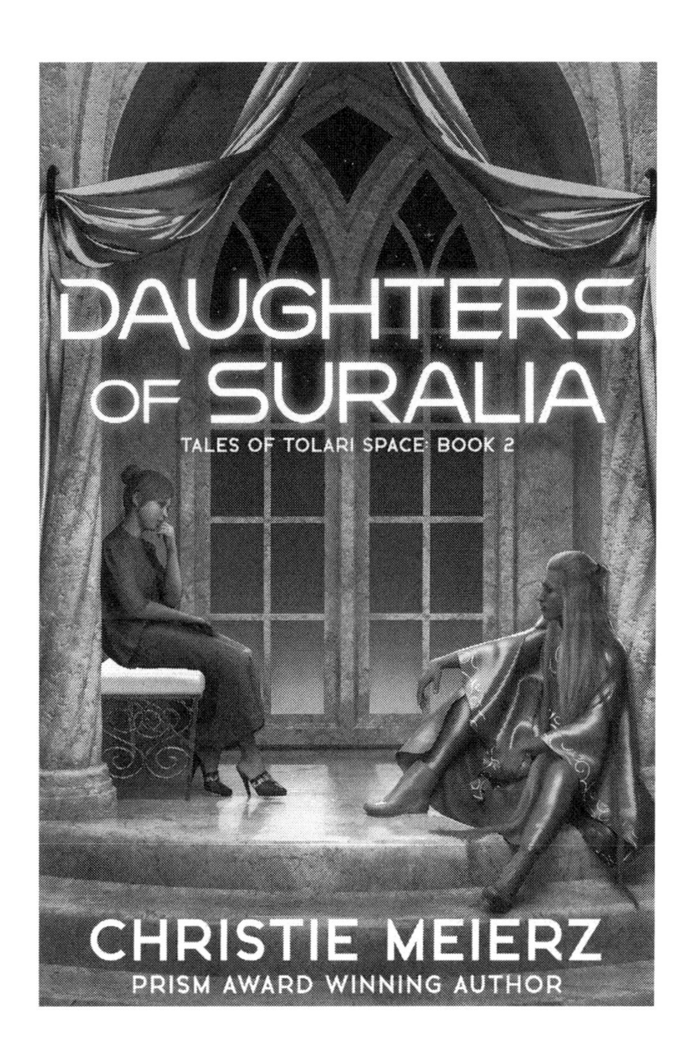

ALSO BY CHRISTIE MEIERZ

The Marann

Daughters of Suralia

The Fall

Farryn's War

Rembrandt's Station

For news about upcoming releases, advance copies, extras, AND a free ebook, sign up for Christie's newsletter at ChristieMeierz.com.

ABOUT THE AUTHOR

Award-winning author Christie Meierz writes space opera and science fiction romance set on a world of empaths at the edge of an advancing human empire. Her published works include her PRISM award-winning debut novel, **The Marann**, four more novels set in Tolari space, and several short stories. She is a member of the Science Fiction & Fantasy Writers Association (SFWA), spent 10 years raising sheep in Broome County, New York, and has been declared capable of learning Yup'ik.

Christie now lives in Rochester, NY, where she and her mathematician husband serve as full-time staff to two parlor panthers known to humans as Banichi the Assassin and Miss Myrtle the Hurricane Cat. (Their true names remain a mystery). When she's not writing, she writes about life and writing on her blog (below), her personal Facebook page, where she welcomes comments and friend requests, and her Facebook Author Page.

WANT SOME FREE BOOKS?

Join the Novus Mundi Newsletter and download FIVE books for free!

Made in the USA
Monee, IL
23 April 2024

e4810650-65c5-40bf-bc91-5aa7ae4a1f04R01